The
Jerusalem
Connection

Choir director Robin Sabine takes a youth choir to Jerusalem for an international competition where she must convince a large number of unpleasant people that she is not a spy. Finally she has to save not only the lives of her teenaged charges, but her own as well.

Janis Susan May

SAB
SEFKHAT-AWBI BOOKS

Dedicated to
CAPT Hiram M. Patterson, USN/Ret
the most wonderful man in the world

Except for actual figures and incidents of history, all the
characters, locations and events portrayed in this story
are fictitious and products solely of the author's
imagination.

Books by Janis Susan May
electronic and/or paperback format

The Avenging Maid
Family of Strangers
The Devil of Dragon House
Legacy of Shades
The Egyptian File
The Jerusalem Connection
Inheritance of Shadows
Lure of the Mummy
Timeless Innocents
Welcome Home
Miss Morrison's Second Chance
Curse of the Exile
Echoes in the Dark
Dark Music
Quartet: Four Slightly Twisted Tales
Lacey
Passion's Choice
The Other Half of Your Heart

Books by Janis Patterson

The Hollow House
Beaded to Death
Murder to Mil-Spec (anthology)

Books by Janis Susan Patterson

Danny and the Dust Bunnies (childrens)

Written with Aletha Barrett May

The Land of Heart's Delight

Chapter One

The old man had never been so persuasive. He had always had a gift for making people do what he wanted them to do, no matter how dead decided they were against it.

Of course at first I told him no. I always did. I was on vacation, I said; teaching a bunch of mutton-headed collegians the glories of music was hard work and I valued my time off. The fact that I didn't want to take the assignment carried no weight whatsoever. When the old man wants something, he wants it and no one I've ever heard of can deny him.

To be absolutely honest, however, there was a certain element of logic in it all. I am a teacher of music, specializing in choirs and singing groups, so the prospect of escorting a group of teenagers to a special choir competition seemed reasonable enough.

"But in Jerusalem!"

He waved my horrified objections aside airily. He was good at that. "It's a lovely place, Robin, and perfectly safe."

School was out, he cajoled; I would have my expenses paid and a little over, as well as some time on my own for sightseeing. Plus, he hinted broadly, I could do him a big favor by picking up a thing or two. When he finally reached the point of it not being just a matter of disadvantaged kids singing and getting to travel and became a part of United States prestige, I knew I was a goner and gave in as gracefully as I could.

It sounded simple enough, after all.

Of course, I didn't know then that I would become entangled with a man like Grey Hamilton-ffoulkes or that the kids were individual contest winners and not a proper choir or that the Crown of the Virgin of Janóch would show up or that I would run into Allen Burke again.

If I had...

I don't know.

I've always hated people who look back at the beginning of an – an incident and know exactly what they would have done had they but known... whatever. Monday morning quarterbacking is easy enough, but to be truthful, in my case I just don't know.

I was told that a sudden illness had prevented the group's original director from accompanying them; by the time we were all finally on the plane I decided it had to have been due to a nervous breakdown. I was positive, because I wanted to have one myself! Teaching college students for a couple of hours a day is a totally different matter from taking complete 24/7 responsibility for six high school students. The difference in age is negligible; the difference in maturity and behavior is incredible.

No matter how much I wanted to, however, I could not desert. Just take my word for it that the old man would never accept a simple nervous breakdown as an excuse for not taking six chronically malcontent, disturbed, hostile and arrogant high school seniors to one of the hot spots of the world! He wanted something and when he wanted something he made up his mind, which really meant he made up everyone else's minds!

"Miss Sabine!"

That's my name – Roberta Barbara Sabine, to be exact, more commonly known as Robin – and until this interminable job I had quite liked it, but hearing it bawled every few seconds from a variety of young throats was quickly getting old.

According to themselves, half these kids had been everywhere and done everything and traveling was a great *ennui* about which they could be told nothing; the other half apparently had never been anywhere at all and were constantly asking questions about everything, from the airport security measures – garnering us some strange looks from the TSA people – to the necessity of passports for Americans. After a harried two days of unproductive rehearsal I was already tired. By the time our flight left for Paris I was exhausted and when the plane finally lifted off from Paris for the last leg of the journey to Ben Gurion Airport I was seriously pondering what happened to women who abandoned their teenaged charges and ran for their lives.

Of course, I wouldn't do that, no matter how attractive the prospect seemed; there was too much at stake. First of all, I had given my word and until the whole thing was over I was royally stuck. Secondly, the old man would never forgive me. Incurring his enmity was never wise; he had a memory like a computer and the wiles of a snake. His rare acts of revenge, though not widely known beyond his co-workers, were legend.

"Miss Sabine!"

I gritted my teeth. I was beginning to think I had made the biggest mistake of my life.

Two days later I was sure of it.

* * * * *

Jerusalem was hot, dusty and noisy. It might have been one of the oldest cities in the world and centerpiece of three great religions, but the part we saw that first day was purely modern tacky. We had been stashed in a little third-rate hotel just off the road to Ramala. It was, our tight-jawed competition coordinator told us, the best that could be managed since we had been so late in registering.

"After all," he all but pouted, "your application did not arrive until after the official deadline and it was only through special intervention that you were accepted at all."

He made it sound decidedly suspect. Knowing the old man and his ways of getting what he wanted, he might have been right.

Maybe he was, but I still think they could have

found us a place a little closer to the center of things. It wasn't all bad, however; hating our lodgings was the first – and almost the only – thing on which my surly charges could agree.

The hotel was a squat, dust-colored three story building set a scant five or six feet back from the sidewalk. That five or six feet was enclosed by a waist-high wall and, I found out later, was the garden so lovingly touted in the hotel brochure. There was no grass, just dirt, a couple of tired plants in enormous pots and one struggling, dusty tree. The owners, Mr. and Mrs. Abramowitz, were immensely proud of that tree. I thought it just about the same size as the ficus in my dining room back home.

When I saw that the front door and every window were covered with a thick ornamental metal grille I worried about fire. I did, that is, until I got inside; then I realized that there was nothing inside to burn. The floors were polished marble; the walls were decorative glazed tiles half-way up to the cavernous ceiling and plain plaster from there. The decor – to be kind – was at most minimal. In my room there was a bed hardly wider than a cot. Other than that most uncomfortable looking piece of furniture, the room held an ancient armoire, a single straight wooden chair, a small mirror with a plain frame on the wall, a thin gauze curtain over the high window and a creaking ceiling fan that only stirred the hot, dusty air.

And that was all.

There was a bathroom on every floor. Accustomed to the unconscious elegance and availability of the average American bathroom, we all found this a shock. Perhaps I should say bathrooms; there was one room for bathing with a tub and a sink. There was another closet-sized cubby that contained a toilet and a miniscule sink impractical for anything more than dampening your fingertips. Neither had any windows, just tiny ventilation slits near the ceiling. The facilities were functional; let's leave it at that.

The girls and I had the top floor, which consisted of only two bedrooms and the bath. They shared a large room in which three of everything had been crammed. My smaller room was across the hall, putting me in the undisputed role of chaperone. The boys were one flight down. At first I was worried about that, until I found out that with their passion for propriety the Abramowitzes had dragooned Mrs. Abramowitz's elderly bachelor brother, a tall, frail-looking scholar named Feldshuh, to sleep opposite the boys. If the kids had had any thoughts of sneaking out and enjoying a riotous nightlife – if such a thing existed in this fanatically religious city – while they were away from parental supervision, they were going to be sadly disappointed.

It was a miracle Mr. and Mrs. Abramowitz were not overwhelmed at having a herd of Americans descend on them. To be totally honest, I would have taken one look at my infamous gang of six and bolted the door. In any case, the décor was not the only thing puritanically stark about this place. Normally it served to shelter visiting rabbinical students and the elderly Orthodox couple who had volunteered it to the competition were obviously as distressed to have a noisy horde of American teenagers foisted on them as we were at living in conditions at least as stringent as the local jail.

The rules were unbelievable to anyone living in the modern world. There was to be no fraternization between the sexes without at least one flinty-eyed adult chaperone present; I hadn't worried about that, because my group had showed no interest in each other at all – except Carla, who showed too much interest in every male, from the airline employees to the competition officials. It was funny, though, and then aggravating to realize that our hosts thought anything beyond an impersonal 'Good morning' or 'Good afternoon' constituted fraternization of an almost lascivious sort.

The house rules were simple, short and graven in stone. We had to take our meals out and could not have any food in our rooms. We could not practice after eight in the evening and not at all during Shabbat, which was from sundown Friday to sundown Saturday. We had to be up and bathed and dressed every morning by eight so the cleaning women could scrub the miles of marble. We had to be in our rooms and preferably in bed by ten in the evening, when the lights were turned out and the doors irrevocably locked. The kids complained loudly and, although it made my looking after them that much easier, I complained too, because the rules were as restrictive on me as on them.

At the moment, the thing which bothered me the most was the ban on practicing after eight and on Shabbat. Of course, there was only one Shabbat during the competition, but with my group every minute counted and we needed every one of them. The remaining guest room on the second floor had been hastily cleaned out and set aside for a rehearsal room. There were six chairs in a row for the kids, one squarely in front of them for me and in front of that – brought to this remote outpost by routes unimaginable – was a battered black metal music stand bearing a yellowing label that read 'Property of Cleveland Symphony – Do Not Remove.'

There was no piano, but luckily we didn't need one. All of the required music for the competition was *a capella*, as were our two elective pieces. The grand finale, Beethoven's vastly overworked *Chorale* from the Ninth D Minor symphony, would be sung by all competing groups and accompanied by the Jerusalem Symphony Orchestra, but with all that mob you could sing *Yankee Doodle* and probably not be heard.

It was the individual competitions which worried me. Most of the groups had been singing together for years; my gang had only met a month or so before. I had worked with them for two days before we left and in spite of myself had been impressed. Seldom in my years as a music teacher had I heard six more glorious solo voices. Good solo voices, however, do not guarantee a good group. Choral singing depends more on blending than on individual technique and everyone in my gang was willing to blend – as long as each of the others blended with them!

To be absolutely honest, I didn't really think this mismatched assortment of voices had a chance in Hades of making the finals, let alone winning. The competition had been instigated to open the much vaunted, internationally funded Hall of World Peace which had been built on one of the high hills in the city. I wondered if I were the only one who found that name ironic in this ancient and blood-soaked city. Although the first of its kind, the competition had drawn the best youth choirs in the world, the caliber of groups that made records and sold out international tours. To challenge them with a hastily put-together group from various corners of rural Texas was sort of like playing St. George with a toothpick.

Well, if a toothpick was all I had to use against the dragon, I would go down with all flags flying. Taking a good breath, I sang the C natural which was the opening tone for Rutter's lovely *All Things Bright and Beautiful*.

Silence.

"Okay, gang, let's go to work." I sang the tone again.

There were the usual groans and gripes. Most of us

were still sleepy under the relentless influence of jet lag, as the interminable twenty-four hour plus trip over had ended just the afternoon before, but we had the opening ceremonies to attend after lunch and I was determined we weren't going to miss a moment of practice. In any case, I had learned to expect the groans and gripes; they had been just as irritating before we left. I had insisted on lots of work then, too; though this bunch of kids was bright – sometimes frighteningly so – they had not yet quite grasped the concept of teamwork. Each was a spectacularly gifted solo artist, but I couldn't make them understand that solo brilliance did not guarantee success in a team effort.

"Hey, Miss Sabine, we've done it a million times already."

That was Tony Manette, foremost among my problem children. The primary problem was that he was no longer a child. When he had showed up I had had to see his credentials before believing it. They certainly hadn't made teenagers like him when I was one – which had not been *that* long ago! Tall and rangy and very handsome in a sullen sort of way, Tony knew how attractive he was and didn't hesitate to use his appearance to further whatever scheme he had going on at the moment, most of which were usually just slightly shady. Aside from having a baritone voice of the size and caliber usually associated with international opera, Tony was almost a blueprint of a juvenile delinquent. Until recently he had taken his criminal apprenticeship in one of the rougher cities on the Eastern coast; his parents, who seemed to be decent enough people, were distracted about him and hoped that their move to Texas would prove beneficial. Tony hated Texas. Tony hated almost everything, most especially any rules that kept him from doing anything he wanted to do. So far, though, he hadn't done anything really bad – or he couldn't have come on this trip – but that was due more to luck than design.

"Yes, indeed. I thought that we were supposed to have some time for sightseeing on this trip. The brochure said..."

That was Gerald. Gerald Fitzgerald Applegate III, to be correct, and I felt quite sure he could quote the brochure word for word. He certainly could everything else, from the Magna Carta to the batting averages of obscure baseball players. A genuine mental giant, Gerald was a cherubic looking little sugar dumpling of a fellow who, though chronologically the oldest, appeared to be about twelve years old. He was constantly trying to show off his knowledge as compensation and a very irritating habit it was, too. Still, nasty little toad that he was, Gerald had the high, clear voice of an angel. I've never been fond of tenors as a breed and agree wholeheartedly with whomever said, "Tenor is not a voice, it is a disease," but Gerald singing *Ave Maria* was almost enough to make me change my mind.

Almost.

"If possible, Gerald. If possible. Now I've arranged

for you all to go on the city tour tomorrow afternoon with the Youth Choir from St. Anselm's."

That brought a general round of grumbling, which I had expected. St. Anselm's was a church school in the high mountains of Switzerland that had a reputation for being stricter than West Point. Apparently possessing unlimited funds, they had one chaperone for every three members. On the flight we shared from Paris I had shamelessly appealed to them for just that reason. It turned out my plea was slightly less than useless; what had done the trick was the fact the old man had talked to the headmaster and been assured that St. Anselm's would be happy to offer any assistance necessary. The choir director had not looked happy, but had agreed without argument.

"And," I continued, just slightly louder, "that is only if you get some solid work done before we go to the reception this afternoon."

"Aw, Miss Sabine!" came from six throats. It was as together as they ever were.

"Now look, kids, we are here as representatives of the United States in this competition and that is our primary job. When – and if – you start sounding like a real singing group, we'll start talking about some real sightseeing."

"Really, Miss Sabine, I've sung *Bright and Beautiful* with a lot of groups. Can't I...?"

Maureen must really want to look around or she wouldn't have opened her mouth; she seldom spoke. Of course, her father was a minister, so she was probably under strict orders to see everything she could. Had the competition been held anywhere but the Holy Land she probably wouldn't have been allowed to come. A mousey little thing, her speaking voice could barely be heard on the few times she had used it, but when she started to sing…! She didn't have a big voice, but her soprano was sweet and true and I hadn't found her top notes yet.

"Maureen… all of you… listen to me, because I'm not going to say it again." Of course I would, whenever necessary, but one could hope! "We are supposed to be a group. We're at a disadvantage because we haven't sung together before and we're going to be singing against groups that have been together for years." I looked around at their closed, sullen faces and felt I could have gotten more response from a brick wall. I gritted my teeth and sang the C natural again, though it sounded more like an enraged buzz saw than music.

"Miss Sabine…"

"Shut up and sing!" I snarled, comforting myself with fantasies of what I would do to the old man once I saw him again.

Chapter Two

In the end it wasn't anything I said that reached the kids; it was the opening party for the competition later that afternoon. It reached me, too, but in a different way.

The First Annual Hall of World Peace International Youth Choir Competition was a class act all the way. The 'informal' party that opened the competition week proved that. The vast marble and stained glass reception area, beautiful in its own right, had been hung with colorful banners and studded with floral arrangements roughly the size of a Mini Cooper. There were long tables covered with white linen, rapidly melting ice sculptures and elaborate canapés that looked much better than they tasted.

Of course, there were also the uniformed soldiers standing everywhere, most appearing little older than the contestants, their eyes always moving, automatic weapons carelessly at the ready, but hardly anybody noticed them. After any time at all in Israel one got used to the sight of uniformed teenagers armed to the teeth.

The thing that impressed the kids most was their

competition. I don't think they had really realized what they were up against until then, how organized and professional the others were. Each group was ceremoniously presented by the Master of Ceremonies, some toothy movie star or another, and although the applause was polite enough for my pathetic little gang, I could have wept for them.

"Gee, Miss Sabine," Carla hissed at me while we stood in line for a paper cup of punch and a handful of tasteless canapés. "You should have warned me! I look so frumpy!"

It would have been Carla who worried most about that. Carla Parkinson was the second soprano and, although a very pretty, healthy-looking girl, she wasn't quite the femme fatale she thought she was. No one with bright red hair and freckles should ever try to be a femme fatale.

"Yes, Miss Sabine," added mezzo Betty Jean Scott, her voice almost as low as a man's. Her teacher had said that the tone of her voice had been a source of dreadful shame to her and her very traditional (read uneducated) family until she had learned she could sing. "It wasn't very fair of you."

"Yeah," growled Tony. It didn't surprise me that he complained; he was all too aware of the effect his dark good looks and on females and was very conscious of his dress.

"Most of them even have uniforms," Larry mumbled good-naturedly, slurping happily at his punch and managing to spill half his canapés in the process. A nice, Nordic-looking lad, Larry Holcombe was our bass. Where he got those booming deep tones I don't know, for although he was tall – two or three inches over six feet – he was as skinny as the proverbial rail and looked as if a good wind would topple him. Also, he didn't quite seem to fit in his own skin. I didn't know what his problem was, but he was a one man walking disaster and seemed perpetually festooned with band-aids and mercurochrome. I noticed a new bandage on his arm since this morning, but the scratch seemed minor and hardly worth mentioning. With Larry anything less than complete amputation seemed almost normal.

I looked at my six charges, clustered around like angry ugly ducklings, and decided it was time for an object lesson.

"Why should I bother? How much attention do you pay what I tell you? Besides, it seems I have told you again and again!"

"Miss Sabine..."

"You haven't exactly made a habit of listening to what I tell you. And, I must say, even if you didn't listen to me I should have thought you would have dressed up for a party."

They hung their heads as I looked from one blue-jeaned body to another. Only Maureen, the minister's daughter who was forbidden to wear any kind of slacks, was clad in anything besides aged denim and her demure dress looked more like a prototype for a nun's habit than a party frock.

"The brochure did say it was informal..." Carla whined. She was so intimidated she hadn't even tried to flirt.

"I wonder what they sound like when they sing?" Tony muttered, eyeing the sleek, uniformed competition, obviously disconcerted for one of the first times in his cocky young life.

"I have a feeling," Larry rumbled, scraping a dribble of caviar from the front of his polo shirt, "that we are going to get creamed."

Despite my antipathy towards the entire assignment, my heart bled for them. It really wasn't fair that they were being used like this; shoving them unprepared into this competition was downright cruel. Inwardly I railed against the powers that be which had decreed it necessary. For the first time these kids were being shoved up against the hard reality that their beautiful voices alone were not an automatic passport to first place. Of course, everyone has to face that in one way or another sometime, but this was downright brutal.

Realizing that there are others as good or better than you is never easy, especially when you have been praised and told you're the best again and again. Luckily for most of us, we don't have to learn it in such a public place. *Never ride too high a horse, my girl,* my grandmother had told me; *there's always someone who'll make you come a cropper.*

Wisely I didn't say anything except to send them out to meet others their own age. If there's one thing I had learned as a teacher, it was when words became superfluous. I handed my plate to a disdainful waiter and shifted my bag from one shoulder to another.

That presumably simple action wasn't as easy as it sounds. Many cruel things have been said about my sizeable canvas totes, but I am one of those people who believes in having all the necessities close to hand at all times. As someone had once said I could have lived very comfortably for a week just with the contents of my purse. This one was new, a present from the old man and made especially for travel with all kinds of inner compartments. The kids regarded my bulging bag with palpable disbelief and not a little caution. Maybe they thought it contained the bones of former students.

Strange how things run in patterns. I hadn't thought of 'he who had laughed about living out of my purse' for a long time; in fact, I thought I had forgotten him. I had certainly tried to! Then, as if my random thoughts had conjured him up like a djinn, I saw him and every drop of blood in my body seemed to solidify.

"Are you all right, madam?" asked one of the other choir leaders. There had been a group of us, chatting superficially while scoping each other out. It had been thoroughly intimidating.

"I'm fine..." I gulped. Wow! Talk about the tricks your mind can play on you. I must be having some sort of a weak moment – the long trip, the emotion, the positively gruesome punch – to create a once-familiar image out of a fleeing resemblance! When I mustered enough courage to look again there was no one who in the slightest resembled the figure of my memories.

"Here she is!"

I whirled as a hard hand clamped on my shoulder.

"I demand that she give us an explanation," continued the same oily voice.

"Miss Sabine..."

I had never met Stanislaus Kaminsky, organizer of the competition, but with his crest of startling white hair and bulbous eyes it was easy to recognize him from his brochure photograph. He looked uncomfortable and I found that somehow alarming. His companion was equally distinctive, though in a far less wholesome way.

Bushy eyebrows met over hard eyes that bored right through me. A sharp chin tucked down until his baby blue *yarmulke*, a sort of mini-skullcap or beanie worn by most religious Israeli men, pointed straight up. His fingers dug into my shoulder like iron bars. "Well, what do you have to say for yourself?"

"About what?" I asked in genuine bewilderment.

"I think you may release Miss Sabine," Maestro Kaminsky said mildly. "She is hardly likely to run away.

"This is a serious contest, Miss Sabine! I protest your daring to insult the Hall of World Peace with your band of ragamuffins!" The blue *yarmulke* wiggled as he shook his head vigorously, but he did let go of my shoulder.

My hackles went straight up. Those six kids might be headaches and distinct pains located a fair space lower, but – *dammit!* – they were my kids and no one could knock them to me! "I beg your pardon?" I asked in tones icy enough to freeze water.

"Miss Sabine, this is Avrom Sternberg," said Maestro Kaminsky with the grave formality for which he was famed. He did have the good grace to look somewhat embarrassed. "He says there might be a question about your group competing."

"I do not say there might be a question about them competing," Sternberg snarled. "There is indubitably a question about their being in the competition!"

My stomach knotted. I had been worried about something like this. "Would you care to explain that remark?"

"Does it need explanation? You submit late..."

"And we were accepted by the committee."

"You submit late, and then you show up with this raggle-taggle bunch of ruffians! I say that there is something fishy here..."

My own brows began to draw together. "I am sorry if you find our appearance not to your liking. I was not aware it was necessary to get wardrobe approval from you."

His color ratcheted up another notch. I was dimly aware of gasps from our ever-growing audience.

"But this..." he floundered, his arms flapping.

I supplied, "Trans-Texas Canticle Society."

We all winced. Even on such short notice they should have been able to come up with a better name than that!

"This Trans-Texas Canticle Society," Mr. Sternberg repeated with a painfully straight face, "is a disgrace to the competition. How dare you," Here his gaze swung towards the obviously embarrassed Maestro Kaminsky, "demean this important occasion with such a bunch of clowns?"

"This choral society has been accepted by the judges, Mr. Sternberg," he said in measured tones. "Just as yours has been."

"My group applied on time and in proper form! We did not have to exert undue influence in order to be accepted!"

And just how, I wondered, *had he found out about that?*

"Neither," Sternberg continued in an increasing voice that was gaining us more and more attention, "are we an embarrassment to this worthy cause!"

"I thought," I said slowly, but in a voice carefully calculated to carry without seeming to shout, "that this competition was meant to open the Hall of World Peace – a cooperative effort between the countries of the world."

"That does not give you the right to turn a classical competition into a circus!" Sternberg all but screamed.

"And when did you take over as director, Mr.

Sternberg?"

The maestro had started to sweat. "Mr. Sternberg does have the right to file a formal complaint. Now I do appreciate your feelings, Miss Sabine, but..."

How I hate that word 'but.' It was nearly always as good as a 'no.' I pulled out my last weapon; it usually worked, but as it was a double-edged sword I drew it reluctantly.

"Very well, Mr. Sternberg, Maestro Kaminsky... I am sure the press will listen most attentively to all your arguments." I smiled blandly.

"The press?"

"Of course. When one has a strong suspicion that an international goodwill contest for musical teenagers is discriminating unfairly against a disadvantaged group, it is only right the world should know, especially when two of the main countries involved are as close as the United States and Israel. Fair play demands it."

I could swear that Kaminsky was stifling a grin, but Sternberg looked almost apoplectic, especially since the much-vaunted relationship between our two countries had been a little rocky lately.

"Miss Sabine, that is not fair! You are the ones who ignored the rules!"

"And the committee accepted us. Why can't you? Do you not want the press to know that you wish us disqualified because our group is unable to meet your sartorial standards?"

"You would not dare..."

"My charges are going to have a fair chance," I declaimed with fine emotion, shamelessly playing to the upper galleries. Heads were turning towards us in an ever-growing circle. "Now you do what you think is right and I will do what I think is right."

To tell the truth I would have been quite reluctant to contact the press – I dislike notoriety and such public scrutiny would not have been to my taste at all – but Sternberg didn't know this. I didn't know who he was or who was behind him, but he didn't seem to realize that the press could be a weapon used equally by both sides.

I was counting on that.

"Well, Mr. Sternberg?" Maestro Kaminsky asked politely. "Do you intend to continue with your protest?"

Sternberg glared at me, then gulped and turned away. "I shall contact you tomorrow with my decision," he declared, gathering the rags of his dignity around him before stalking away into the crowd. Kaminsky gave me a bow that was just slightly deeper than it needed to have been, signifying that the point was mine before he too walked away.

Well, the old man wouldn't be happy with this! Instead of being just one in a crowd, I'd managed to make a humdinger of a scene the very first night! Maybe if I just stayed out of sight... I turned away, only to stop suddenly as my purse made solid contact with an immovable object.

"I say, is that some form of new secret weapon or

merely a family embarrassment?"

I stopped still. The voice was male and baritone with a distinctly upper crust British accent, and it was one of the most beautiful voices around. I couldn't help wondering how good a singer he was.

Turning, I looked up into the darkest blue eyes I had ever seen. They were of such a startling color that it was a moment before I realized they were set in a distinctly handsome face crowned with dark blond hair very gracefully laced with silver. He was smiling.

A woman would have to be deaf, dumb, blind and dead not to respond.

"I call it the equalizer," I said with a smile. "It gets me respect in crowds."

He tugged experimentally at one of the straps, testing the weight. "That, and not a few lawsuits, I should suppose. Do you have to register that as a lethal weapon?"

That made me laugh outright. "Someone mentioned it once. I've got the papers somewhere in my purse."

He chuckled at that, his blue eyes twinkling devastatingly. Deftly he commandeered two tall glasses from a passing waiter. "So much for legal protection. Why do you think that tiresome ass Sternberg wants you out of the competition?"

His timing was perfect. I had just finished sipping when his question ended and my opinion almost automatically spilled out; however, I did manage to restrain myself. As I had been told often, out-spokenness was a bad habit.

"This is really champagne," I gasped. Most of the surprise was genuine. I had been expecting some more of that weak and sickly punch.

"Rank – and age – do have their privileges, and you are avoiding my question."

Boy, he was a smooth one. I smiled and sipped again. It was not only real champagne, it was extremely good champagne.

"To rate champagne like this, you must have a very high rank because you're not very old."

"Hardly, you hardened flatterer. I'm really sort of a forgettable type fellow," he said in palpable untruth. "The trick is not in having rank oneself, but in knowing those who do. Do you not intend to answer my question?"

I ignored his tenacity. "The Hall is certainly gorgeous."

"Determined to be mysterious, are you?" He had a *devastating* chuckle!

"No," I admitted with a becoming hint of reluctance. "Maybe he just wanted to harass someone. I don't think he'll follow through."

"Just as well. You bested him fairly this time and did so very well. Anyway, it was a Heaven-sent opportunity."

"What?"

"I've been standing here concocting half a dozen

schemes of how to detach you from that bunch of bores." With a graceful economy of motion he gestured to the growing party bibble-babble behind us.

"Really? And you expect me to believe that out of all these beautiful and worldly women you have chosen me? Now I suppose you'll tell me you're perfectly harmless."

He laughed again and raised his glass in salute. "I admit to exaggerating, dear lady, but never in telling direct lies. My name is Greystoke Hamilton-ffoulkes, more commonly known as Grey, and I am nothing more than a lowly member of Her Majesty's diplomatic service."

Diplomatic service member he might be, but lowly... never! It would be a crime against nature. Really, I had seen very few men as handsome as Mr. (Mr? He hadn't mentioned a title) Greystoke Hamilton-ffoulkes. On the surface he seemed to be the kind of man about whom women dream.

Unfortunately, I don't believe dreams come true that easily.

Especially to everyday-looking women like me. I have no illusions about my looks. My reddish-blonde hair is neatly cut, my eyes are an ordinary sort of blue, my figure shows the effect of exercise; for a woman in her early thirties I look pretty good. But not, I think, good enough to elicit the interest of a man like Grey Hamilton-ffoulkes across the traditional crowded room.

Cynicism, they say, is a mark of maturity.

"How do you do? I'm Robin Sabine. I have a six-voice choir somewhere in there."

He nodded. "I heard your eloquent defense of them. They're lucky to have you. I saw them during the introduction." His tone left little doubt as to his reaction.

Though I felt the same way about my charges I irrationally resented his patronizing them. "It's unfortunate that they haven't proper uniforms or any of that sort of thing, but that isn't what they judge on, after all. They have won a number of contests," I said in perfect truth. After all, every one of them had won at least one individual competition – that was how they had been chosen. They had just never sung together.

Blue eyes sobered a moment, then his face creased into a smile. "You care about your charges. That's good. May I take you to dinner tonight, Miss Sabine? After they're safely tucked up, of course."

"I'd love it," I answered with real regret, "but I must decline."

He looked startled, as if being turned down was a rare occurrence. Not being a femme fatale type myself I found his startled expression most pleasurable, but an innate honesty compelled me to explain a little of our situation and the humor came back into his eyes.

"So you must be locked in right and tight by ten, eh?"

"Not only in, but in bed, or we have to grope our

way in the dark."

"Barbaric customs, what? Locked in with half-a-dozen teenagers," he mused, rubbing the back of his neck. He made it seem an elegant gesture. "I can think of few worse fates. Lunch tomorrow?"

Sadly, I had plans for tomorrow. I smiled and shook my head. "Sorry. Not possible."

"I say, Miss Sabine, are you playing hard to get?"

"Not voluntarily, I assure you."

"Well, that's a relief. We must see what can be done to expedite your problems. Perhaps I can count on taking you to dinner tomorrow night – and your purse, if you feel you need the protection of a deadly weapon."

"No promises, but we'd be happy to discuss the possibilities," I said lightly, never expecting to see or hear from him again. Gorgeous men simply do not materialize in the middle of parties and make promises they actually intend to keep.

In any case, meeting a man like Grey Hamilton-ffoulkes had been a lovely extra in an assignment that appeared to be determinedly dreary. Giving in gracefully – and perhaps with a sigh of relief? – he procured me another glass of champagne before we said our final goodbyes and he vanished into the crowd.

It was sad that I couldn't accept his invitation for lunch tomorrow; maybe there would have been time for a quick bite... but unfortunately I was here to do a job and that had to come first.

"Robin?"

My heart stopped.

It was a voice that I knew and that I feared. So I hadn't been wrong about what I saw. Slowly I turned around to look straight into my past.

"Hello, Allen."

Chapter Three

They tell you that first loves are the worst. That isn't necessarily true. Without the aid of photographs I can barely remember the face of the man I almost married in college, the man who – at the time – I thought I should love forever.

Allen Burke was not my first love, but to this day I can call up his features without the slightest bit of effort. I can see the set of his shoulders in a passing stranger, hear the tones of his voice in a television newscast. They had never left me since that awful night at Ravenhurst Castle when he had accused me of trying to break into Lord Mugoran's safe.

So now we stood face to face again and it truly had been he whom I had glimpsed across the room. In my heart of hearts I had known that we would see each other again, one more time at least, that the story between us was not yet finished, but why oh why did it have to be here and now?

"You're looking well," he said.

"You are too," I answered.

Prim words exchanged between people who have nothing – or everything – to say to each other.

Amazing. It had been over a year, but he was unchanged, as if I had just seen him yesterday. Still eternally boyish, still vaguely rumpled as if perpetually ten minutes behind, still... Allen. He wore a no-color sports jacket with leather patches at the elbows, corduroy trousers and the long-sleeved shirt that was his trademark. He even wore the same pair of battered old cufflinks. His hazel eyes behind their tortoise-rimmed glasses weren't as warm as I remembered them, but most of their warmth had come from the love that had once blazed there. On the other hand, there was none of that cold hostility which had filled them at our last, explosive meeting.

"I saw your confrontation with the brass," he said with his usual bulldozer tact. "I thought I'd give you a minute to get over it. That, plus I didn't know how you'd react to seeing me again."

I'd forgotten how perceptive he was. That was one of the reasons he was so good at his job.

And one of the reasons we had parted so viciously.

"I had a one-up, you see," he went on. "I knew you would be here. The competition committee gave lists of all groups and their leaders to the press. That way I knew to watch out for you."

Of course. I had forgotten the efficiency of the publicity machines.

It was my turn to say something. What could I say? How it felt as if I had been punched in the stomach to see him standing there, rumpled and appealing as ever, the same battered leather camera bag dangling over his shoulder? How he still haunted my dreams? How I longed to explain, but there was never the opportunity, even if I could?

"I saw that piece you did on Afghanistan," I said at last, babbling the first neutral thing that came into my mind. "It should have gotten the Pulitzer."

"Thank you. And now you wonder what I'm doing covering a Mickey Mouse music competition? I – I'm sorry," he amended hastily. "I didn't mean to imply...."

Same old Allen. Foot in mouth as usual. Once I had thought it appealing. The damnable thing was, I still did.

"I know. It is a valid question, though; are you just marking time here until something hot breaks in this area? Seems something usually does, sooner or later."

He pulled off his glasses and polished them with a disreputable handkerchief. It was a heart-stabbingly familiar gesture; he always did that when he was off-balance, uncertain. I was uncharitably glad to know that I wasn't the only one who felt that way.

"Something like that." The polishing completed, he jammed the handkerchief back in his hip pocket and hung his glasses from his jacket breast pocket by one shaft. They swayed precariously, as they always had, yet I had never seen them fall. "Wish I'd gotten over here sooner."

Several bitter replies leapt to my lips, but I swallowed them down manfully. "Oh," I choked, "why?"

Hazel eyes, kaleidoscopic in their emotions, pierced mine. "I know we didn't part on the best of terms, Robin, but I don't want you to get in trouble or fall in bad company again."

Curse it, he sounded so sincere!

"Very kind of you."

He must be really upset, because he put on his glasses, then took them off again and shook them at me. "Look, Robin, you can take what I say seriously or ignore it, but you need to know that things here aren't like they were in England. The people here play by different rules. They play hardball and they play for keeps."

"How sporting." I tried to keep my voice light even as my nails dug trenches in my palms.

"Dammit, woman, I wasn't going to let you make me mad!" His hands clenched into fists.

I thought about telling him I wasn't doing anything, but that would only add fuel to the fire. "I'm sorry, Allen. We always did have the ability to get under each other's skin."

That, at least, was unalloyed truth.

"Just watch yourself, will you? I saw you talking to Hamilton-ffoulkes. He's got a reputation, Robin, and it's not very good."

"I'm a big girl, Allen." It wasn't a very original response, but it was the best I could do at the moment without resorting to unadulterated profanity. He was a fine one to be preaching about reputations, especially after the way we had behaved – once upon a time.

"That's not what I mean and you know it. This is a hot spot, Robin, and I just want you to be careful about the kind of people you associate with." He looked so sincere it tore at my heart, ripping away hard-won scar tissue.

I even almost believed him.

* * * * *

We took a taxi home. It was a squeeze getting the seven of us into the dilapidated old sedan, but we managed, though I for one cast some very uncharitable glances towards those more fortunate groups who had their own buses or limousines. If gloom were a quality to be weighed and measured, the taxi never would have made it back to the hotel. I was certainly in no mood to talk and the kids were uncharacteristically quiet.

Except for Carla. Oh, she was quiet enough, but there was a smug complacence about her that, had I been less involved with my own upheavals, I should have noticed. As it was, I merely said, "What did you find to smile so about, Carla?"

"I never knew that so many good-looking men would be here."

"Oh, yeah," Larry rumbled, "and they're all just dying to meet you."

"Little Miss Sexy strikes again," jeered Tony, which infuriated Carla.

"You're just little boys," she hissed. "What do you know about the way real people act?"

"What do you call real, Miss Hot-Pants?"

"I'm sure," said Maureen, a born peacemaker, "that Carla would never consider doing anything questionable."

"Unless, of course, it suited her purposes." Gerald spoke around a mouth full of food. Heaven only knew how many of those tasteless hors d'ouevres he had stuffed in his pockets. "Both history and literature abound in examples of..."

"Shut up, Gerald."

"But it's true, Miss Sabine!"

I sighed and dreamed of my small Dallas apartment half a world away as if it were some unobtainable Shangri-La. "Simply because something is true is no reason to broadcast it, Gerald."

"See, smart-ass?"

"Shut up, Tony," I said wearily.

We stopped for some falafel sandwiches – strange concoctions of pita bread, fried chickpea paste and shredded cabbage with a thin, slightly sour dressing, but sort of good in spite of all that – at the tiny café across the street before heading back to our comfortless hotel. No one was truly hungry after the largess of the reception, but I knew that they would be ravenous before morning and there was no imagining Mrs. Abramowitz allowing them to raid her refrigerator.

It was a compromise that pleased no one. First of all, none of my kids were especially adventuresome gastronomically; secondly, you have to be awfully hungry to enjoy a falafel sandwich the first time. Or the second. I suppose they are an acquired taste, like ripe olives or anchovies.

Still, everyone managed to get one down – Gerald ate two – and then we sat in the dismal, dusty open air café sipping Cokes and watching the scanty traffic until we could wait no longer.

We walked through the gates of the hotel at ten minutes until ten, where Mr. Abramowitz was waiting to lock the doors behind us. He seemed to regard allowing us inside as a great favor.

The lights went out at ten, so we stumbled into bed more by feel than anything else, and I was glad of it. I had had just about all the conversation, chaperonage and company I could stand. I wanted nothing more than to lie in the dark and think of the day's events.

Of Grey Hamilton-ffoulkes, to whom I would probably never speak to again.

Even more so of Allen Burke, who so dramatically reappeared after all this time.

And finally of the nondescript little sedan that had circled our hotel repeatedly that evening.

* * * * *

Getting rid of the kids without protest was a great deal easier than I had dreamed. By the time we had taken a quick breakfast at a bigger café down the street, come back for a couple of hours of solid practice and then crowded into a cab for the competition luncheon, they were as anxious to be rid of me as I was of them.

From a purely musical point of view we were making progress; considering from where we started, we had to! From a personal point of view, we had perforce gotten to know each other better and I don't think any of us liked what we saw. An afternoon apart could only be beneficial.

The luncheon had been set up in an outdoor restaurant not far from the Hall of World Peace, but what a difference there was between this one and the shabby cafes around our hotel! There was an enormous wall surrounding a paved area covered with tables and any number of large and shady trees. The trees were mostly in flower and the thick sweetness of their scent was sort of like an additional spice to the meal.

Even as large as the place was it was crammed with all the contestants and their entourages, sometimes with almost no space between the tables. My group was near the center; at least I didn't have to worry about them ducking out. I doubted if they could even stand up. I was seated at the humbler end of the directors' table, a long affair set under the porch overhang. Maestro Stanislaus Kaminsky had the center seat at this table of honor and – somewhat to my dismay – Avrom Sternberg, my tormentor of the night before, was seated to his right. He knew where I was, too, because after one lengthy, contemptuous look he spent a great deal of energy not looking at me.

"I think it's shameful," said the large, hard-faced woman to my left.

"I beg your pardon?"

"That Sternberg creature. I saw the display he made last night." A flipper-like hand was shoved at me. "I am Hildegarde O'Connell. Canada."

"Robin Sabine. USA."

"It was absolutely unforgivable the way he accosted you," she went on, sending a fierce glance his way. "Old age has not mellowed him, I see."

"Do you know him well?" I picked at my wilted fruit cocktail.

"Unfortunately. I have been at many contests where he has competed."

"Do you think he can get my group put out?" I found to my surprise that it was very important to me.

A smile rearranged her heavy features. "Lord love you, no! This is one of his favorite tricks. He loves to make a stir."

"But why? What can it gain him?"

"Attention. A reputation. Don't you realize that all geniuses are supposed to be temperamental? He chooses a group that... that..." She floundered, an unexpectedly girlish blush rising from her collar.

"A ratty group with no chances?" I supplied.

Her smile widened. "Perhaps not so harsh a description. A group which does not meet his own exalted standards, but which might have a chance to come in close against his. Then he throws a fit and has to be placated. It is an old game."

I had heard about other, similar fits of temper from

other musicians. Strange how something as beautiful as music could bring out the more warped aspects of some minds. "So you don't think we have a problem?"

"Your group has many problems, my dear," she said with brutal honesty, "but I do not think Avrom Sternberg is one of them."

She didn't know the half of it.

There were speeches, of course; Kaminsky gave a doozey that lasted some twenty minutes. I can't recall a word of it. Then Moses Barrientos, the director of the Hall of World Peace, gave a short talk. I can't recall a word of it, either. I just remember that I couldn't get a refill on coffee and I couldn't wait until this was over and I could get away.

Finally the luncheon ended simply because all things must end sometime, then I had to endure the rush to the restrooms and the hassle of getting my group together and herded toward the St. Anselm's bus. After actually seeing my group the chaperones seemed a little less anxious for them to share the tour with their scrubbed, disciplined and seemingly identical little darlings, but charity – and the old man's influence – prevailed. In short order the chaperones got everyone boarded with no nonsense. I stood and waved until the bus was out of sight down the narrow street, dismayed at just how elated I was to see them go.

It was all just a part of the job, I told myself.

Then I grabbed my purse and made a beeline for the Old City.

Chapter Four

I couldn't help it.

I did some shopping of my own first.

The Old City of Jerusalem is a fascinating mélange of shops and apartments and places of worship. Most of them are so ancient it takes the breath away. When you come in by the Jaffa Gate, a stone portal opening off of Jaffa Road – which is still the main street of the city, old and new – you walk directly into a fascinating shopping quarter. Each side of the street is lined with tiny little shops, some no bigger than a good-sized walk-in closet, all filled and overflowing with colorful goods. Rugs and vests and dresses and shirts hang over the street itself, creating a fluttering canopy that filters the vicious sun.

By itself that would have been hard to resist, but when the shopkeepers entreat your attention with a variety of dulcet and strident sales pitches in almost every language known to man, sometimes even pulling you into the shop physically, all the while promising the bargain of the century, it would have taken a stronger person than I to resist.

At first it was a white leather Bible with an

intricately carved mother-of-pearl cover. My mother would love it. Then it was a gauzy scarf, impractical as anything, decorated with jingling fake coins. Then a vest embroidered with gold and silver and colors and hung with more coins; I didn't know where I would wear any of this stuff once I got home, but I certainly couldn't go home without it.

And the jewelry! Great hunks of amber and knots of turned silver, painted china trade beads and great flat sheets of mother-of-pearl, semi-precious stones and precious gold... My wallet writhed while my credit cards whimpered in sheer terror.

Actually, it was the jewelry which pulled me back down to earth. Not the prices – though they helped – but their real purpose as personal adornment. I had other things to do. There would be time for more shopping before I went home. Physically pulling myself away from the siren song of a bib necklace of silver coins hung with malachite medallions, and ignoring the whining wails of the shop owner, I slipped back into the street.

It was no easy thing to ignore the lures of the seemingly endless shops, but I persevered and by dint of constantly comparing the scrawled bit of Arabic I had to the tile street signs set into the stone high above my head I finally found the Street of the Khan. It had been more difficult than I had thought; even if the enticing stores had all been shuttered finding this little side street would have been hard.

The Old City was made like a rabbit warren of intertwining streets. They were little more than stone channels some ten feet wide and perhaps three times that high, crowded with people and merchandise, none of which helped my latent claustrophobia. Only by occasionally looking straight up at the clear blue sky did I keep from completely losing it.

In this area the shops were smaller, more enclosed. In places huge pieces of tin had been hung some ten feet over the street, turning it into a dim tunnel. Part of the way was a section of the Via Dolorosa, the Way of Tears; every so often there was a luridly colored picture set into the wall depicting which station of the Cross should be said there. I threaded my way through knots of the devout saying their prayers. It was more easily said than done and I received more than one dirty glance, leading me to suspect they thought the world should stop while they followed their faith.

Around the corner from the station of St. Veronica and the handkerchief (I think!) I slid into a tiny shop. The front was mostly plate glass, which made it different, more subdued and businesslike than the spilling-over exuberance of the Jaffa Gate area. The door was tiny and a bell tinkled as it opened.

"May I help you, madame?"

It was the first time I had seen a woman serving in a shop in the Old City. Her eyes and complexion stamped her as Arab, but her look was pure Paris... understated, simple and devastatingly elegant. She made me feel overheated, grubby and unappetizingly suburban. I disliked her on sight.

The shop itself was stark. There were two chairs near the door, two Western-style glass showcases set in an L and a sublimely sad-looking potted plant. The showcases themselves were nearly empty, holding only a few pieces – though those few were spectacular. I wasn't interested in any of them.

"Good afternoon. I'm looking for a gift."

"Anything in particular?"

"Maybe something for the hair?"

She didn't even glance at the cases. "I'm sorry. We do not have anything like that."

I hadn't anticipated that! "You don't? Not at all?"

"I am sorry."

"It's something special. For my boss' wife. She loves something unusual."

Those exquisite obsidian eyes flickered. "Did you have anything particular in mind?"

I had memorized what the old man told me. "Something shiny. Lots of stones. She likes glitter. Something like nothing else."

She nodded slowly. "We do not have anything like that at the moment. I believe we might receive something that might suit you on Friday. If you would care to return..."

We were competing on Friday. At least, we were if we got past the first round of judging.

"I'm sorry, but Friday is out of the question. I must

find something for her today."

She shrugged, making even that homely gesture elegant. "If you must have it now you might wish to look in the shop of my husband's cousin. He carries that sort of thing."

Coming out of her lips it sounded as if I were looking for something unwholesome. However, I couldn't afford the luxury of personal reactions, so I merely smiled, stretching clenched lips over gritted teeth.

"Perhaps I might take a look. Where is this shop of your husband's cousin?"

She gave me directions. I asked her to write them down, but she refused rather haughtily, almost implying that no one of adequate mental capacity would need to have them written down. In the end I wrote them down myself – on the back of the piece of paper with this shop's address on it, which she didn't like. I was glad I had, since finding the shop of her husband's cousin was decidedly difficult.

Difficult, perhaps, but worth the effort. It was in the oldest, darkest, narrowest part of town, where the ancient walls almost seemed to lean against each other in their decrepitude. Here the strip of sky above the street was almost obscured by the huddling buildings and the splintery old pierced wood balconies. Here there were fewer signs in English, more shops that sold things catering to the native populations. I could have lingered hours, rattling among the unfamiliar kitchen implements or sniffing the enormous, suitcase-sized bags of loose spices.

Once I got there the shop itself was like something out of the Arabian nights. Bolts of silk spilled over usable utensils of hand-hammered copper. Painstakingly embroidered dresses hung from the ceiling like fantastically colored stalactites. Figures of carved olive wood lay in profusion on every level surface, waiting to grab at an unwary ankle or elbow. Or purse. I pulled it and my various sacks in and held them close.

So much merchandise was displayed that it was a challenge to enter the shop itself. Carefully positioning myself, I eased inside, going carefully and alert for the first sign of something overbalancing.

"May I help you, madame?"

Now here was a shopkeeper suitable for the shop! A hawk-faced Arab of indeterminate age, he wore a traditional dish-dash – the long, dress-like garment more common in Egypt and Saudi, but found on men all over the Arab world. Only the gold Rolex on his right wrist, which was either genuine or a very good fake, gave positive identification that he belonged in this century. Being of somewhat romantic nature I could easily imagine him with a triangular *kaffiyeh* on his head and a scimitar at his side, riding out to fight invading Crusaders. Or somebody. My knowledge of history is notoriously sketchy.

"Madame?"

"I'm sorry... I was just overwhelmed. There are so many lovely things..."

"I try to keep a good stock. I am happy that madame finds it pleasing. Would you care for some coffee or tea?"

I knew of the custom of shopkeepers offering refreshments, but this was the first time I had run into it in this day of frenzied shopping. Which to have? The thick, sweet coffee, full of grounds and whipped to a reluctant froth, or the delicate tea, divinely sweet and flavored with a stalk of *merimilla*?

"Tea, please," I said, sinking onto the decorated camel leather pouf he indicated, "with *merimilla*."

The dark eyes, hooded as a falcon's, brightened. "Ah! So madame is familiar with our customs! That makes life so much more pleasant!" Clapping his hands, he gave a quick order in Arabic to an urchin who appeared seemingly out of the ground, then settled himself easily on another pouf exactly the correct distance away. It was as if I were being entertained in the home of a friend.

"How are you enjoying our city, madame?"

"I find it fascinating. The new part..." I shrugged. "The new part is much like new parts of cities anywhere, but the old... It is magnificent!"

"I am glad it pleases you," he said and somehow I had the feeling he might have arranged it all just for my amusement.

As suddenly as he had appeared the first time the

urchin was back, this time bearing an ornate brass tray with two cups. I knew that almost every commercial street in the Old City had coffee vendors every few yards, incredibly tiny cubbys where an aged man dispensed tea and coffee for the shopkeepers in his area. My host, like almost everyone else, must have run a daily tab, for after he had served me with the aplomb of an English butler the urchin vanished.

"Oh, this is good!"

"It is not as good as earlier in the spring, but if it gives you pleasure it has justified its existence."

I laughed. "Please! I'm an American. We aren't used to such flowery speeches."

"Does it not please you?"

"It pleases me too much. I have to return home and over there..." My words trailed away and I shrugged.

"Then American men do not know the pleasure of light conversation."

"Neither, unfortunately, do American women, so please do not spoil me."

"But madame... I cannot help myself." Then —and I'm not quite sure how he did it – but without rising he managed a very credible bow. "Would you deny me the pleasure?"

I glanced at my watch. I had spent too much time enjoying myself.

"I'm afraid I shall have to. Time grows short."

"Then I must aid you in any way I can." Rising, he took our empty cups and stuffed them into a corner.

"What would please you, madame?"

Taking his outstretched hand, I struggled ungracefully up from the pouf. It was lower and more comfortable than it had appeared. I was not pleased about appearing so gauche and clumsy.

"I need a gift. For my boss' wife."

Something rippled in those dark eyes. "A gift? What kind of a gift?"

"Something for her hair, I think."

"A barrette made of olive wood, perhaps?" He slid behind the glass case which was almost hidden beneath piles of fabric.

I followed him more slowly. Even though the distance was no more than a few feet it was significantly darker in this part of the shop. I regarded the dim, anonymous lumps at my feet with caution.

"No... Something shiny. Lots of stones. She likes glitter. Something like nothing else." I took a breath, then quoted, "'...make me a crown of shining gold...'" and laughed self-consciously.

His eyes closed to slits as he nodded, then finished the line. "'...spangle it with gems of unearthly style...' But, madame, there are those who say, 'There are many crowns within man's reach – '"

"'– And many lines,'" I answered, "'and a man's life in each – '"

"'– A heap of flags, a heap of bones –'" he returned, with no apparent sense of irony about quoting the grisly words in this city of perpetual battle.

"' – And in the end, naught left but stones.'"

He nodded as if pleased, then for a moment vanished behind the case. "Perhaps," he said, popping up again like a jack-in-the-box, "this will please the lady. It is not everyone who would appreciate such a piece." In this light his smile looked wolfish as he placed before me a messy package of dark cloth.

Then, when he began peeling away layers of the coarse fabric, I forgot him altogether. It was exactly the kind of thing the old man had described, although it was much bigger, much more expensive looking than I would have expected. Even in this dim light it seemed to glow with its own unholy fire.

"Will this not do, madame?"

"Yes," I managed to gasp. "How much?"

"For you, madame, a very special price..."

I accepted the first price he quoted – generally a mistake in a native market – and counted off a surprisingly low number of bills from the wad the old man had given me. Of course, who knew what had been paid for this originally? By the time it got to this juncture... Not daring to pick it up, I laid a gentle finger on the cold metal edge and wondered at how such a thing came to be here.

"Your receipt, madame." He held a small sheet of flimsy paper out with a flourish. "Be sure to keep it to show to the customs agents when you return."

"Thank you."

He rewrapped the dark cloth, then wrapped that in

a thick coating of cheap newsprint. "And, madame, a small gift for you." Another largish wad of newsprint was added to the parcel and the whole thing whisked into an expandable string bag.

I took the bag, dumped my other, inconsequential purchases on top and, listing slightly, edged my way out of the shop.

Now where?

The shops called to me with a siren song, but the kids should be back from the tour in no more than an hour or an hour and a half. By then I should be deep in the paperwork that I had told them would occupy me the entire afternoon. Getting out of the Old City and finding a taxi should take at least half an hour. That was going to be cutting it close.

Forget the paperwork. This afternoon had changed everything and I needed time to think it out.

"Ah, so Fortune is indeed kind! How are you this afternoon, Miss Sabine?"

With a sinking heart I looked up into the handsome face of Grey Hamilton-ffoulkes.

"What are you doing here?"

He looked completely unabashed at my rude outburst. "Just come on an errand. You?"

I have never been able to control my face. 'You have a face of plain glass,' my grandfather had said. 'Don't you ever try to play poker... you'll lose your shirt!'

"Been doing a bit of shopping, I see, and..." Grey

looked at me appraisingly. "I'll bet you're playing hookey!"

I took the lifeline like a trouper and nodded.

"Run out on a rehearsal?"

"No... the kids are on a city tour with another group. I'm supposed to be doing paperwork."

"Can't say I blame you. Paperwork is the modern bane. Since I couldn't inveigle you into lunch, will you join me for a cup of coffee?"

"I should get back... it's hard to get a taxi..."

"No need to worry about that. I've a car and driver waiting just outside the Jaffa Gate. We can enjoy our coffee and still have you home before you could find a taxi."

It was obvious why he was in the diplomatic corps. In spite of my firm resolution he had me into a hard wooden chair in a small café and in a minute or two a plate of fanciful pastries and two American style coffees appeared in front of us.

"I hope you don't mind," he said, unrolling his paper napkin with gusto. "Simply cannot resist the things and they're awfully good here."

Lunch seemed a long way away. I gulped at the scalding coffee, then took an experimental stab at a whipped cream covered pastry. Grey was right; it was very good.

"No need to ask what brings you here." He glanced at the bulging string bag which, along with my equally bulging purse, took up most of the room under the tiny table. "The shops in the Old City are fascinating. Did you find some bargains?"

"A few," I admitted. "What brings you down here? Or are you playing hookey too?"

"No, just dreary business. There was a rumor that the Crown of the Virgin of Janóch might be floating around down here. Thought I'd come check it out, though I think the whole idea's ridiculous. You know about it, of course?"

Of course I knew. It had been front page news back home for almost a week. Janóch was a small town in the backwaters of Middle Europe that had lain quiet and dull for over half a century of Communist occupation. Then, with the dissolution of the Communist empire it suddenly recalled its long ago status as a place of Christian pilgrimage. From the early Middle Ages until the time of the Communists there had been a shrine there with a statue of the Virgin which, according to those who believed, had been created and blessed by a manifestation of no less than St. Michael himself.

Well, there was no way to prove that St. Michael had had a hand in the affair, but there were irrefutable records of a jeweled Madonna which had stood in the old church and, according to those same records, had worked a fair share of miracles.

Then the Communists had come, the church had been destroyed, and the Madonna and the miracles had vanished. Until...

Only a few months ago there had been international news about the rediscovery of the Virgin of Janóch. Hidden by the last priest of the church and kept secret for generations, the Virgin had reposed in seclusion until She was brought back into the light. There had been celebrations and pilgrimages and promises of a new era. The whole thing had been a big lift for the entire world.

Then, not six weeks ago, the fabulously jeweled Crown had simply disappeared. It had been impossible for it to have been stolen, but it had vanished nonetheless.

And now they thought it was here in Jerusalem.

Grey didn't believe it.

I did. It was safely wrapped in dark cloth and newspaper and sitting in a bulging string bag right next to my foot.

Chapter Five

We sat chatting at the little café until long after my self-imposed deadline, but thanks to the proximity of Grey's car – and the suicidal tendencies of Grey's driver – I arrived back at the Hall of World Peace well before my charges. Grey went on immediately, claiming that his duties at the embassy called him. I was almost sorry to see him go; I had had such a good time I didn't want the afternoon to end, even in spite of the thing that crouched at my feet.

I waved merrily as Grey drove away, then went up to the mezzanine, where there were always empty offices to be found. During the short time of coffee and pastry and Grey's lightweight, amusing banter I had forgotten my problem – surely a testament to the man's charm – but as soon as we had started back it seemed to throb right though the confines of cloth, newspaper and string bag.

How had the Crown of the Virgin of Janóch gotten into a shabby little souvenir shop in the backstreets of the Old City of Jerusalem?

Furthermore, what was it doing in my shopping bag?

I locked the door of the first empty office available, sat down at the naked desk, and stared at the lumpy sack without touching it. Wild, improbable scenarios filled my head, only to be replaced by a mind-numbing fear. Somewhere I had read that the value of the gold and jewels alone – not counting the intangibles of religious affiliation, antiquity and workmanship – was well over a million dollars. I know a million dollars isn't worth quite what it used to be, but there are men who would kill without compunction for a quarter of it.

That did not make me feel secure.

Ruthlessly I dumped out the contents of my purse and unzipped the bottom security compartment. It was a tight fit for the thickly wrapped Crown and the equally padded gift, but at last the zipper closed and I tossed the rest of my stuff back in. Now the weight was the only difference. I just hoped I didn't have to carry it any distance.

I barely got finished and back down to the lobby before the kids began spilling in, hot, dusty and simply bristling with hostility. The St. Anselm's group stayed on the bus as mine disembarked, but didn't look any too happy either. The leader, after escorting my group to within six feet of me, greeted me with the curt announcement that we had to have a conference. I promised her one later, which, brimming with indignation, she had to accept, as I simply walked away from her towards my kids.

"Hey, what's this?" I asked, looking from one sour

face to another with growing dismay. I thought of taking them back up to that enticingly empty little office, but decided against it. It was always best to strike while the emotion was hot. Instead I headed toward to the isolated area behind the sweeping staircase. "Come over here."

"Aw, Miss Sabine!"

"Nothing, Miss Sabine."

"Tell me!"

"It's that little creep," Tony snapped after a long moment of decision. "You'd think he was some sort of friggin' professor or something."

"Tony! Language!" It popped out before I could stop it.

"Those who do not wish to learn do not have to listen," Gerald said with lofty disdain that sounded ridiculous coming from someone who looked like an apprentice garden gnome. "Unfortunately, those who need to learn the most care to listen the least."

Luckily Larry was standing close enough to grab and restrain Tony from what would have been at least manslaughter. Larry sported two new bandages, one on his elbow and one on the side of his hand. Had I the money, I would buy stock in the medical supply business. All by himself Larry must contribute handsomely to their bottom line.

"It was just so unbelievably embarrassing, Miss Sabine," complained Carla. "I mean, everyone was trying to avoid us! First Gerald won't shut up and then

Maureen here has to get into an argument with one of the priests at one of the churches."

Maureen flushed brightly but stood her ground. "He was saying that *all* Christians believed – "

I didn't want to know the details. Considering the attitudes of her rather narrow sect and narrower father it would be easy to imagine the conflict she would have with any priest. "That's enough, Maureen. We don't need a replay."

"At least Maureen didn't keep disappearing," said Betty Jean. She spoke so seldom that her husky voice was a surprise.

"Shut up, Betty Jean!" Carla turned on her like a tigress.

"Disappearing? Would you like to explain that, Betty Jean?" I asked with a sinking heart. Thank Heavens I had had this afternoon. After this I wouldn't dare to leave them alone for a minute! "Who kept disappearing?"

"Carla."

"I didn't disappear! I was always there when the bus was ready to leave!"

"Don't equivocate!" I snapped. "Did you leave the group?"

"Only when there was a man around," Tony smirked and this time it was he who had to duck, since Carla went for him with shrieks and clawed nails.

"Quiet!"

Normally I am softly spoken, but umpteen years of

vocal training create a capacity for sound. I didn't use it often, but when I did – as now – it stopped everything dead, reverberating off the marble walls of the multi-story entry like a fusillade of gunshots. Each of the kids paused mid-breath, shocked into momentary good behavior.

If I had wanted no one to notice us, that had blown it. A security guard, his rifle snapped to the ready, came flying across the floor.

"What is wrong?"

"Nothing," I replied soothingly. "Just a small disciplinary problem. Nothing for you to worry about."

For a moment he looked unconvinced, then as I continued to smile, he relented, swung his gun over his back and walked away, glancing back suspiciously a time or two.

I had control again. "Now," I said, looking each of the kids over with as much contempt as I could manage, "I can see I am going to have to rethink things. It's obvious that you are not mature enough to handle nor worthy of the trust I put in you."

It was almost possible to watch them shrink before my eyes. I wasn't enjoying this – really, I wasn't – but discipline had to be maintained.

"So," I continued, "from now on we are as one. We will eat together, sing together and do everything else together. There will be no sightseeing and no free time until I say so. Is that clear?"

"Miss Sabine!" came from five anguished throats.

From the sixth : "Might I assume that you infer..."

"Shut up, Gerald. Shut up, all of you. You know exactly what I mean. I thought you all were mature enough to handle some independence. Apparently I was wrong. Now we are going directly back to the hotel, where you will have exactly ten minutes to clean up and get ready to rehearse. We have at least two hours we can use before dinner."

"Miss Sabine!" came from six anguished throats.

"Tony, get us a cab."

The trip back to the hotel was remarkable only for its cramped discomfort and its silence. No one said a word on the trip or as we trooped through the hotel. I went up last, realizing how much I felt like – and probably resembled – a sheep dog herding its mindless charges. I had only reached the landing when Mrs. Abramowitz stepped out from their private quarters, her face set and stormy.

"Miss Sabine!"

"Yes, Mrs. Abramowitz?"

"You have a visitor. A man." She made it sound obscene. "In the garden."

I stopped on the stairs, wishing I dared rush up long enough to freshen up. Could Grey have come back so soon? Or was it...?

Right there on the landing I dug out my makeup case and, to Mrs. Abramowitz's horror, ran a comb through my unruly locks and put on a smear of lipstick. It was a new one, bought especially for the trip – a bright pink called Jezebel, which had somehow seemed appropriate for a trip to the Holy Land. I didn't think I was going to like it.

As I had expected, Allen was waiting for me in the garden. He was sitting at the small, somewhat ratty metal table under the struggling tree and looking morosely across the street at the veiled women going in and out of the tiny grocery next to the café. I was surprised he didn't have his camera out; he had always had an appreciation for local color. He had always seemed to be smiling too, in that first, happy time, but in this last year and a half we had both changed.

We had met during the cool delightful green dampness of an English spring, which was just about as different from the dusty heat of a late Middle Eastern summer as imaginable. So many things were just about as different as imaginable...

I gulped, but the sudden flood of memory would not be stopped.

There had been a musical festival held on the grounds of Ravenhurst Castle. I had been there singing with a group that specialized in madrigals. Now madrigals have never been my favorite form of music, but the attendant lures had been too much to resist. I wanted a free trip to England and they had wanted a competent soprano with unquestionably perfect pitch.

The festival had lasted several days and, due to a shortage of lodgings in the neighborhood, a lucky few of us had been housed in the castle itself. That week of the festival was one of the most memorable in my life – for several reasons. I had never lived in such splendor, even sharing a room with three other women, and I had never had such a blazing romance.

Allen Burke had been assigned to cover the festival. It wasn't his usual beat; he was much more at home in crisis situations, and his byline was becoming familiar all over the world. However, apparently his superiors decided that he needed a break and assigned him to the festival, a fact for which we had both declared ourselves grateful.

How do people fall in love? I don't know. All I can remember sounds suspiciously like one of those cheap drugstore paperbacks – sparks when we met, every free moment spent together, stolen hours alone in his hotel room, not-so-secret glances in public, long lovely walks in the fairy-tale gardens of the castle.

So what had gone wrong? I can't say. Later there was a world-wide scandal about Lord Mugoran being a turncoat, about proof of his treachery being in his safe during the festival, about his collaboration with fascist groups – allegations that were hard to reconcile with the short and pudgy music lover who had sponsored the festival for years. I never denied that I was alone in the library the last night of the festival, but Allen would never believe me when I tried to convince him I was not breaking into Lord Mugoran's safe. After a short, bitter confrontation he had left, stalking away into the night to look for his lordship.

I had never seen nor heard from Allen Burke again until last night.

Now he was sitting there, waiting for me, staring at nothing, his mind obviously far away. Was he remembering too?

"Hello. I'm sorry I didn't see you when we came in."

He jumped to his feet, sending up little puffs of pinkish dust. "Hello, Robin." He looked uncomfortable, as if unsure of his welcome. Well, that was just fine with me!

I sat in the chair he held out for me, dropping my purse at my feet.

"Is that thing attached to you?"

"I feel secure when it's near."

"A rather ugly security object."

"We were told this was an unsettled area and advised to keep our money and papers with us at all times," I answered primly.

"So you can run at the slightest hint of trouble?" He shrugged. "Not bad advice."

"It's seemed so calm," I went on at last, since the conversation had dropped to a standstill. "Except for the infighting at the competition."

"Don't be deceived. It's never calm here. Sometimes it's just quiet, that's all. All it needs is a match. One incident. Then the whole place goes up like a dry haystack."

"You're being gloomy."

"Just honest."

The silence descended again, so deep and uncomfortable that I could hear the dusty leaves rubbing together in the fitful breeze and the roar of engines down on Ramala Road.

"What do you want?"

"You sound so hostile, Robin." He looked at me as if seeing me afresh, then pushed his glasses back up his nose. I had done that for him, in other times, other situations.

"I'm not hostile, I'm just curious. The view isn't very interesting, the conversation certainly isn't scintillating and if it doesn't get any better than this, I've got work to do upstairs."

"I'm worried about you."

"What?"

"I thought you were going with your kids on the city tour today. Then I ran into the tour at the Garden Tomb and found out you weren't on it."

"Allen Burke, have you been checking up on me?"

"Not really... I just asked where you were and found out that you had stayed home to work. I came straight over here, but you weren't here either."

I stood up, shivering with fury. "That sounds like checking up to me. How dare you!"

"Dammit, Robin, someone has to! I came by here and found that you hadn't come back and I didn't have any idea of where you might have gone – "

"And who appointed you my keeper?"

"– and then you come back very chummy with Grey Hamilton-ffoulkes!"

"You always seem to think the worst of me," I snapped, "so what difference does it make to you?"

His mouth opened and closed a time or two as if he were biting back foul-tasting words, then he slammed his hand down so hard that the metal table bent. "Robin Sabine, I have never known any other woman who could make me so mad! I – I just can't stand by and watch – "

"Watch what? What do you have against Grey?"

"Oh, so it's 'Grey' now. He's a smooth one, they were right about that."

"They who? What are you blathering about?" I asked in spite of myself. I would have liked nothing more than to stalk inside and end this embarrassment, but the siren song of curiosity lured me on.

"The oh-so-proper Mr. Hamilton-ffoulkes is a very suspicious character."

"Don't be silly. He works for the British government."

"So he would have you believe, Robin. There are tales – "

I snatched up my purse, enough adrenaline flowing through my veins that I didn't even notice the weight, and looked him straight in the eye. "There could be tales about me, too, tales you helped start. Or have you forgotten?"

"Robin, I never..."

I didn't listen to him, but at the door I stopped and turned. "Let's get one thing very clear, Allen. What I do is no business of yours. Do you understand?" Then I stalked inside.

Somehow after all this time that should have felt very good.

It didn't.

* * * * *

I walked up the stairs slowly, feeling every ounce of the purse's weight, then nodded politely to Mr. Feldshuh, who was peeking out of his room like a turtle out of a shell. Strange; I never would have picked him for short, round Mrs. Abramowitz's brother. He was all long angles and bones. However, my elder brother and I were equally dissimilar, so who knew what someone would think of us half a century hence.

Back in my room I put on some more lipstick — some of my standard It's Raining Rubies instead of the violently pink Jezebel — then as a final act of dutch courage, sprayed on some cologne. I thought about it, then decided to take my purse down to the practice room with me. Somehow I had the feeling that lipstick, cologne and courage would all need refreshing.

I won't be boring and relate the details of that evening. Enough to say that at practice we seemed to be going backward and by the time we went off to supper I was happily entertaining thoughts of abandoning my charges and running home as fast as I could go.

Of course I didn't do any such thing, no matter how

much pleasure the fantasies gave me. We finished practice, then took a cab to a restaurant called the Petra which Miss O'Connell had recommended most highly.

At least one thing worked out well that day, for the Petra was indeed better than average. The fare was typical Middle Eastern, with the wide array of *salatas* – a sort of appetizer or snack course – one learned to expect and the grilled lamb I at least had learned to love. The kids, of course, dreamed of hamburgers. I intended to let them go on dreaming, since one of the leaders had told me at the opening reception that the only place she had found hamburgers was at one of the big hotel grills – and those at $35.00+ American money!

Unfortunately, others had heard of the Petra as well, for as we were in the process of leaving, Allen Burke walked in. We didn't speak, but as we were going out the door I caught him looking after us solemnly.

My mood did not improve with our arrival back at the hotel. One of the advantages of such a Spartan lifestyle is that there are so few things to watch.

I didn't really notice anything until I was sure that the kids were securely tucked in for the night, but in the few minutes between closing my door on the world and the lights going out I finally saw. The slight ripples in the bed's pristine surface fired my curiosity; after that there were a number of things that shouldn't be there – the almost imperceptible disorder in my lingerie drawer, the tiny crack where the armoire door hadn't been completely shut, the disarray in my toiletries bag. There was only one rather distasteful conclusion.

While we were out my room had been very professionally and very thoroughly searched.

Chapter Six

It was a fake, of course.

The lights had gone out just as I had pulled the Crown from the depths of my purse and unwrapped it, but I am prepared for such emergencies. Digging in the depths of the bag so many despised I found my flashlight and, using it as a candle, examined the Crown thoroughly.

Even I could tell it was a fake, though it was a pretty good one. The Virgin of Janóch was approximately one-half life size, and the Crown had been made to proportion. Dish-shaped with a hole for the head, it would simulate the traditional shape of a halo. Most of it was gold (gold plated? coated brass?), decorated with bas-relief scenes of the martyrdoms of the saints. At least, that was what the magazine articles had said; here they looked more like vaguely anthropomorphic lumps.

Between the lumps were sunbursts, each containing a brilliantly colored jewel. Most of these were cabochons, which attested to the original's great age, but a few were roughly faceted. Even the poor light of my tiny flash brought fire from their depths and for one wild moment I wondered if the Crown – or at least the jewels – could possibly be real.

There were several lines of thought; if the jewels themselves were real, wouldn't it be rather foolish to try and transport them in a duplicate of an artifact that everyone on three continents was seeking? Wouldn't it have been better to ship them as something totally different, like decorations on a vulgar country and western singer's outfit or game pieces or something like that?

The gold itself looked real, except for one spot on the back where the plating hadn't taken and the grayish gleam of base metal shone through. It was the first clue I had that this was a fake.

Though perhaps it was not a fake, not in the criminal sense; in the flush of capitalism which had swept through Middle Europe and brought forth the re-birth of the Virgin of Janóch, could not some enterprising businessman have made copies of the Crown as souvenirs? I thought about it for a while and then discarded the idea. First of all, the idea of a life-sized copy of the Crown would probably be distasteful to those who went in for pilgrimages and shrines and that sort of thing. Secondly, even if it weren't, a copy this good would be much too expensive for just about everybody. Suncatchers and keychains and t-shirts would probably sell like hotcakes; something this large and fine would have a very limited market.

That brought up further possibilities. I shut off the

flashlight and sat crosslegged on the bed, my fingers running over and over the cold metal Crown as if they could divine some information my eyes had missed. Maybe whoever had stolen the real Crown had more buyers than he could accommodate; that would explain a copy – though I couldn't see a real collector being hoodwinked by an obvious copy like this, even excluding where the gold plating hadn't taken. Had this been a trial piece, perhaps stolen by the artisan for a little extra cash?

There were just too many alternatives! I could sit up all night creating scenarios and still not hit the one that accounted for this piece's presence in my possession. Rewrapping it carefully, I turned over and went to sleep. It wasn't my problem.

* * * * *

Morning brought its own problems which – unfortunately – were mine to deal with. Our first round of competition was at eleven. We had been trying to ignore it, but the time had finally come and the effect on my little group was incredible. They were as quiet and subdued as any director could wish, which I found surprisingly unnerving. It was sort of like waiting for a bomb to go off.

"Miss Sabine, I'm so nervous..."

I patted whoever's outstretched hand was on mine. "I know it's scary, but this is why you're here, after all."

Maureen looked up with swimming eyes. "It's so awful... I just can't bear to fail, not here."

Anger bubbled through me. It just wasn't fair to put these kids through this! They were each good performers, but they were nowhere ready to sing in a competition like this. They had no chance of winning, probably not even of making the first round, and the experience of such an unequal competition could scar them for life. Their uniform of plain black trousers, white shirts and black bolo ties with cheap metal Texas-shaped slides practically screamed that they didn't even have real uniforms and were therefore negligible. I could think of a dozen things I wanted to tell the uncaring powers that be who had put this thoughtless plan into motion.

"You will not fail, Maureen! None of you will! Now I doubt if we can take the prize, but not doing that does not mean you fail," I pontificated with heartfelt if ungrammatical fervor. "We will fail only if we don't try!"

That sugary sentiment had come straight off one of those inspirational posters which seem to sprout in public schools. I halfway expected my group to scorn such homely platitudes, but apparently they were so frightened any hint of understanding was welcomed.

The first round of competitions was held simultaneously – small groups in the office area, medium groups in the orchestra room, big groups in the auditorium. First there were the preliminaries, when about a third of the groups would be weeded out; then the semi-finals, which would take care of the rest except for three finalists in each category. These nine (up to eleven, at the discretion of the judges) groups would then compete in the main auditorium before a vast, black-tie crowd. There would be one first for each category; after that was awarded, every group that had entered would stand and join with the Jerusalem Symphony Orchestra and a couple of famous opera singers in a massive rendition of Beethoven's Ninth. Even in the brochure it had sounded deadly. Of course, they had official names for all of the events and categories, but that's what it boiled down to.

All the groups waiting to sing were herded together in the big foyer where the reception had been held. Several hundred nervous, artistic teenagers in one room, however big, created a scene I would rather forget.

"I wish we could get this over with," Tony growled.

I could almost hear each of them wishing that they had practiced more, that they had had more time to prepare. I could almost hear every group in the room thinking it, but somehow my pathetic little band seemed so much more poignant.

Even a real uniform would have helped. Getting Maureen into trousers had required the diplomacy of a world-class negotiator and a sacred oath that her father would never find out she wore them. The saddest thing was that after seeing the other groups' stylish and colorful outfits neither she nor any of the others said a word about the trousers, apparently accepting that no one except the first round judges and a couple of competing groups would ever see her in them. There would be no pictures of the Trans-Texas Canticle society beamed out over the world. I vowed then that if there were anything I could do to help these kids, to keep this group together and make them a real contender for the next year's competition, I would do it.

No matter what the old man said.

"Miss Sabine," growled Larry hesitantly, "I can't sing. My throat hurts."

At least I didn't have to put a bandage on that. He already looked like one of the walking wounded.

"It's just nerves," I said firmly. "Don't you dare get sick on me now."

"No, Miss Sabine."

A loudspeaker crackled to life as it had been doing every few minutes ever since our arrival. "The Trans-Texas Canticle Society, five minutes, please. Five minutes."

The next half hour is not one I like to remember. It comes back in static pieces, like photographs, but photographs prickly with emotion.

The feeling of fear that gripped us at the five minute call, the stark terror that followed as we walked to the room, the shuffling of feet as the kids got into position, the pull of my arms as I lifted them to conduct, the tingling in my throat as I sounded the C natural to open Natalie Sleeth's *God of Great and God of Small*, the first required piece... I don't think I shall ever forget any of it.

The funny thing, though, is that I remember nothing else. I don't remember the kids singing *All Things Bright and Beautiful*. I don't remember us doing Hal Hobson's *The Gift of Love*, our first day elective piece. I don't remember getting out of the room. I don't remember anything until we were back down in the main foyer, surrounded by a horde of nervous teenagers whose agitation was as abrasive as sandpaper.

"How did we do, Miss Sabine? Were we good?" or some variant came from six dry throats.

I pasted a broad smile on my face and reached out to all of them with a giant hug. "You were great!"

It might not have been a fib.

"Ah, so it's all over, is it?"

As out of place as an eagle among sparrows, Grey Hamilton-ffoulkes forced his way through the crowd. The image of eagle startled me, for had I thought about it surely some other softer, more colorful bird would have seemed more suitable. What had made me connect him with a bird of prey?

"Mr. Hamilton-ffoulkes."

He looked abashed. "So formal? I swear I remember you calling me Grey when you refused my invitation to lunch yesterday."

My glares seemed to do no good, so the next best thing seemed to be play it as it laid. I introduced him to each of my kids in a manner of which even Emily Post would have approved. They seemed somewhat overawed by him, which didn't surprise me; I was too. The girls were staring at him in gape-faced wonder and I could almost see the nascent vamp rising out of Carla's pores – *that young woman was born for trouble*, my mother would have said – while the boys... I don't know what the boys felt, but they were quiet and subdued, which is all I could have asked for.

"So," Grey continued, having handled the round of introductions with the aplomb of a born diplomat, "I decided to test my luck again and see if today were any better."

"Lunch? Today?"

"Why not? It's lunch time."

"I'm sorry," I answered with real regret, "but I can't abandon these guys – "

"We can look out for ourselves," growled Tony, always quick to dispute any notions that he was not as grown up and macho as he thought he was.

Grey's gulp was almost imperceptible, and his smile was sunny. "Who says you have to? I'm inviting all of you."

"Grey – I couldn't let you –"

"Oh, Miss Sabine!" rose from six throats.

"You see, my dear Miss Sabine, you're outvoted. Make it official?"

When he was being forthright Grey Hamilton-ffoulkes was very appealing; when he tried to be appealing he was irresistible.

"All right. Thank you."

"Are you done for the day? Do we have any kind of time schedule?"

"No, though we have to do some rehearsal for tomorrow."

"Considering the quality of the competing groups and our performance today, I consider it highly unlikely that we will be requested to participate in the second round. A basic performance..."

"Shut up, Gerald!" came six angry voices. One of them was mine.

"Well, that shouldn't be too hard to arrange, but lunch first, what? A performance group of international caliber needs fuel."

"You don't have to lie to make us feel better," Tony said pugnaciously.

"Yes," added Betty Jean, surprisingly. "You shouldn't patronize us."

Grey looked startled. Obviously he wasn't used to the directness or honesty of American teenagers. Neither, for that matter, was I. At the moment I would have welcomed some soothing support, patronizing or not.

"Patronize! My dear fellows, I meant nothing of the sort! You just must look at the whole thing from an unprejudiced view. You are undoubtedly a performing group. You are obviously of international standards, because you are here, along with a number of other groups from other countries. Are there no performing choirs left in the United States?"

He was reaching, obviously, but the polished diplomacy worked. Those kids must have grown at least an inch each as I watched. They might go no further in the contest, but Grey had helped make them winners more than I ever could. I didn't care if everything Allen had said about him were doubly true; for that kindness to an unlovely band of gangly teenagers I could have forgiven him almost anything.

"Well, now that we're straight on that, let's go to the car, shall we?"

I don't know if he brought the car – a different one from the day before – with the intent of taking us all to lunch or if he were just thinking to impress me (which he did anyway) but it was almost big enough for us and St. Anselm's as well. A stretch Mercedes with British diplomatic plates and little flags fluttering on the fenders, it took up most of the 'No Parking' area in front of the Hall of World Peace, as well as garnishing more than a fair share of stares.

It was almost sinful how much I enjoyed shepherding my gang into this imposing piece of machinery under the mostly incredulous eyes of a number of competition-related people. Including, I am overjoyed to say, an open-mouthed Mr. Avrom Sternberg. I was less pleased to see a sad-faced Allen Burke standing in the shadows of the main entrance.

* * * * *

Despite the specter of Allen's last-minute,

disapproving appearance, the afternoon started out splendidly. Grey disposed all the gang in the back seats of the car, then put me in front, dismissed the driver and crawled behind the wheel himself.

"This isn't quite the afternoon I had planned, but one of the trademarks of the diplomatic corps is adaptability," Grey said with a grin.

"You're really very sweet to put up with all this," I answered, trying to keep my voice down to a small roar. Flush with Grey's flattery, the choir was sounding more like a riot than a musical group.

"It seemed I couldn't get to take you out otherwise," he said. "Besides, modern science is wonderful. Good bye, children," he shouted, pushing a button on the central console. "Don't tear things up!"

From the back of the front seat, just behind our heads, rose a thick pane of glass that effectively cut off the noise from the back. The kids laughed, then smirked, then went back to talking among themselves; at least I suppose so, for it was entirely silent.

"It is not only soundproof, it's bulletproof. One cannot be too careful these days. Especially with teenagers," Grey intoned solemnly, making me laugh.

The motor started with the barest wisp of sound, as if it too were behind bulletproof glass.

"That's better," he said. "Do you know that's the first time I've seen you laugh?"

"I didn't know you were waiting for it. If I had I would have tried to oblige."

"And taken the sport out of the chase? Dear girl, would you spoil my fun?"

"Strange fun," I replied.

There were advantages to traveling in a diplomatic car. The normally hectic Jerusalem traffic simply seemed to part for us and though the pace was horrific, as it always was, those cute little flags – one blue and white Israeli and one Union Jack – on our fenders seemed to act like magic wands. It was just about the least hair-raising ride I had had since coming to Jerusalem.

It never occurred to me that those diplomatic flags could just as easily make us a target.

Chapter Seven

Lunch, as it turned out, was a good forty-five minutes away.

"Jericho? We are actually going to Jericho?"

"Why not? It's less than an hour away and a charming little town. Quite different from Jerusalem, too. Since I have to go there anyway I thought you and the children might like it."

"Don't let them hear you call them children. They'd be highly insulted."

He glanced in the rearview mirror, craning to see into the back. "What do you call them, then? Adolescents?"

"No," I laughed, "at least not in their hearing. Usually I just call them kids."

"Kids?" Grey feigned horror. "Like goats?"

"Don't ask me to explain. It's just one of those untranslatable Americanisms."

"And people think we speak the same language!" He glanced in the rearview mirror again and smiled. "It may not be too far off, though."

Alarmed, I turned around just in time to see what appeared to be Tony trying to strangle Gerald; however, by the time I could get my mouth open to shout Maureen had separated them, so I let it ride. Surely they were intelligent enough to realize that homicide – even of Gerald Fitzgerald Applegate III – was illegal here, too.

At first I felt a flutter of alarm when we zoomed out of the city and then past the suburbs, but Grey's description of the joys awaiting us quickly allayed any nerves I might have. Allen's warning words echoed dimly in my head, to be sure, but I was having such a good time I ignored them. Surely nothing bad could happen in the protection of a charming diplomat in a car belonging to the British Embassy.

Silly me.

The country changed almost as soon as we left Jerusalem. For the first few miles it was rolling, rocky land, sparsely covered with low, dusty-looking plants. Here and there were late-blooming clusters of poppies. Grey said that a few weeks before the whole area had been a carpet of brilliantly red poppies, Spring's yearly display.

Remembering what I could of the history of this disputed land, I thought they looked like gouts of blood.

Then the land changed. From sparsely vegetated rocky land it turned into bare and forbidding rock. The relatively gentle hills became sheer escarpments of barren stone through which the road twisted and wound. I asked Grey to roll down the window so the kids could share his comments about the land, but he refused.

"What? After I've worked this hard to be alone with you for just a few minutes I should allow a scrubby gang of children – excuse me, kids – to interfere?" Then he laughed merrily and, picking up the intercom microphone, gave a very good imitation of a tour bus driver for the last few miles into Jericho. A single glance in the back showed that they seemed to enjoy it as much as he.

The land surrounding Jericho was again different. The rocks gave way to flattish sand which, where irrigated, was startlingly fertile. As soon as we reached the town itself Grey switched off the air conditioning and – over my protests – rolled down all the windows. The hot, desert wind breathed through the car, but it was not as scorching as I had feared. Yes, it was uncomfortably warm, but bearable, and it carried the most delightful scent of flowers, sweeter than any perfume I had ever smelled.

"It's wonderful!"

"Jericho is a garden town in more ways than one. Wait until you see where we are going to have lunch!"

In a weird way, Jericho reminded me somewhat of Mexico. Nice squat houses reposed in the middle of lush gardens which were surrounded by high and uncompromising walls. These blank guardians gave us only the faintest glimpses of the treasures inside through tall filigreed metal gates or more traditional solid wooden ones left open.

For a city in the desert the foliage was lush. Thick vines trailed along the tops of walls. Trees, forty and fifty feet tall, were solid masses of purple or pink or white blooms. Grey didn't know the name of them; neither did I. I always meant to ask, but... well, things intervened. I still remember them, though, and how beautiful they were. It seemed strange that there were no people around to appreciate it. Once we entered the town itself we saw only a few people, most on bicycles or in dilapidated cars.

It was obvious that Grey was a well-known visitor at the little garden restaurant where we finally stopped. It too was surrounded by a high wall, but this wall was scalloped. The top points must have been seven or eight feet high, but the bottom of the wrought iron filigree-filled half moons were less than four feet high, presumably so that the people on the street could glance in and see what a good time people were having inside.

The sizable space inside the wall was mainly under wisteria-covered latticework, creating a surprisingly cool island of shade. In the center there were meticulous beds of crushed stone, each containing one or two carefully tended flowering shrubs. The scent was heavenly.

We were seated at a long table beneath a drooping cloud of wisteria, which from time to time dropped single petals into our plates in the manner of an offering. After a long and involved greeting, which included our being introduced individually to the short, smiling Arab owner. Grey and the proprietor and an incredibly rotund man who must have been the cook had a long and very colloquial discussion in Arabic, finally culminating in smiles all around.

I watched Maureen closely. One of the objections her minister father had had to her coming on the trip was that the Holy Land simply teemed with Arabs, and he obviously regarded the entire race as nothing more than vermin. There were apparently a lot of people who thought like that since 9/11. Maureen was patently terrified of them. She was a brave little thing, though, and in spite of the fact she was pale and stiff as a stick she stood quietly by my side.

"I hope you don't mind, but I ordered for all of us," Grey said with one of his patented smiles. "The best things are freshly prepared, and that depends on what they have in the kitchen."

"What are we having?"

"Lamb," he replied and we both laughed even as the kids groaned.

"Lamb! Again!" pouted Carla in her best soignée manner. I can't tell you what it looked like on a pudgy, carrot-topped teenager. "That's all we've had to eat since we came to this country!"

"Hardly surprising, since this is a desert area." That was Gerald. Of course. "Ecologically speaking, the wholesale raising of beef – such as the scale we practice in the United States – would not only be impractical, it would be suicidal. In terms of pounds of meat obtained proportionate to the area of land available..."

"Shut up, Gerald," growled Tony.

"Have you read the report a cooperative team of British-Israeli ecologists did about two years ago?" Grey asked imperturbably, directing his question to a delighted Gerald.

"Oh, Lord, we've got another one!" Larry moaned and both he and Tony would have stalked away in dramatic dudgeon had not the inevitable *salatas* begun to arrive in an unimaginable variety and supply.

It was a most companionable meal! Not only was the lamb (marinated in spices and lime juice, then kebobbed over open coals) superb, but everything seemed perfect – the rest of the food, the slight breeze, the heady scent of flowers... and Grey. Grey put himself out to be the perfect host. It was easy to see what he was doing in the diplomatic corps; what I couldn't understand was why he wasn't head of one of the major posts.

He managed to talk with each of the kids, really talk with, not at, showing a tact and a real interest that I'm sad to say I had lacked. They responded to him, too, after they were sure he was neither shallow nor patronizing. Of course he and Gerald found instant common intellectual ground, but he was able to discuss ancient music with the normally reticent Betty Jean, baseball versus cricket with Tony, and the practical –

ie, commercial – applications of space travel with Larry. He even managed to discover a passion within Maureen for modern languages, an interest I had never even suspected existed.

It was a humbling experience.

The only one with whom he did not score a complete triumph was Carla, and I suspect that was because he did not respond to her very thinly veiled attempts at flirtation. Not that he laughed at her, though the boys snickered openly at her ploys; Grey kept the conversation on the same forthright, companionable level as with the others, mainly about music. It was the only slightly sour note in an otherwise perfect outing, one so perfect that I hated to be the one who had to break it up.

"Grey, this has been lovely, but you said you had some work to do here today. Shouldn't you be doing it?"

He looked startled. "Aren't you enjoying yourself?"

"I'm having a wonderful time!"

"Then why are you trying to rush things?"

"I don't mean to, but you said you had to be down here today and we need to think about getting back so we can practice."

"I wouldn't worry too much about that, Miss Sabine," Tony said in sulky tones, then Gerald continued, "Given the caliber of groups competing and estimating our performance this morning I would venture to say…" and Carla interrupted, "Say it straight.

We blew it. We've got no chance to get into the semi-finals, so why should we even try?"

"Now wait a minute, gang," I snapped. "We have just as good a chance as any other group in our category and I won't have you throwing it away just because... Because..." By now I was on my feet, gesticulating wildly, and with no idea of what to say next.

Very carefully Grey set upright the flimsy metal chair which I had overturned in my fervor. "One should never give up the battle until the final bugle, chaps. As for my business here, Robin, I only had to ask old Fuad here if he would let the place be used for a film location next week."

You could almost see Carla start to glow. "Do you do location scouting for films?"

"Just one of the many duties of a minor member of Her Majesty's Government. As the bad joke goes, someone has to do it."

"That's what you came all the way out here for?"

He smiled and tried very unsuccessfully to look sheepish. "It was the best way I could think of to take all of you to lunch. Besides, haven't you enjoyed Jericho?"

"Very much, but we've got to get in some practice."

"But I thought we'd take a look at the excavations just outside town and then perhaps run down to the Dead Sea, do a little sightseeing..."

It was so tempting, and looking at Maureen's longing eyes didn't make it any easier, but there was the competition to consider. I was determined that these kids were going to have the best shot at winning – or, more likely, placing – that they could, no matter under what circumstances they had started.

"We need to practice."

"Why not here?" Grey asked, devils of mischief dancing in his dark blue eyes.

"Here?" I was astonished. "But that's impossible."

"Miss Sabine!" Six anguished howls tore at my resolve.

Grey shrugged. "Why? It's a beautiful place, and old Fuad is hardly overrun with customers."

"Okay," I said slowly when I couldn't think of another argument. "Compromise. We run through every number and if you get them all good, we don't have to go back until it's time to dress for the announcement ceremony tonight."

They weren't very happy with that. I could almost see them protesting that they wouldn't make the semi-finals, so why should they go to the ceremony announcing the winners; on the other hand, they seemed to realize that it would be the best they would get. Grey might be persuasive, but officially I was still the boss.

"Okay."

"All right," Grey said, ever obliging, "I'm sure there is a piano to be found..."

"We don't need it," I answered.

"You use just a pitch pipe?"

"In a way."

"Actually, Miss Sabine is one of the rare people who has inborn perfect pitch. I believe the odds of this happening are..."

"Shut up, Gerald."

At my gesture we stood and took our performing positions. I hummed the C natural and hit the downbeat for a rather *bel canto* version of *All Things Bright and Beautiful*, our best piece. One by one we went through every song in our repertoire, including the three alternatives we had barely touched since I had joined the group.

The kids had never sounded better. In fact, they sounded magical. I know part of it had to be that charming patio restaurant with a sky made of wisteria and flowers, but even cynically discounting that, it was wonderful. Just how wonderful I didn't realize until it was over, until the self-contained absorption of making music was broken and we looked around.

In that seemingly deserted town we had attracted an audience. The courtyard contained at least two dozen people, including the entire restaurant staff. Each scallop of the fence framed several eager heads, all looking startlingly disembodied atop the pink plaster. Beyond the fence itself there were other knots of people, all standing in listening silence.

Then they began to applaud! That, of course, was comprised of more than just clapping. They shouted, they laughed, they called to us in joyous Arabic and half a dozen other languages. It had ceased to become a performance and became an event.

It rejuvenated my choir. I looked at their glowing faces and blessed whatever gods there might be for this gift. They might win no awards in the competition, but they had won the people.

I glanced at the kids for confirmation. "Please tell them we'll do two more, then we must go. I don't want to overwork their voices."

Grey's announcement was received with a fresh round of joy, then – as I raised my hands – it was silenced with a positive snakepit of hissing and shushing.

"Let's give them something happy. What about the climax of the Ninth? The Joy?" I asked, then gave them the opening tone.

Beethoven's celebration of joy is a vast piece meant for an enormous choir. With six voices, however good they were, it sounded a little thin. Well, we didn't care and apparently neither did our audience. The sheer exuberance of the piece – and the delight shining in my young charges' faces – more than made up for any musical deficiency.

Then I took a big risk. Admittedly I wanted to give a good show, but I also wanted to see just how far my kids had come towards being a seasoned group. I wanted them to see it, too.

"OK, gang, let's try the Herschel *Lord's Prayer*. I know we've never done it together, but I know you all know it pretty well. Maureen, what's the pitch?"

I knew the pitch as well as she, but I had to do something to calm the sudden spurt of terror filling her eyes. Perhaps part of that fear came from the extemporaneous performance of an unpolished piece, but there was doubtless another reason. Even during our short association her terror of Arabs had been obvious. Part of her father's belief was a morbid conviction that all followers of Islam were the immediate servants of the Devil and recent world headlines had done little to dispel such a notion. I paid no attention to such beliefs myself, nor much to any religion, but it had been impossible not to notice Maureen's intense fear of every Arab who came near. This pleasant afternoon was the first time she had relaxed even the smallest bit. Now I could imagine she was afraid that singing a statement of the Christian faith like a version of the Lord's Prayer to such an audience would bring about at least a demonic attack with pitchforks and lightning bolts.

Well, who knows where religion ends and superstition begins? I would not dream of mocking her faith, but neither did I see anything wrong with broadening her horizons.

As far as performances go, the *Prayer* would have won no competitions; in fact, it might have gotten us disqualified from a few, but our audience liked it, going wild in their applause. The kids acquitted themselves better than I had expected; I think they even surprised themselves.

Grey didn't applaud. He merely sat in his uncomfortable folding metal chair at the head of the table, his arms crossed and a very serious expression on his face, and began to intone in his glorious voice, "'Everyone suddenly burst out singing; And the world was brim with delight; Everyone raised their voices high, To celebrate the glorious light. My heart filled joy to hear the wordless song, May never the singing be done.'"

I jumped as if he had bitten me.

Chapter Eight

Whatdid you say?"

He looked up at me with innocent eyes. "Sorry. Poetry is a very bad, very old habit of mine. Has been since my schooldays. That was a little piece by Lauren. Edgar, that is, not the designer fellow. Are you familiar with it?"

"No." I shook my head briskly. "I don't know anything about poetry."

Diversion came in the form of our host, for he ran forward, grabbed my hands and kissed them with European exuberance, all the while babbling in Arabic.

"He is thanking you for bringing music to his restaurant."

The man was still talking.

"That's all?"

"Oh, he's complimenting you and your family."

"My family!"

"Yes, and all the way back to Java Man from the way he's going at it. Hey, Fuad, old fellow..." Then Grey switched to Arabic and it must have pleased the proprietor, because he kept bowing all the way back to the building.

"What on earth did you tell him?"

"Oh, just that you're in the Hall of World Peace competition and that you'd all come back sometime and sing some more. Come on, if you're determined to leave, we'd better get gone before he asks exactly when."

Our departure from the restaurant turned into something of a circus. The impromptu audience was still applauding as we piled into the limousine – feeling rather like visiting royalty as we did so – and as we drove away several of the parties which had cars nearby simply joined the parade.

For a while it degenerated into pure farce. Grey could not find the correct turnings to the archaeological site of Ancient Jericho, so he finally pulled over to the side and motioned the closest car to pull up alongside. Then they became our guides and the little procession set out.

Grey had seen Maureen's joy at the proposed visit, so he tried to prepare her for the reality. The actual dig had been closed long before, leaving the barren hills that covered the ancient site looking very much like the barren hills which surrounded it for miles.

It didn't make much difference to Maureen. She stood pressed against the wire fence that edged the site and the look in her eyes was too intense for me to watch. When one of the locals – a policeman, Grey said – held the strands of wire apart and motioned for her to go through, you would have thought it had been the gates of Heaven instead of several rusty strands of farm wire. She didn't even seem to notice that he was an Arab.

Exhibiting a tact that I hadn't known they possessed, the rest of the kids let Maureen walk across the field of Ancient Jericho alone, seemingly content to stand back with the rest of us. I imagine that was one of the high points of Maureen's trip, despite all the rest, for it was a different girl who walked back to us from the one who had walked away. Her smile simply glowed and I was very proud of the way she said a special thank you to the local policeman who had held open the wire fence.

Even the sunshine was golden at that moment. Later I tried to hold onto that feeling.

Our entourage accompanied us for quite a way out of Jericho, finally turning back with a great farewell of trumpeting horns and vigorous wavings. Elated with their success, the kids bounced around in the back like demented puppies, so Grey merely raised the glass shield and didn't even try to give them a commentary about the changing terrain.

As Grey described it to me, our journey today was roughly triangular, with Jerusalem sort of in the middle, Jericho above and the Dead Sea below. After we left Jericho we drove through miles of irrigated farm land. Every so often there were people working the lush fields, their kaffiyehs tied up into great knots on top of their heads.

Then, without warning, the land changed. The comforting farms vanished, replaced by a country that grew rougher and more barren every foot. The road, never more than a two-lane strip of blacktop, dropped off over an edge of land so sharp that it might have been defined with a chisel and we began the descent into the huge basin of the Dead Sea.

It was like going down into another world. There were faint evidences of man – the road itself, a resort hotel where tourists went out and smeared themselves all over with the black, sticky mud – but even these seemed small and temporary intruders, momentarily tolerated by the timeless land. The country was red and rough; craggy walls shot straight up from the narrow shore. Pylons of stone, isolated from the wave of the stone cliffs, stood at various intervals along the shore like columns of a vanished temple.

The strangeness intensified when Grey pulled off the road and rolled down all the windows. He had chosen a place where no mark of human intervention was visible except for the faint black scar of the road. I admit even then I had a thrill of apprehension; Allen had warned me about this man. What if he dashed off, abandoning us here in this desolate wasteland?

That was foolish, of course. Grey just wanted us to hear the contrast of pure silence when he turned off the motor. When that almost inaudible mechanical purr ceased, it was as if we suddenly could no longer hear. We might have been transported to before time began.

Even the kids were affected; they were speechless. The silence was deep and almost tangible, not so much quietness as the complete absence of sound. Finally a soft sigh of wind, so faint it would never have been heard under other circumstances, squeaked passed the tortured rocks and reassured us that we had not been magically stricken deaf.

It was hard to believe that we were standing by a large sea. There was the water, of course, spreading out to the faraway mountains, but that almost seemed an optical illusion. There were none of the things that we have come to associate with bodies of water. No algae or flotsam at the shore, just water fingering the rocks. No wheeling birds. No splash of waves or fish. There were only the rough rocks gradually disappearing under the clear water. There was nothing growing within sight. We might have been on the moon.

"It's easy to see why it's always been called the Dead Sea," Grey said at last and even his beautiful voice was almost an obscenity in that pristine stillness.

"It's spooky," said Carla with a theatrical shiver.

"It's like we're on the moon," murmured Tony.

"Hardly. First of all, since the moon has no atmosphere – even assuming we had protective clothing – there could be neither water nor color. The inhospitality of the terrain, however..."

"Shut up, Gerald!"

After that the silence descended again, broken only by the sound of a distant motor. Nothing passed us, however, so I assumed that whoever it was had simply stopped at a deserted spot as we had, the better to savor the desolation.

Gradually the kids drifted down the half-dozen yards to the silent shore and began to wade, Larry stumbling over the hard-edged rocks only once. There was no spurting blood or familiar yelp of pain, so I didn't bother digging in my purse for bandages. Maureen was the last to strip off her shoes, but she waded out the farthest. Once again I thanked Grey for giving the kids – and most especially Maureen – this experience.

"I had been planning to take them on some kind of a tour before we left, but I don't think any of them would have been as special as today."

"The proper thing for me to say would be that it was nothing, but I think that would be insulting to all of us. I really didn't intend on taking all of them out with us, today, you know."

Grey and I were drifting aimlessly along the shore, the tiny rocks of the beach scrunching under our feet.

"Somehow I had come to that conclusion," I said. "You've been so kind, and I appreciate..."

"No, don't. I didn't plan to include them, but as it has turned out, I am the one who has benefited. Sometimes we can become so deadened to that which we see frequently. I am so delighted to re-see all this through the children's eyes. And yours too, of course."

"This is something we'll never forget," I said with

heartfelt gratitude, never dreaming of how true that was going to be.

"What is it you have to get back for tonight?"

"There's a dinner of some kind and a ceremony to announce those groups which got into the semi-finals."

"You don't have to worry about that, surely?"

I shrugged. "I don't know. If the judges had heard them this afternoon, but... I don't know."

"Well, I'm sure it will be all right. What time to you need to be there?"

"Dinner starts at eight, but there's some sort of a press thing at seven. And we'll need at least two hours to get ready. Probably more," I added, remembering the dressing habits of teen-aged girls, a problem exacerbated by having only one bathroom.

"Then we need to leave in a few minutes. They certainly are making a media circus of the competition, aren't they?"

"Yes. I keep trying to tell myself it's for a good cause, but I wonder."

"You don't believe in what the Hall of World Peace stands for?"

"Well, here especially you must agree it's sort of like believing in the tooth fairy. I think it would have been better if they had made the peace first, then built the Hall, not build the Hall in hope it might help."

"You don't believe in lighting candles in the dark?"

"Not if the dark is a thunderstorm. I think positive action is a lot more practical than pretty gestures."

"Well, you certainly do think differently from most of the fuzzy-headed do-gooders running around," he said, a note of respect in his voice. "Now tell me how you would create this peace."

"Don't be provoking," I laughed. "We could argue about that for hours. Really, Grey, it's been wonderful, don't you think we should be starting back? I'd like for the kids to get a little rest before tonight if they can."

"We might as well. After the first few minutes there really isn't much to do down here," he replied with a smile. "I hope the next time I take you out we can find something a bit more exciting to do. And perhaps just the two of us?"

My heart began to thud in sheer anticipation. "I would like that very much."

We turned around and headed back towards the car. The silence on the way back, though easy, was deafening.

Apparently the desolation was affecting my citybred charges, too. With the exception of Maureen, who still stood ankle-deep and entranced in the thick-looking water, they had all gravitated back to the car, much as savages must have once huddled near some familiar totem for reassurance when the expanse of nature became too overwhelming.

"Maureen!" I called, motioning her in. My voice seemed to carry forever. "Time to go!"

"Sometimes," Grey said, leaning on the shiny metal roof, his eyes fixed on the distance, "I think of what it must have been like here in ancient times, when people traveled by foot, making only a couple of miles on a good day, when a man could live and die and never go over ten miles from the place where he was born."

"It must have been very uncomfortable." Surprisingly that was Maureen, who had obediently come back to join us.

"I think it must have been frightening," said Betty Jean with an almost fearful glance around. "It seems so hostile."

"I wonder how they made a living here," Larry asked. "It looks like a wasteland."

"It is. This is sort of the land of the dead, in more ways than one. The pastoral tribes ran their flocks back up on the plateau, where there was grazing. Current theory indicates that based on the estimated population during the Bronze Age..."

"Gerald," Grey said gently, "don't you think some things are better understood with the heart than with statistics?"

Tony snorted as Gerald sank into thoughtful silence. "Thanks, Mr. Hamilton-ffoulkes. Living with him has been like living with a damn walking encyclopedia!"

"Tony!" I cried, inwardly agreeing even as I cringed at the hurt which flashed in Gerald's unlovely eyes. "That was unkind."

Tony shuffled and hum-hawed and looked away. I ached for both of them.

Ever a diplomat, Grey stepped in to cover the breech. "Maureen, I'm sure you know a lot about the various historical theories surrounding this place. There are a number of rock-cut tombs and caves back in those *wadis* that were used for burials and safe storage and, who knows, maybe for rituals." His arm gestured toward the rough and fissured cliffs. "In fact, *Wadi Q'mran* is not too far over there."

Both Maureen and Gerald's eyes shone.

"Where the Dead Sea scrolls were found..." Maureen breathed.

"Could we possibly go explore there?" Gerald asked with more enthusiasm than he had ever shown.

Grey shrugged. "It's dreadfully rough back in there. I'm not sure the area is open to tourists."

Carla gave an exaggerated shiver of distaste. "Why would anyone want to go up there? I'll bet it's all dusty and horrible."

"But you could arrange it," Maureen said gently, her eyes fixed on Grey. "Oh, please, please... would you try?"

"Hey, gang, don't worry Mr. Hamilton-ffoulkes. I think he's done more than enough in giving us this afternoon's treat. Now we've got to think about getting back for the semi-final announcement dinner."

"Why bother?" Tony growled. "They aren't going to choose us."

"You don't know that." Valiantly I grabbed at straws. "Besides, there's going to be a nice party."

They grumbled at that, their idea of a nice party apparently being totally different from mine, but obediently they piled into the car and we started back to Jerusalem.

Purring softly, the car scooted along the road and easily pulled up the occasionally steepish rises to the top of the plateau. Almost as soon as we reached the top signs of life began appearing again. In almost any other situation I doubted if I would have noticed them – tiny, ground-hugging plants; a bird wheeling in the sky; the faraway outlines of a crumbling building. After the desolation below they were almost like reaffirmations that we had returned to the land of the living. Here there were rocks and cliffs on either side of the road, too, but although the terrain was rough and stark by anyone's standards it was a living land instead of dead.

At first I thought a rock had fallen against the windscreen. Even when the car swerved sharply, throwing me against the door and scrambling the kids in the back I didn't understand. What finally made me realize that this was not just some ordinary road hazard was Grey's voice. He was muttering under his breath, his voice very tight and hard, and he was swearing with deliberate and prodigious precision.

"Grey?"

Another impact spidered the windscreen and Grey jerked the car to the other side of the road and then back in a weaving motion.

"Be quiet and cover your face!"

"The kids!"

"It's bulletproof. The glass won't break, but there might be splinters. They'll be all right. And so will we." He spared a brief, tight smile. "Cover your face!"

I took one quick glance in the back. The kids looked terrified and they were hanging on for dear life, but they didn't look hurt. There was nothing I could do, so I scrunched down in the seat and buried my face in my purse just as another bullet hit.

That didn't last long. It was bad enough to have someone taking pot shots at you, but it was infinitely worse not to see. Shielding my face against possible glass splinters, I eased upward.

I wished I hadn't. There were two large trucks ahead, both going fairly slow. Grey kept the gas floorboarded and, as the Mercedes swayed wildly, passed them both. On the outside. Of a curve.

"My God, Grey!"

"We're almost out of range."

Half a mile or so past the lumbering trucks Grey slowed down – though not much – and lowered the window to the back. As it came down a babble of tears and curses and shrill excitement poured through the gap like rushing water.

"Quiet!" I bellowed and the noise stopped as neatly as a shut-off tap. "Is anyone hurt?"

A ripple of shaking heads answered my question. They looked at me with wide, questioning eyes and I felt my stomach contract. These kids were my responsibility; it was my duty to keep them safe. To what sort of danger had I exposed them? For a moment I wondered if I were going to be sick, right then and there.

"Is everything all right back there?" Aside from a slight tightness, Grey's voice sounded normal.

"We've got a few bumps," Tony said. For some reason he sounded very grown up. "But we're all right. What happened?"

Grey didn't take his eyes from the road, for which I was glad. The speedometer was hanging just a little over ninety. Miles, not kilometers.

"I'll be honest with you. I think there was a sniper up in the hills."

"A sniper!" That produced another babble of alarm. I would have stopped it, but Grey grabbed my hand and shook his head slightly. It frustrated me to wait, but maybe he was right; let them work off some of the emotions, then we could talk more coherently. Also, he could watch his driving; he was allowing the car to slow somewhat, but the speedometer was still fluttering over eighty. Still miles.

"Shouldn't we slow down?" I muttered.

"And give them a chance to catch up?" Noticing the flagging speed, Grey lowered his foot again and we roared around a clutch of cars as if they had been standing still. The Mercedes swayed like a small boat in a storm.

"Who do you think it was, Mr. Hamilton-ffoulkes? Terrorists or some individual with a fancied grievance?" Gerald looked positively green, but he sounded the same. Perhaps the intellect does control all.

"No idea. I haven't heard of any unrest in the last few days, at least any more than normal. As soon as I drop you off I'm going directly back to the Embassy to report this incident." Grey cleared his throat. He sounded uncomfortable. "I'm afraid I owe all of you an apology. I just thought we'd have a nice afternoon's excursion. I simply cannot believe anyone would just up and attack a British diplomatic car for no reason at all!"

Neither could I.

Chapter Nine

After the incident on the road, everything else seemed anticlimactic. An apologetic Grey dropped us off at the hotel. As the kids piled out of the back he took my hand.

"I'm sorry, Robin."

"You had nothing to do with it," I said softly. "You saved our lives."

"I don't know what's going on, but I want you and the children to be safe. Would you like me to have a guard assigned to you?"

For a moment the idea sounded wonderful. Then I realized how impossible it would be. I shook my head regretfully. "No, you don't have to do that. But thank you for wanting to."

Grey did not look convinced. "Robin – "

"We'll be all right, Grey." No matter how I felt personally my voice left no room for negotiation.

Grey nodded. "Very well. But stay in touch with me, and be very careful. Do you want me to pick you up for the affair tonight?"

I shook my head. "We'll just take a cab."

Grey nodded again, this time more slowly. "All

right, Robin. Please take care of yourself."

And then he was gone. I had to fight myself to keep from calling him back. But it wouldn't do. It simply wouldn't do.

"Okay, gang." I turned to face their disbelieving stares. "Go up and get some rest. Let's be ready to go in an hour and a half, all right?"

"Miss Sabine..."

"Now!"

Unusually subdued, my group trooped upstairs.

I wasn't so lucky.

"May I have a word with you, Miss Sabine?"

"Of course, Mr. Abramowitz."

He had been waiting for us in front of the hotel and, after speaking to me, turned and walked into the tiny office, apparently sure that I would follow. It was the first time that I had seen any part of this place that was not stark and so pin-neat it was almost sterilized.

Hardly more than a closet off the lobby, the office was dominated and nearly filled by a scarred and ancient wooden desk and a single chair. Everything else was paper. There were stacks of papers on the floor, tied into bundles of varying sizes with string; there were stacks of papers cross-hatched on the desk; a narrow bookshelf jammed against the far wall was full of papers. These were mostly letter-sized sheets of paper as far as I could tell, not newspapers or books or folios. I wondered what on earth they all were.

He looked uncomfortable. "I wanted to talk to you

about tomorrow and the next day, Miss Sabine."

"It's Shabbat, isn't it? I know we aren't supposed to practice here. We'll just go down to the Hall of World Peace. There are some facilities there."

"None of your group is Jewish, I gather."

"No."

He sighed and his expression became almost hostile. "We began this hotel as a haven for those of our faith. If things had not been so pressured..." He rubbed his balding head and regarded me with watery brown eyes. "You are the first non-Orthodox to stay here."

Reaction to the shooting was setting in. I didn't have the time or the temperament to be polite about his waffling. "Mr. Abramowitz, why don't you just say what you want to tell me?"

"Very well. Tomorrow at sundown begins Shabbat. From then until sundown the day after it is a time of worship. My wife and I follow the old ways, which means we are forbidden to do work of any kind."

"If you're trying to say our rooms aren't going to be cleaned, that's fine."

"That is part of it, Miss Sabine, but not all."

I could have strangled him. Maybe that way I could squeeze the words out of him.

"We must ask you and your group to observe silence, Miss Sabine, and if you go out tomorrow to be back before sunset. If you absolutely must go out the next day, please do not return until after sundown."

It took a moment for his effrontery to sift through.

Then I started to get mad. After the strain of the
competition and the fear of the sniper attack this
afternoon I was in no mood to deal with a strict
fundamentalist of any religion.

"Are you telling me you expect us to go by the rules
of Shabbat?"

His face cleared. "Yes, that is right."

"No, that is wrong! This is a hotel, Mr. Abramowitz,
not a church or a temple or whatever. We did not
choose to stay here, we were placed here by the
competition and I would assume that when you made
this hotel available to the competition it must have
crossed your mind that there was a chance the groups
assigned you would not be ultra-Orthodox!"

He was starting to look uncomfortable again, then
mumbled something in a language I didn't understand.
"Miss Sabine..."

"I am still here, Mr. Abramowitz. Now I respect
your right to religion and we have agreed to practice
elsewhere on Shabbat, which I am sure none of the
other contestants have been forced to do, but as this is
a hotel provided by a non-sectarian competition I do
not see any reason we should be expected to observe
your rituals."

I had to stop for breath.

"But how will we manage?" he cried in real
distress. "The doors, the locks..."

I had heard of certain sects of the Jewish faith who
observed their law of not working on Holy Days so

strictly that they would not make fires by turning on lights or opening doors and a bunch of other things that made no sense to most of the rest of the world, but I had never thought I would meet one. How on earth had a world-wide, non-religious competition ever decided to place a group here?

"I think you should have thought of that before you made your hotel available to the competition."

"That's true, that's true... Maybe Feldshuh can help. I will talk to him," he muttered and then just walked off.

Good Heavens, it had been a day!

* * * * *

Neither was it over.

The semi-finals announcement dinner was held with all proper ceremony in the cavernous ballroom of the Hall of World Peace. The group was still subdued from our frightening experience and I was still boiling from my skirmish with Mr. Abramowitz. The kids were, of course, seated on the back fringes of the room; the popular groups, the sure winners, were clustered in the center, directly in front of the speaker's podium. There was status in the directors' tables, too; there were four of them in a straight line in front of the head table. I was at the furthest one, with the directors of all the other groups considered negligible in the competition.

I suppose there is some sort of cosmic law about large banquets, be they in Jerusalem, Buenos Aires or Duluth, since invariably they seem to be cursed with the same tasteless chicken, bland vegetables and tough bread. Maybe I'm being unfair. I was hardly in a mood to notice.

If the dinner were dull, the company was duller and the first speaker positively deadly. Indisputably an American well past the first bloom of middle age, she was poured into a dress not only inappropriate for a youth-oriented music competition, but for almost any legal pursuit in any civilized country. Her dress was paint-tight and her bodice apparently held up by little more than friction.

"Music is a magical thing," she began, tossing her tousled, unnaturally black hair like a cooing starlet.

"Who is that?" I hissed to my closest neighbor, a dour Swede who had said less than half a dozen words during dinner.

"Her name is Dorothy Crowe," came his thickly accented whisper. "A wealthy American. Oil money, I think."

"She underwrote most of this competition," muttered the woman on the other side, a tiny Japanese wearing a distinctive Hanae Mori print. "Which means she thinks she bought it."

"And we must believe in this idea of peace, just as we must believe in the idea of Israel," Mrs. Crowe continued, batting false eyelashes that resembled nothing so much as a pair of dead tarantulas. "That's why I have committed so much – more than most people know – to this competition and to the Hall of

World Peace itself. Those of us who bear the responsibilities – "

She said a lot more, but very few people listened. All the teenagers in the place were squirming like worms and their directors – myself included – were not much better. In fact, they were worse, for the table next to us was getting up a pool on when she would pop out of one side or the other of her dress.

Apparently Maestro Kaminsky thought the same, for he waited until she took a breath, then said, "Thank you, dear Mrs. Crowe."

For a moment I didn't think she would give up the podium, but Kaminsky was not above using his bulk to ease her over.

"He already has her money, so he doesn't have to put up with her foolishness now," said the Japanese lady with an evil grin.

"That is good for us," said the Swede.

The pool at the next table seemed disappointed.

"I think now it is time to let all of these talented young people know the list of semi-final winners," smiled Maestro Kaminsky, handing a scowling Mrs. Crowe over to an aide and bringing forth a short and bespectacled politician with a voice so plumy and delicious it could have been bottled.

"Thank you, my dear Maestro. Now, young people, I want you to realize that just by being at this competition you are all winners..." He went on for several minutes in the same sugary vein until the closest aide – Kaminsky was nowhere to be seen – coughed portentously. Rattling the paper and clearing his throat, the politician began to read. "First of all, we have the Celestial Voices of the Cathedral of Arnulf, director Doctor Eilert Franck…"

There were thirty Celestial Voices, all impeccable in their pressed navy and green uniforms, and they stood as if they had been attached to the same string. They had just finished their second record and were considered just about a shoo-in for Best of Show. That wasn't the correct title, but the way I felt at the moment it fit.

The politician read down the list of names, pointedly pausing each time for a round of applause. A time or two in the beginning there were some awkward pauses, but then the audience realized what was expected of it and each group – requested to stand as their names were called – got its polite spattering of claps.

"The Trans-Texas Canticle Society, director Miss Robin Sabine."

I didn't see my kids stand up. My eyes were too full of tears. The only way I got on my feet was that the dour Swede next to me simply grabbed my elbow and shoved upward. It was like the sentimental ending of a cheap movie – corny, unrealistic and simply wonderful. For a moment or two I was as happy as I had ever been in my entire life.

It didn't last, of course.

We all remained standing until each semi-finalist group had been recognized, then – as we were all taking our seats again in expectation of more speeches – a smiling aide in the competition's official blazer tapped me on the shoulder.

"If you please, Miss Sabine, Maestro Kaminsky would like to speak to you in the foyer."

We had had our moment. I had seen my kids vindicated. Now I was just as happy to miss a bunch of boring speeches. Somehow all after-dinner speakers sounded alike and I wondered if they came from some central supply, like the chicken dinners.

Stanislaus Kaminsky was sweating, even though there was a cool draft blowing through the enormous marble chamber. There were some nervous stutterings, then he blurted, "Miss Sabine, I have some bad news for you. Arvom Sternberg has lodged a formal complaint against your group."

"What?"

"Not only that," he said, swabbing at his damp forehead "but he has requested that you and your singers be expelled from the country, as you entered under false pretenses."

I could not say a word. Oh, I could have, but the words I was thinking at that moment would not only have blistered paint, they would have totally destroyed any shreds of dignity I had left. So would my secondary impulse of slugging him with my purse.

"I'm so sorry, but..."

"You aren't going to pay any attention, are you?"

"We have to pay attention, Miss Sabine. With the reputation of the competition at stake..." He looked as if he were being roasted alive. At the moment I would have gleefully helped with the basting.

"What about my kids? What about how they feel? What does that low-down snake think he's doing?"

"Mr. Sternberg feels that your group is not a true group at all. Admittedly the members have beautiful voices, but we both realize that beautiful voices alone do not make a true choir," he said in an unconscious echo of my own early doubts. It made me furious.

He even tried to smile; the result was ghastly. "Mr. Sternberg has based his protest on the fact that your group's entry in the competition was made after the deadline – in fact, your whole acceptance was rather irregular – and he feels that since you came into the country on a false premise, for the good of the competition you and your charges should be made an example of... and deported first thing tomorrow morning."

"You must be joking!" I all but shouted as soon as I could draw breath again. "Surely you aren't taking any of this seriously!"

"We must think of the good of the competition and what it stands for, Miss Sabine. The Hall of World Peace..."

In cartoons people's faces turn red and steam rises from their ears. I might not have looked like that on the outside, but I sure felt like it on the inside! I didn't know if such high-handed actions were possible, and at the moment I didn't really care. "Might I remind you that your precious Hall of World Peace International Youth Choir Competition Committee accepted and admitted my group in spite of any irregularities in their application, which to my mind negates them. That same committee has just announced to the world that the Trans-Texas Canticle Society is good enough to place among the semi-finalists."

Apparently Kaminsky hadn't heard that, for he went from boiling red to white. "What?"

"Indeed, Mr. Kaminsky. Now how is it going to look if your precious competition announces that we were not entered correctly, even though your committee accepted us and allowed us to compete, and that we are not a real group, but your judges thought us good enough to reach the semi-finals, which means that we are roughly in the top one-third of all the entrants?"

If his color faded much more he'd pass out right there on the floor. "Miss Sabine..."

"Not only that, but we're stuck off in some weird little religious hotel where they don't even want us to talk or even move around on Shabbat, even after we agreed to go practice somewhere else! I don't think anyone else is being forced to live under such restrictive conditions. Now that's going to sound an awful lot like someone has been juggling the circumstances and to me that sounds like a fixed contest."

"Please…" He was almost pleading.

"I meant what I told that worm Sternberg at the reception, Maestro Kaminsky. Unless my kids are treated just like every other group in the competition, with every courtesy and every fairness, I am going to hold the biggest press conference this dratted Hall of World Peace project has ever seen! And then I'm going to start talking to anyone in Washington who will listen. Can you imagine what it will do to your image when I start telling everyone that I have reason to believe this contest is fixed?"

The maestro's mouth opened and closed a time or two before words finally dribbled out. "I will talk to Mr. Sternberg."

"Good. You just do that. Things will be fair, Mr. Kaminsky. And, I want us moved to a regular hotel, one where some of the other groups are staying."

"That may not be possible," he said, but his heart was not in it. "This late date…"

"By twelve noon tomorrow, Mr. Kaminsky. I think it's extremely funny we were stuck way out off Ramala Road in a strictly Orthodox hostel when every other group is staying in European-style hotels not too far from here." That was a shot in the dark, but from the look on his face apparently a correct one. "Yes, I'll be sure to tell everyone that, too. People don't like rigged contests, Mr. Kaminsky. This could taint the Hall of World Peace forever."

He didn't say a word, but the sweat was pouring

from him. Nodding weakly, he slipped away through a door in the paneling, leaving me alone in that great empty hall.

As often happens when great emotion departs, there was a correspondingly great hollowness and I wondered if I might collapse in on myself. Where on earth had all that come from? My friends say that I can always be relied on to be a peacemaker; my enemies have said that I am a wimp. I could not recall ever having raised my voice in anger in a public place, to say nothing of threatening a great musician known the world over.

Good grief, what on earth had I done?

Before the door closed behind the fleeing Kaminsky, while the ghosts of my angry words still shimmered in the air, there was another sound, a slow, measured, vaguely insulting clapping.

"Bravo."

I should have expected it from the absolutely miserable way this evening was going. Still clapping, Allen Burke walked slowly across the vast expanse of marble floor.

"Hello, Allen."

"I should at least say, Hail Boadicea! I never knew you to be such a warrior."

"When there's a good cause. That man had the nerve to tell me..."

He raised a languid hand. "I heard. Actually, I couldn't help but hear. This place is like a sound chamber."

Sudden panic. "Do you think...?"

"No, they didn't hear. Most of the time there was some speaker or another booming through the sound system. That's why I came out here."

"Thank Heavens for that."

"Will you go through with it all? Your threats?"

"Of course. I don't have a choice. It's all too ridiculous, and my kids deserve what they've earned."

He was standing beside me now. I could smell his cologne. It was different than the kind he had worn before, milder, less pungently spicy, and I had a quick, painful stab of emotion wondering if someone had given it to him. Someone female.

"Maybe it would be a good thing if you gave in." One hand lazily stroked back a loose strand of hair. It was the first time we had touched in well over a year, but there was still that spark, that charge, that visceral attraction between us. I could almost feel the point of contact glowing.

I almost had to force myself to speak. "What are you saying? They have no right...!"

"My God, Robin, there are other things than right and wrong."

"Such as?"

"Such as saving your life! Don't you think you're in a little bit of a strange situation? Especially after what happened this afternoon?"

"How do you know about what happened this

afternoon?"

"You didn't really think that in a hot news spot like this someone could start taking pot shots at a British diplomatic limousine without it creating all kinds of news? And when the passengers are an American singing group which seems to be here under somewhat unusual circumstances? I don't know what kind of shady deal you're involved with this time, Robin, but–"

"I'm not!"

"Robin, Robin..." His gentle eyes were clouded with emotion. "Oh, my foolish Robin, you don't think I've forgotten about Lord Mugoran and his safe, do you? Now whatever you're in, get out of it! These are the big leagues and you could get killed."

Why, oh why, of all times and all places, did I have to run into him again here and now?

"Allen, I'm not – "

"Dammitall, Robin, don't you realize? Look, I know there are some bad feelings between us, but I still care about you. You can trust me. Let me help you."

His face was so very close to mine. That face had haunted me constantly for months, still did sometimes, and for one weak moment I might have thrown everything over if he had just taken me in his arms and kissed me the way he used to do. I wished I could have told him everything, except I didn't know the reasons behind this tangle.

In any case, I would still have liked the kiss and his face was so close, his eyes so tender, that it might have happened, except at that exact moment the doors from the ballroom opened and quite literally a thundering herd of teenagers flooded out.

For once the competition officials and choir directors were wise enough not to try and regulate their behavior. I don't know even if they could, because all the kids were emotional about the semi-finals list and over-energetic about having had to sit still for so long. They exploded into the foyer with a shrill but joyous cacophony of languages and laughter that was literally an assault upon the ear and almost upon the body.

Allen was swept away from me at the first wave and I was almost glad. I had come too close to revealing myself, to letting my emotions take over. I got busy locating my gang. They were elated and our mutual congratulations and expressions of joy were just as noisy as all the other groups who had been chosen for the semi-finals.

It took me a moment to realize that Carla was not with the group, but I didn't start to panic until we had made a deliberate search and could find no trace of her.

Chapter Ten

B ut where can she be?" I asked frantically. We had just reconvened in the alcove by the stained glass window of the olive tree. When we finally realized that Carla was not among us, the group had scattered, discreetly – I hoped! – looking to see if she were in the ballroom or at the other end of the lengthy foyer or in the ladies' room or even in the dusty open courtyard in the middle of the building.

She wasn't.

"It would be logical to assume that she has either eluded our search, which was admittedly perfunctory, or she has left the building."

For once no one told Gerald to shut up.

"But why? And where would she go?"

Tony snorted. "You have to ask that with all the men around here?"

"That's unkind, Tony," began Maureen the peacemaker, but she was silenced by Tony's growling, "And you're too nice. Carla is a hot-pants little tramp."

"You shut up!" Larry startled us all by swinging at Tony. He would have connected, too, if Tony hadn't been as quick as a fish. "Or I'll smash your face!"

"Larry!" I snapped. "The question is, what are we going to do?"

Normally I should have called the police, though I doubt they would have paid me much attention this quickly, but right now I didn't want to attract any more notice – official or otherwise – to my beleaguered little band.

"Do any of you know if Carla knows anyone here?"

Five heads shook in the negative.

"But the day we were on the tour with St. Anselm's..."

"Yes, Betty Jean?"

She looked uncomfortable. In fact, Betty Jean always looked uncomfortable. If she had her way, she would simply blend into the wallpaper when she wasn't singing, an attitude I would blame most heartily on her family. From what I had been told they were determinedly ignorant, hostile people from whom Betty Jean had to be rescued by her voice teacher, who now had legal custody. To look at the girl was nothing – muddy blonde hair and a rabbity face – but her figure alone had earned her Carla's instant enmity. Even with half a dozen surgeries pudgy little Carla could never aspire to the calendar-girl figure Nature had so lavishly given Betty Jean Scott.

Betty Jean also had a secret. I didn't think any of the others knew, but I had noticed and ached for her. She hid it well, but poor, plain little Betty Jean was madly in love with Tony Manette.

"When we were on the tour, when she was always disappearing, I think I saw her talking to a man."

"Is that all?" Tony scoffed and she seemed to wither.

"A man? Who?" My stomach sank. I knew Carla was boy-crazy, but I never believed she would actually go so far as to get involved during the competition. She had said again and again just how important her career (she was going to be a world-famous singer and recording artist, of course) was to her. On the other hand, when the hormones started bubbling it was easy to forget something simple like rules or decency or a career.

"I don't know. But I saw her talking to him at least twice."

"Was he someone from the competition? Would you know him again if you saw him?"

"No." Betty Jean shook her head slowly, probably regretting she had opened the whole can of worms. "I just had a quick glimpse or two and they were from the back."

Gerald nodded complacently. "I saw him once, but I know it would be impossible to recognize him again. It was as if they were trying to hide their association and conceal his identity."

"Well, I didn't see her with anyone, and I think it's kind of stinky of you to jump on Carla when she's not here to defend herself." Larry's lanky body was stiff with anger.

"If she were here," said Gerald with a precise pedantry guaranteed to send his social stock plummeting even further down, if possible, "there would be no reason to question."

"Shut up, you...!"

"Larry!"

All we needed to complete our expulsion from the contest and probably the country too was a full-blown fist fight in the foyer of the Hall of World Peace! Luckily Tony was more alert in the matters of physical combat than I, for he stepped immediately in between Larry and the frozen Gerald. He said nothing, made no gesture, but his face was eloquent and in a moment Larry's flaming color began to subside. The whole thing happened in seconds, just enough time for me to pull my shattered control back together.

"Thank you, Tony. Larry, that was not called for. Physical violence is never a solution for anything."

"He didn't have to say those things about Carla."

"Perhaps," a rapidly revivified Gerald sprung back with a devilish gleam in his eye, "I am unaware of my exact words. Could you tell me precisely what it was..."

"Shut up, Gerald!"

"Well, what he implied!" Larry growled, looking away and angrily picking at one of his bandages.

"Larry," Maureen said gently, "I'm sure Carla would appreciate your championship, but it doesn't change the point that she isn't here."

Her sensibility brought rationality back and the

group turned to me with pleading faces. "What are we going to do, Miss Sabine?"

I wished I knew.

Smiling with a fine false courage, I dared not let them see that I was just as fearful and confused as they. "Well, our look around was a little haphazard. Maybe we missed her."

"You're saying we should have another look? She might just have been delayed talking to someone." That was Larry, his very hopefulness painful.

"It won't do any good if she doesn't want to be found." That was Tony, cynical as ever.

"We don't know that." That was I, trying desperately to retain control. "She might just have gotten separated when everyone rushed out of the ballroom. Think how frightened she must be, all lost and alone."

It was weak, but it worked. Once again they separated, sliding casually through the thinning crowds. As I had before, I waited where I was. It was difficult; I personally would rather have been running through the crowds, peeking into every corner and screaming Carla's name until she showed up.

On the other hand, that would have been rather attention getting to say nothing of silly; it would only have complicated things if all of us got lost and had no definite base. So, like it or not, I was the base, meaning I had to stay in one place, pretending like everything was normal, and allow the kids to bring her back.

Only they didn't. One by one they dribbled back and as each returned their faces fell more and more. Visions of where and how Carla might be tore at me. Oh, Lord, had I made the insufferable mistake of pride in not calling the police immediately?

The foyer was clearing out; fully half the groups had left and it looked like the rest were preparing to go almost immediately. That meant I had to make my mind up right now... Call the police this minute and risk our expulsion from the competition and probably the country or wait and depend on luck and Carla's good sense, which meant that there was no real decision at all.

"That's it, then. Where's that security man? We've got to call the police."

"That's a bit drastic, isn't it?" Grey's voice came from a surprising distance away.

I didn't realize my voice had carried so far, then none of it mattered, because clinging to his arm was a blatantly unrepentant Carla.

"Where have you been?" I snapped, relief making me harsh.

"Looking for you. Where did you all go? I've been so frightened!" she said in a remarkably level voice. She didn't turn loose of Grey's arm.

"I found her out on the front walk looking very lost indeed," Grey said easily. "Told her I'd stay with her until she found you again."

"I must admit I find it strange that the rest of us

managed not only to get here together, but to re-convene at least twice after looking all over the building for you."

Carla frowned a little at that, glaring at Gerald's seraphic face. "Oh, shut up, you little toad!"

"Now that you are safely restored to your family again, my dear, allow me a few words with your leader." Dexterously Grey removed his arm from her grip, then reached out to me, leaving Carla to the tender mercies of her peers. We walked just far enough away that we could speak without their hearing but near enough to keep them under close visual surveillance.

"Grey, I can't thank you enough!" I said with heartfelt gratitude. "I didn't know you were even coming tonight."

"I hadn't planned to. Robin, what are you thinking of letting that girl go about by herself?"

"I didn't! She simply just wasn't there! We've been looking for her ever since the banquet let out."

He nodded in thought. "I thought so."

"What did she tell you?"

"I'll tell you later. Nothing important. Right now I want to talk to you about that sniper incident today."

"You've caught whoever it was?"

"No, worse luck. We don't even really know who's responsible, and that's suspicious. Usually whenever there's that sort of incident there's some megalomaniac claiming credit for it. That's as much why they do it as a political statement."

I started to feel very cold. "So you have no idea who it was?"

"None. Now I've been able to keep a complete news lock on the incident so far, but it's not going to last much longer. The boys in the garage were all babbling about the bullet holes."

"I'm afraid the news is out. Someone mentioned it here tonight."

His face grew even more grim. "Already? That tears it."

"What must we do?"

"I'm afraid the press boys will be on the scent almost immediately. I'll take care of the official statement, but they'll probably make your life miserable. Yours and the children's."

"Oh, great! That's all it takes to make the day perfect," I exclaimed bitterly. One more unpleasantness to deal with. I didn't think I could do it. I wanted someone – anyone, though Grey would have been nice – to put their arms around me and tell me everything would be all right.

"Robin, what's the matter? You look ghastly."

"Well, I've earned the right! I've fought with our landlord, who wants us to keep the rules of Shabbat, and been told by the great Kaminsky that we're not only being thrown out of the contest but out of the country!"

"What? I thought you made the semi-finals?"

"We did. But according to Kaminsky, who is having his strings pulled by Avrom Sternberg, by the way, we

are not a real group and there were some irregularities
in our application, but in spite of our being accepted by
the committee we are in the country illegally and
should be deported! Tomorrow morning, no less!"

"Good God."

I shifted my purse from one shoulder to the other.
Maybe I was getting old; it felt heavy and was starting
to make deep dents in my flesh. "And if we don't get
started home right now, we're going to be locked out of
our hotel. Assuming they haven't thrown us out
already."

"My car is outside. It'll be a squeeze, but we'll be
able to make it without too much trouble."

"Do you make a habit of playing white knight, Mr.
Hamilton-ffoulkes?"

"Not until lately," he replied with a quicksilver grin
that faded almost instantly. "I have never met anyone
who needed it so much."

* * * * *

It was, I realized with a sinking heart, almost
fourteen minutes after ten when we pulled up in front
of the dark hotel. Even though Grey had driven like a
madman, the fiendish Jerusalem traffic had stopped us
at almost every corner until we got almost to the hotel,
when it evaporated completely, leaving us in a quiet,
deserted neighborhood.

Here even the night seemed ugly. Any moonlight
there might have been was displaced by the bright pink
streetlights that took the color from everything and

gave no beauty in return. All the buildings were shuttered, closed in upon themselves, with no hint of light or life about them.

"We're going to be locked out," someone muttered and then someone else replied, "Yeah, all because Carla had to have her evening's flirt!"

"Quiet!" I snapped. "We won't have any of that."

They had spoken in hoarse whispers, disguising their voices effectively. I could guess who had said what and administered appropriate punishment, but it wouldn't have done any good and, besides, I felt pretty much the same way.

"Well, we'll just have to knock them up and have them let you in."

It was what had to be done – if it could be done – but I wasn't looking forward to it. Neither were the kids; we hung behind Grey as he strode up to the closed doors of metal filigree and wood and pounded on them with casual elegance.

I don't know quite what I had expected, perhaps a nasty confrontation, or a threat to call the police, or even boiling oil poured from the second floor, but it just proved that you can't ever second-guess a situation. The doors opened so quickly from Grey's first knock that it would seem they had been attached to the same string.

"Ah," said Mr. Feldshuh, "you are back, Miss Sabine. We had begun to worry."

The words were nice to hear, though the darkened

house and locked door – not to mention the oft-repeated house rules about closing time – seemed to make this a strange turnaround. On the other hand, perhaps I was becoming so accustomed to seeing potential obstacles in every little thing that I was becoming Don Quixote, not only letting fly at windmills, but inventing my own windmills.

"I know about the house rules and we are late, but the banquet and the speeches went a little long. I'm sorry."

A thin hand waved the problem away. "Not to worry. One must make allowances. But, if you would be very quiet going upstairs? The Abramowitzes are asleep."

One by one the kids filed past him and all but floated up the stairs on tiptoe. I think they had been so afraid of a dreadful scene that they would have crawled on their hands and knees to escape to their rooms.

I may not always behave like it, but I did have a good upbringing and company manners are really nothing but stylized ways of getting through difficult situations. Very properly I introduced Grey and Mr. Feldshuh, then – seeing Grey regarding him very closely – explained that he was our hostess' brother.

Apparently Mr. Feldshuh could accept the impropriety of a slightly late arrival, but there was no way he was going to foster the immorality of a private farewell. I said a proper good-bye-and-thank-you to Grey, gave him a remote handshake and then started creeping up the stairs as Feldshuh locked the door after him. He might be permissive in the face of an outsider, a diplomat, another man, but I was in no mood to linger in case he might fancy a private argument.

Even the electricity had been left on for us. That was a bad break for someone (*who?*) for as soon as I stepped into my room it was obvious that it had been searched again, this time more carelessly than before. Nothing was missing and nothing had been harmed, but it just gave me an incredibly creepy feeling to know that someone whom I didn't know had been handling my clothes and digging through my cosmetics.

I had had enough! Throwing my purse on the bed I dug out the packages that had made it so heavy. In traditional Middle-Eastern shops it is the custom for the shopkeeper to give the customer a small gift; I'm sure that even in these tourist-haunted days there are some who still practice that lovely custom. I am just as sure that my Arab shopkeeper was not among them. Before I had hardly glanced at the newspaper-wrapped gift he had pressed on me and thought it nothing more than a rather tasteless joke.

Now I examined it more carefully and it wasn't funny at all. The blue steel gleamed under a thin coating of protective oil. It was large, noisy and very deadly. I know about guns, as every sensible person should, and thanks to my father and brother I can handle them with a fair amount of skill. That doesn't mean I particularly like them.

On the other hand, the fact that I didn't like them didn't mean I was going to leave it lying around my room for just anyone to come in and find. Re-wrapping it in newspaper, I stuffed it back into the security compartment in the bottom of my purse.

Apparently according to the law of Abramowitz we had had enough time to get into bed, for the lights maniacally chose that minute to go out. I scrabbled for my flashlight and went on with what I had to do.

There had been some good moments, but on the whole today had been one of the worst days of my life. I had been shot at, yelled at, lost one of my kids, threatened with professional disgrace, deportation and unwanted publicity, and had my private belongings searched for at least the second time.

Grimly I unwrapped the Crown again and stared fixedly. It glittered magnificently in the light of my flash. Fake it might be, but it was still beautiful.

Why would anyone go to such extreme lengths over such an obvious fake?

Chapter Eleven

I f I had thought getting up early would save me a confrontation with our landlords, I was wrong. We were not tiptoeing down the stairs, no matter what anyone might think, we were just trying to be quiet, but as soon as my feet touched the marble flooring of the hall Feldshuh popped out of the tiny office like a jack-in-the-box.

"Good morning, Miss Sabine. I hope you slept well."

"Fine, thank you, Mr. Feldshuh."

"If you please, Miss Sabine, may I have a word with you?"

To be honest, a word with him was just about the last thing which would have pleased me. Still, it had to be done and I was tired of running away.

"If it won't take too long. We're on our way down to the Hall of World Peace."

"Queen Shabbat does not come until sundown," he said in perfect misunderstanding.

"And we have a great deal to do before then. Kids, go out and get a taxi. I'll be out in just a minute. And don't let Carla out of your sight!"

It made me feel better, but my words sent Carla into a snit. She had almost been to the door, then she turned and stomped back, her feet sounding like a fusillade on the marble.

"I am not a child, Miss Sabine," she snapped, shoving her face just inches from mine.

"After last night I don't intend to take any more chances, Carla. It isn't fair to the rest of the group."

"So now you're going to watch me like... like I was some sort of baby?"

"Until you demonstrate that you are responsible enough not to need it. I hope you can recognize that whatever you do affects everyone and the others don't deserve to suffer for your whims. If you behave, things will be nice for everyone."

"I'm not a child!" she repeated. She didn't quite stamp her foot, but doubtless she wanted to.

"Then don't act like one. Go with the others and get us a taxi. And nothing else!"

Mr. Feldshuh had the delicacy to wait until she had slammed out the door before he coughed delicately to draw my attention back to him, then gracefully gestured toward the tiny office. I didn't really like that place – it set every claustrophobic nerve I had quivering in hideous anticipation.

"Can't we talk here? I want to keep an eye on the kids..." I moved toward the door. They were at the taxi stand across the street. Carla was still with them and Larry was hovering over her like some sort of gawky shadow. So far so good.

"If you wish. I wanted to talk to you about the unfortunate misunderstanding you had with my brother-in-law yesterday."

"Misunderstanding?"

"About your having to keep the rules of Shabbat. Of course this is a hotel and as guests you should not be required to follow our faith. It would devastate us to lose you and those charming adolescents." He actually managed to say that with a straight face. "It is just that my sister and her husband are so devoted to their religion they tend to be a little idealistic…"

"Their religion? Surely yours too?"

He looked startled. "Yes, of course, mine too. I am just a little more worldly than they. As much as we would all like to keep the Laws to the letter we must live in the world as it is. You understand."

"Of course."

His reasoning sounded good, but I had difficulty swallowing it. Making ends meet in a small specialty hotel like this must be difficult. Seven customers for almost a week was a fair amount of income they wouldn't want to lose. I couldn't quite accept that, though. Surely it was Abramowitz who owned the place, so his rule should be law. Why had he accepted non-Orthodox guests from the competition in the first place?

And there was the small matter of my room having been searched at least twice. Could they *(who?)* have been looking for non-kosher food? One of the other directors at the pre-competition luncheon had said that had happened to her on a previous visit, and she had been staying at one of the major European-style hotels. On the other hand, neither of the kids' rooms had been bothered; I had been careful to find that out first thing this morning – but subtly, very subtly.

Should I bring that up? No, we'd be gone this afternoon – one way or another – and I didn't want to cause any more commotion than absolutely necessary. Whoever had searched my room had not found anything – because there was nothing untoward there, non-kosher or otherwise. Under normal circumstances, whatever they were, I would have been squawking like a banshee. With the possibility of my group being thrown out of the competition and the country and who knew what else, I had other priorities. Everything else simply would have to wait its turn.

"Taxi's ready, Miss Sabine," Tony called through the door.

"I'm coming. Good-bye, Mr. Feldshuh."

"I hope your day is pleasant, Miss Sabine. I will be here when you return tonight." He even gave a courtly little bow.

I all but ran out of the hotel.

* * * * *

Two pairs of eyes, one steely with ill-suppressed anger, the other uncomfortable, looked straight at me.

I stared right back.

"We have been considering your case, Miss Sabine." That was Maestro Kaminsky. His voice was soft.

"It is blackmail, pure and simple!" The words popped out of Sternberg's rigid lips like little puffs of dark smoke.

We were seated in the luxurious office temporarily assigned to the competition. I had left the kids under the supervision of a contest official; ostensibly they were vocalizing, but I could tell they were resentful at being 'sat with' like little children. I couldn't really blame them, but at this moment I couldn't afford one more worry. Or incident.

"Please, Mr. Sternberg, Miss Sabine does have a valid case. In fact, after looking over things the committee and I find no reason to uphold your accusations." Kaminsky looked relieved once his verdict was out.

Sternberg didn't. In fact, he looked almost apoplectic. "But this is an outrage! An insult to music and to the honor of the rest of the competition. If you let this happen the reputation of the competition will forever be smirched!"

"I am curious about something, Mr. Sternberg."

"You are curious?" he roared, looking at me as if I were some kind of big, ugly bug.

"It is common knowledge among the directors that at the beginning of most competitions you throw a fit like this – "

"A fit!" he spluttered, looking as if one were imminent.

I ignored him. " – but you usually just rant and rave and it eventually dies down. This is the first time you have persevered to the point of making charges. One can't help but wonder why. Are you really so afraid that my group will take the title away from yours?"

Even Kaminsky spluttered at that outrageous idea, while Sternberg looked as if he were going to explode. It took almost a full half minute before he could regain enough breath for coherent speech.

"My group? Your pathetic ragamuffins a threat to my group? That is – " Then he switched to German, a language of which I am not particularly fond even when it is not being spat at me like machine-gun bullets. He babbled in that for a moment, probably beyond caring that I didn't understand a word he was saying, before stamping out the door and slamming it behind him so hard that the pictures rattled against the walls.

There was silence for a moment, then a tiny sound trickled into the void. It took a moment to realize that it was Kaminsky chuckling.

"You have my congratulations, Miss Sabine. That is the first time I have ever seen Avrom Sternberg completely lose his temper."

"But it is still a good question. Why my group?"

"I don't know. But you have nothing to worry about. The committee has certified your accreditation most definitely." He smiled benignly, as if it had all been his idea from the very beginning.

"I never had a doubt they would. Now, about our hotel…"

The sunny face clouded. "That is another question, Miss Sabine, and unfortunately one we cannot solve so quickly. There simply is no more space."

"Surely in a town this size…"

"The competition is on a budget, and unfortunately most accommodations here are quite costly. It is a fact that your late entry caused a problem regarding rooms. We did the best we could."

My stomach started to plummet. Just the idea that we couldn't get out of that place made me not even want to go back to pick up our stuff. "Then there's no chance?"

He shook his head mournfully. "I am most sorry. I have made note of your complaint, though, and you can rest assured that place will never be used again."

Fat lot of good that did us!

"Thank you," I said graciously. Stanislaus Kaminsky was of the old European aristocracy. I didn't think he'd understand if I told him there was more than one way to skin a cat!

* * * * *

I should have known things were going too smoothly when I stepped out of the elevator coming down from the rarified atmosphere of higher management to the mezzanine. Towards the left was the corridor leading to the meeting rooms commandeered as rehearsal halls while towards the right was the magnificent sweeping staircase which lead to the foyer on the ground floor, ending in front of the main doors. Between me and both of them was a gaggle of reporters.

Now I am of the television generation and have watched reporters interview current newsworthies for years. I had never before noticed how much they look like a pack of carnivorous beasts, circling, watching, waiting for a weakness.

"Miss Sabine!"

"Would you give a few words...?"

"What were your impressions...?"

"Were any of the young people injured?"

"What do you think...?"

"Do you blame...?"

"Do you think...?"

"Who do you feel is responsible...?"

All at once.

There were microphones shoved at my face like strange misshapen flowers, strobes flashed and, had the elevator not closed behind me, I would have jumped back into it without the slightest bit of compunction.

"I have nothing to say."

There was a derisive groan at that and one reporter, a predatory-looking female with a shrill voice, leaned close to my face.

"Is there a personal relationship between you and

Greystoke Hamilton-ffoulkes?"

Oh, Lord!

"No. We are simply acquaintances."

Another reporter, male this time with a foxy face, shoved forward until he was almost standing on my toes. "Do you have any idea about who is responsible for the attack on you yesterday?"

"I take it you have all spoken to the British Embassy?" I asked and then pointedly waited until most of them had nodded. "Then you know just as much if not more than I. Please let me pass."

There were more groans at that, of course, but they didn't move. Another voice called out, "When do we get to talk to the choir?"

My plate-glass face did me in again, for my anger blazed so clearly that the predatory female and the foxy faced man both took an involuntarily step back.

"I absolutely forbid any of you to speak to my choir members!"

They detected a new scent. The alertness ran through the group like a stiff breeze.

"What are you hiding, Miss Sabine?"

"Why don't you want us to talk to them?"

Physical violence never solved anything. I tried very hard to remember that.

"I am not hiding anything," I said in a hard voice pitched to carry to the entire crowd. "Neither the group nor I know anything to hide, but what I do know is that I have six artistic, nervous teenagers who are competing for just about the biggest thing in their lives and I will not have them upset or the experience ruined for them simply because they happened to be in the wrong place at the wrong time!"

"But what can it hurt...?" began one while another bleated the old refrain, "The people have a right to know..."

"No! While we are here I stand in place of their parents and speaking as their guardian I am telling you to leave them alone or suffer the consequences!" I snapped. I didn't even know if there were consequences for creatures like them, but it sounded good.

It was the wrong tack to take. Maybe a conciliatory, pleading tone would have been better, but I don't do conciliatory or pleading well. I was too angry with those nosy vampires and now it was too late to go back. I wanted to keep things quiet and look what had happened! Sternberg would be transported with joy and might even renew his complaints.

Well, whatever happened I would keep these bloodsucking newshounds away from the kids for as long as I possibly could and hopefully the scent of some other event would draw them off from us.

I threw caution to the winds and plunged against their solid line. It broke and almost immediately reformed in my wake as I swept over to the stairs.

Every woman who has ever seen a romantic movie has probably wanted at some time or another to sweep down a majestically curving stairway. I had, and I did, so I did it, but it wasn't very much fun surrounded by a clump of reporters every bit as harrying and annoying as a cloud of mosquitoes.

Neither did I have any idea of what to do once I reached the ground floor. My main impulse had been to lead the reporters in the totally opposite direction from the kids up in the rehearsal rooms and I had done that, but what did I do with them now?

Grand stages demand grand gestures, an old voice teacher of mine had once said. I don't quite think this was what she had in mind, but it was as good as anything else.

I swept to the main door and held it open as if it were the front door of my residence, thanked them very kindly for coming and wished them a better news story with their next assignment. I apologized most sincerely that security was not there to open the doors for them, but that a guard could be summoned momentarily.

They understood. They didn't like it, but they went away, only after throwing a few more questions – these more insinuating and vulgar than the ones before – against the stone wall of my anger. I didn't even respond.

Wearily I closed the door after the last one and leaned against it. Dear Heaven, what next?

"Miss Sabine?"

I looked up into the expressionless face of Stanislaus Kaminsky. Oh boy.

"Were those reporters?"

"Yes, Maestro Kaminsky. I suppose I should have told you before, but..."

He waved a hand airily in the same gesture that could bring a hundred violins throbbing to life. "Of course you should have, but I realize that your first concern is your group, which is as it should be."

"You know," I said in sudden comprehension. "How?"

"I am a very old friend of the British Ambassador. When any of my people are involved in anything he would of course notify me. He called me last night, at home."

"And you're letting us stay in the competition?"

"Naturally. In fact, the committee and I got together this morning and prepared a little statement to give the press later this afternoon. When I was notified that there were reporters in the building looking for you, I came down immediately. I hope they did not bother you too much, but I must say you handled them magnificently. It was just what I would have done."

I opened my mouth, then closed it again. There were no words. I don't believe in Santa Claus, the Easter Bunny or the Tooth Fairy. At least, I hadn't until now. I was always open to a revision of opinion.

"I don't know what to say, Maestro. I didn't expect..."

He smiled benignly. He really was a handsome old man! "Think nothing of it, Miss Sabine. If nothing else, the way you handled Avrom Sternberg this morning was worth it. Oh, and if you see that young devil Grey Hamilton-ffoulkes around, tell him I approve." Smiling until his twinkling blue eyes almost disappeared into a cluster of soft wrinkles, he nodded and walked away.

Luckily there were lots of benches in the foyer. They're all made of marble – what else? – and not at all comfortable, but at the moment I didn't care. I had to sit down and think this out. There were a lot of things niggling at me and Maestro Stanislaus Kaminsky's sudden metamorphosis into a benign grandfather was just about the least of them.

My sodden brain had finally clicked into action. Allen had told me last night that it was all over town that we had been sniped at, yet Grey had said he had put a news lock on it. The fact that the reporters hadn't found us until now either meant that they weren't very good at their jobs – which I found difficult to believe – or that Grey had kept his word. What was curious was that there had been a fair sampling of the newsgathering media there, but not a sign of Allen Burke. Had he been sent somewhere else? Had he not wanted to see me again? And, most importantly of all, how had he known about the incident last night? Of course, he always had his own ways of doing things, but why hadn't he pumped me for information last night? I couldn't see Allen paying the slightest attention to Grey's news lock.

"Robin?"

I jumped.

"Where were you? Are you all right?"

"I'm fine, Grey. I'm just thinking." I wasn't even surprised to see him. My thoughts had conjured him up, that was all. I needed his help, so he just appeared. Apparently Santa Claus was still on the job.

Grey settled on the bench beside me and if I had not been quite so absorbed I would have noticed his frown immediately. When I did, it was mainly to notice how much his frown changed him. He looked older, grimmer, more dangerous.

He looked like a wholly different person.

"What's the matter?"

"Have you talked to Kaminsky this morning?"

"Yes. Twice. He told me to tell you he approved."

"What on earth did he mean by that?" Grey asked, momentarily startled. "Oh, well, I'll ask him myself. Did you talk to him about changing your lodgings?"

I nodded morosely. "No hope. We're stuck there."

"Well, that certainly won't do. We've got to get you out of there."

"Why?" Something in his voice touched me and despite the midday heat that leached through the walls and windows I felt a chill.

"When you introduced me to that man..."

"Mr. Feldshuh?"

"Yes. I knew I had seen him somewhere before. I can't remember exactly where, but I do know it wasn't something pleasant and his name wasn't Feldshuh."

"Grey, you're frightening me."

He scrubbed at his eyes, then yawned. "I'm sorry. I didn't get much sleep last night, so I overslept this morning, and that's why I'm so late in getting here. Robin, I've got all our resources looking to identify who that man is, but we know for sure that he isn't Mrs. Abramowitz's brother. Both she and her husband are doing a lot of research into those lost during the Holocaust, mainly because they both lost all their family in the camps. But, the really interesting thing is that Mrs. Abramowitz was an only child. She never had a brother."

Chapter Twelve

What?"

"The man's a fake, Robin. I don't know what he's doing there, but I'll wager it's nothing good. I just wish I could remember where I've seen him before."

Another complication, but it could be turned to my advantage. I had planned on asking Grey's help anyway; now I could be pretty sure of getting it.

"What do you think it means?"

"I don't know, but I'm sure Stanley doesn't know about it."

"Stanley? Oh – Maestro Kaminsky. Is he an old friend of yours?"

"More of the family. I'd better go talk to him. He simply must get you out of that place."

"That would be wonderful. Grey, why are you being so nice to us?"

He looked a bit startled. "Let's just say I root for the underdog."

"Thanks!"

"That, plus you seem to need it at the moment. After all, isn't that what we embassy types are for, to help innocents abroad?"

"But we aren't British."

"Chalk it up to international good will, then. Anyway, I'd best go talk to Stanley before he gets away. See you later?"

"We'll be in the rehearsal rooms."

"That's right. When is the next competition?"

"Tomorrow. Today there are supposed to be tours and banquets and that sort of thing. And theoretically time to rehearse Lots of PR opportunities," I added bitterly. It certainly wasn't the way I would have run a competition. The kids should compete while they were up, while they were on edge, instead of being made to wait an entire day.

Speaking of the kids, they had been left alone long enough; I had all the confidence in the world in the competition official with whom I had left them, but I was getting very nervous unless they were right under my eyes. Dear Heaven, was this what being a parent was like? How did anyone bear it? I stood, hiking my purse strap over my shoulder.

Grey stood as I did. "Are you surgically attached to that thing?"

"Just about. The kids call it my life-support system."

"It looks more like a fitness course."

We stepped into the elevator, which was just off the hallway behind the door in the paneling through which Kaminsky had disappeared the night before. I got off at the mezzanine, while he continued up to the top floor. He had offered to walk me to the rehearsal room, but I had declined, saying his time would be better spent with Kaminsky.

When the hands reached out from the deserted office and jerked me inside I wished I could have changed my mind.

"Don't scream! I'm not going to hurt you."

Useless advice, since my entire midsection was paralyzed by his crushing grip. I was going to have to concentrate just on breathing for a moment.

"Allen!" I finally hissed when I had enough breath. "What in the name of...?"

"Don't get upset. I had to talk to you."

"Did you ever consider just walking up and saying hello? You've done it before." With deliberate motions I disentangled myself from his embrace and stepped back, leaving an arm's length of space between us.

"I've tried. You've had all those kids with you or that damned Englishman's been around or he's had some of his goons watching you. I had to get you alone."

The overhead lights in the office were on, pale fluorescent ones that turned everything slightly greenish, but it was bright enough to see him clearly. His features were tense, the eyes hard, the jaw tight.

"Allen, what are you talking about?"

"You don't even know, do you? Robin, there's something very wrong going on here. I'm afraid you're in some sort of trouble. Danger. I want to tell you whatever you're doing, stop it!"

"You're off on that kick again – " I began in anger, but he interrupted me."

"It doesn't make any difference. I don't care what you're doing, but if you aren't careful, you're going to get yourself killed."

Long banked anger spoke for me. "And how does that concern you? As I recall, you once said I could go to the devil for all you cared."

"Yes," he replied softly, sadly. "I said that. I even tried to believe it. But even if I don't approve of what you're doing – "

"I'm not doing anything!" I snapped.

" – that doesn't mean I still don't worry about you." He spat the words back at me and seemed embarrassed for saying them. "Don't you see what's happening?"

"No, but there's something I'd like to know. You knew about that sniper incident last night, but Grey said he'd put a news lock on it until today. How did you find out?"

"Well, there are a few things left in this town that Greystoke Hamilton-ffoulkes doesn't control yet. I have some contacts."

"You make him sound like some sort of villain."

"How do you know he isn't?"

The question was like a slap in my face. "How...? He's been nothing but helpful to me."

"Oh God, Robin, open your eyes and *see*, will you?

What better way to gain your confidence than to play the rescuing white knight?"

His unconscious use of my very words struck home. In an unconscious echo of our old closeness he seemed to pick up on my hesitation and pressed on.

"Look, what better way for him to get into your confidence than to be a helpful friend? How many times has he come to the rescue? And how does he always manage to be there at the right time?"

I didn't answer, but I did think. I had wondered why Grey was being so helpful. It was horrible to consider, but Allen was starting to make sense.

"But why? What earthly motive could he have?"

"What are you involved in, Robin? What are you doing here?"

I shook impotent fists at the Heavens. "I am not involved in anything! I am here to conduct a small choir in the Hall of World Peace competition and do a little shopping! That's all."

"Okay, okay, maybe that's true. But what if he doesn't know it? What if he does think you're involved in something?"

"In what?"

He looked flustered. He always looked particularly adorable when he was flustered. His glasses slid further and further down his nose as he ran his fingers through his hair until it stood on end. Even now, even in the middle of this, I had to restrain myself from reaching out and smoothing down those tousled locks. It was hard not to; this man had haunted my dreams for over a year.

"Robin..." he said with gentle sadness. "I was there, remember? I saw you working on Lord Mugoran's safe! I'm a newsman. I know what was being said about him and I know what happened after, even though they tried to hush it up."

"That's the silliest thing you've ever thought," I said with desperation. "It wasn't like that at all. If we just could have talked. If you just would have believed me."

He must have sensed the swampy emotional ground ahead, for he looked away and changed the subject. "Robin, even if we take it that you aren't involved in anything, it doesn't make any difference, because if he thinks you are you're still in danger."

"But why?"

"I don't know, but you must admit the circumstances are damned queer!"

"In what way?"

The look he gave me was brimming with exasperation, as if I were being deliberately obtuse. "All right, we'll take it line by line. First of all, you're late in registering for this contest."

"That was all done before I was even hired. I'm a replacement, remember?"

"Which makes it all the more unusual, don't you think?"

"I guess you think choir directors never get sick or have accidents like normal people, don't you? Things happen, Allen."

He sighed and went on as if I hadn't spoken. "Second, your group, which was touted as not having a snowball's chance in Hell, makes it to the semi-finals against some of the best youth choirs in the world."

Admittedly I was having trouble with that, too. Either the other groups were unbelievably bad, or miracles did happen. I mean, my kids were good singers, but even they knew that as a group they weren't up to the status of the others. However, I would never admit that to him!

"Which only proves people shouldn't make snap judgments. We won fair and square. My kids are good, and I'm a good director."

"So good that someone would take pot shots at you?"

"Whoever it was was shooting at the embassy car."

A pained expression crossed his face and he took my shoulders in his hands as if he were going to shake me. He didn't but the memories did. That was the way... well, suffice it to say that it pulled up a bunch of intimate memories which I'd just as soon forget.

"There hasn't been an attack on a British Embassy car for years. Do you honestly believe that some unnamed sniper would just happen to take a couple of pot shots at it while you just happened to be in it?"

"But Grey..."

"Of course Hamilton-ffoulkes played the hero. And I'll bet he's been right there playing the helpful English gentleman every time you've had trouble. I've heard it's one of his best roles. It usually works with you romantic types."

"Don't be so – " I had the word silly in mind, but he interrupted me.

"Jealous? Okay, I admit it. In spite of everything I still have feelings for you. I haven't forgotten last year. I'm not made of stone, Robin!"

"Allen..."

"Robin..." he said in a tone totally different from mine.

Then it was as if neither one of us were in control. His lips descended against mine and – as corny as it sounds – I felt a jolt like electricity. For one moment I forgot the kids, the competition, my job, my problems, everything. What I was thinking about is nobody's business but my own. To be in Allen's arms again, to have his lips claiming mine with a passionate urgency was the fulfillment of a dream. For a moment I forgot everything and simply gloried in living my fantasy.

Unfortunately, reality is always lurking, and it pounced with a vengeance when we stopped for air. Appalled at my moment of weakness, I pushed him away as if contact would contaminate. After the way he had treated me, after considering all my responsibilities, I shouldn't even speak to him, let alone be thinking the romantic thoughts I had!

"That's enough, Allen."

"Spoiled to that Englishman's kisses?" he sneered.

"Grey has never touched me."

"Just wait. Robin, Robin, I'm sorry that happened. No, no, I'm not," he amended. He was stalking the short width of the room now, both hands clawing his hair into a witches' nest. "But I've got to make you see! You've got to leave. Today. Now."

There was such sincerity in his voice. I wanted to tell him, to make him believe that there was no problem, but I couldn't do that even with myself. The one thing that was definite, though, was that I was not going to trust Allen Burke with any part of my life, no matter how tempting it might be. I had done that once before with only heartbreak and disaster for results.

"Leave? Why?"

"You say you're not involved in anything. Okay. I believe you, but there are others who might not. It doesn't make any difference what you're not doing as long as they think you are. Why can't you see that?"

I did see it, and although it had occurred to me before, it still was not cheering.

He must have seen that his words touched me, for he doubled his fervor. As he spoke he came closer and closer, until he could not help but take hold of me again. It didn't seem to bother him as much as it did me.

"Think, Robin. People only believe what they want to believe. And it's not just you. That sniper could have hit any one of the kids just as easily as he could you."

That had occurred to me too. It wasn't cheering,

either.

"Let me help you."

"You? How?"

"I've got a car and driver downstairs. Come with me. You probably haven't brought much with you, so we can just abandon your luggage."

"Allen..."

"Listen to me!" We can just go downstairs and I can drive you directly to the airport. You get on the first plane out and then you're safe."

"You think I'd be safe if I just left? Allen, even if I believed your taradiddle, I couldn't just leave. The kids..."

"They'll be all right. No one wants to hurt them and there are people in the competition to see that they get home all right."

"And what about their competing? Really, Allen, I think you've been reading too many bad paperbacks."

"You'd risk your own life? You'd risk the lives of the children entrusted to you?"

"Risk? What risk? You haven't proved a thing." I yanked my arms free and turned toward the door.

"What about your request for a different hotel?" he asked and I stopped dead in my tracks.

"How did you find out about that?"

"Like I said, I have a few sources that Mr. Greystoke Hamilton-ffoulkes hasn't managed to dry up."

"Why are you so down on Grey? What has he done?

What has he done to you?"

His hands flew up in frustration. "That's just it. People can know things and still not be able to prove them."

"Or, like you, they can *think* that they know things," I said bitterly. The shaft went true, for he blanched as if I had struck him physically. "That's not a good argument."

"What's the trouble with your hotel?" he asked in a small voice.

"It just isn't comfortable."

"Where are they going to put you?"

"They aren't. I just talked to Kaminsky. He said there's no budget."

"So good old Grey is going to talk to him and see what he can arrange?"

I whirled. "How did you know that? You couldn't possibly have overheard."

"I didn't overhear. Dammit, Robin, what else could it be? Now Hamilton-ffoukes is going to go play the good guy and get something done and you're too damned stupid to see that it's a set-up!"

"Enlighten me," I said through gritted teeth.

"All the competition did was make reservations for the hotels. The bills are paid by the groups, or by their sponsors. The competition budget has nothing to do with it, but I'll bet you money that Hamilton-ffoulkes will come down with everything settled and by tonight you'll be in a hotel of his choosing. Robin... Robin..."

Very slowly I opened the door, walked through and closed it definitely behind me, as if by doing so I could close out my chaotic thoughts or the sound of Allen rhythmically slamming his fist against the desk.

The next office was empty, too; I ducked in and leaned against the door, feeling as if I were hiding from a thousand devils. Absurd as it all was, Allen's weird theory almost sounded as if it made sense. He was all wrong, of course, but there was enough there to make a nervous person start looking over her shoulder.

Well, I was not really the nervous type, but even if everything were all wrong Allen might not be the only one to believe it.

Did I believe it?

No. I knew the truth. At least, I thought so.

What was I going to do about it?

Opening the door carefully, I peeked from side to side to make sure the hallway was deserted, then skittered out. I didn't want to risk waiting for the elevator, so I dashed down the stairs – no thought of romantic elegance now – and out the front door. I didn't stop running until I was across the decorative front esplanade and safely anonymous in the thick braids of pedestrians moving along the sidewalks.

Chapter Thirteen

Everyone was mad at me.

In a way I couldn't blame them.

The competition official was angry because I had said she would only have to babysit for an hour; in actuality, it was closer to three.

The kids were furious because (1) I was late taking them to lunch, and considering their appetites, that was practically a capital offense; and (2) because I wasn't there they had missed getting to take the tour to the Sea of Galilee.

Grey... it was hard to tell how he really felt behind that well-bred barrier of British reserve and good manners. Still, when I told him I had seen to the hotel problem myself, there was a ripple of some sort of emotion, like underwater currents wrinkling the surface of a calm pool.

"I told you that I was going to talk to Stanley, Robin."

"You've been a dear, Grey, but I really am capable of handling my own problems. Besides, I didn't think there was anything the competition could do. After all, they just reserved the space; our sponsors are paying the bills." *And that*, I thought, *was something the old man should have told me in the beginning!*

"I don't understand," he muttered, slowly rubbing the back of his neck. Then I shivered as he went on, saying words directly out of Allen's nightmare scenario. "I've arranged the whole thing. Rooms for all seven of you and a rehearsal room. The hotel owner's an acquaintance of mine. Stanley even approved it."

"Well," I said, forcing myself to speak lightly, "I just hope he'll feel as kindly towards my choice."

"Robin..."

"Please, Grey, I appreciate your interest, but I can't let you take care of everything. When you went up to speak to Maestro Kaminsky I was sure you'd get the same response that I did, so I took care of it myself. I'm sorry you went to all that trouble."

"No trouble, really, I just made a telephone call. I just..."

"I'm glad it didn't put you out," I said with unmistakable finality, "because I have taken care of everything."

Stanislaus Kaminsky – and through him the competition committee – weren't mad at me yet, simply because they didn't know. As soon as I had returned to the Hall of World Peace I had been very scrupulous about going directly to his office and, since he was out, leaving a note explaining the move. I had been tempted to forget to mention the name of the hotel, but decided that was too risky. At this point I didn't dare do anything – more than I had already done – to antagonize the competition committee, and it was obvious they would need to know how to reach me if some need arose.

It sounded so simple, but putting everything into a succinct note took me a few difficult minutes. I didn't go into personal details – like Allen's suspicions of Grey, or even Allen himself – but just told him that I still felt strongly about the hotel where we had been placed and that while I had credit cards there was no need for my group to feel penalized, that the monetary balance could be straightened out later with the sponsors. Then I hoped he didn't hit the ceiling when he read it.

Why had he allowed me to think that the competition was responsible for paying our hotel? I couldn't think of a single good reason.

Very rarely did I draw attention to myself by taking hold of things with my own unsure hands, but when I did, I did it completely. My missing time from the Hall of World Peace had been well spent. I had walked for two blocks, then when I reached Jaffa Road had taken the first taxi I could catch down to the Old City. I had decided already that when I moved us it would be into an Arab hotel that had no connection in any way with the competition and did not impose any religious restrictions on its guests. As if our own experiences hadn't been enough, I had heard enough horror stories from the other directors to instill a deep – though probably overwrought – apprehension of trying to find anything in the new part of the city, even if there were something I could afford. Just wait until I got my hands on the old man. Just wait until I turned in my expense voucher! Secondly, the hotel had to understand about our singing at any reasonable hour.

How to accomplish this had been my main problem. Sometimes the hotels didn't even look like hotels and since my Arabic consisted of just two words – *min fodlok* (please) and *shukran* (thank you) – I decided I needed help, preferably that of someone not connected in the slightest way with the competition. I didn't want to go back to that icy woman in the shop on the Via Dolorosa, so my next best choice had been the last gift shop.

It was closed when I got there. The big metal pulldown door was closed, but the flaring black soot stains against the honey-colored stone gave mute testimony to what had happened. My first thought was anger, pure fury that all the beautiful things in that shop, the things of beauty I remembered and the unknown promise in all those mysterious cloth bundles had been reduced to useless, anonymous ash.

"May I help you, madame?" The question was asked in stilted but perfect English. It was the owner of the kitchenware shop which had fascinated me on my last stolen trip to the Old City. He was short, balding and wore a gaudy Western-style sport shirt and slacks; he inspired no fantasies of ancient battles.

"When...?"

"Two nights ago. We are lucky it was after closing, or the whole street might have gone." He gestured to the profusion of goods that spilled from the shops onto the narrow street.

I could see what he meant. It would be easy to imagine the flames gushing forth from that stone mouth like a blast from Hell itself. Apparently the stone had contained the flames from the rest of the building above the shop, but shooting across the street they could have caught the overspill from several other shops. It was all too easy to imagine the entire stone channel of a street turning into an inferno.

"What a shame! There were so many beautiful things in there. I hope the owner was insured."

The shopkeeper looked at me with expressionless, obsidian eyes. "It would make no difference, madame."

"What...?" I gulped. "You mean he was in there?"

"The fire brigade found his body when they put the fire out."

My stomach lurched in horror and I had to lean against the wall to keep from falling over. Alarmed, the shopkeeper shouted something in Arabic and, bracing me sturdily, led me back through his shop to the office beyond. Almost on our heels came the little street urchin with coffee.

Only after I had been seated in the ancient wooden armchair and been helped to sip the tiny cup of coffee did the shopkeeper speak.

"My most sincere apologies, madame. I had no idea you knew Selim."

I shook my head slowly, as much to clear away the encroaching cobwebs as to answer him. "I didn't, not really. I had been in the shop – "

I had been in the shop two days ago.

The afternoon before the fire.

I had just left the shop when I ran into Grey.

Suddenly Allen's little scenario didn't sound quite so wild. Was there another player in the game?

" – to buy some souvenirs. There was something I decided to come back for. I have a horror of fire," I ended lamely.

"A normal reaction, madame. May I do anything else for you?"

I twirled the thimble-sized earthenware cup in its pierced brass holder. The thick sludge in the bottom scarcely moved. As sick as Selim's ghastly death made me, I had come to the Old City for information from someone unconnected with the competition. This wasn't what I had planned, but it would have to do.

"Yes," I said. "I'm planning to move to another hotel and I need a recommendation."

The shopkeeper was very helpful and within an hour I had us registered in a small, family-style hotel not far from the Jaffa Gate. It didn't have the icy perfection of our current lodgings – in fact, if we were back home I might have thought it none too clean – but it was more than acceptable and very welcoming. That, plus it was not connected with anyone or anything connected with the competition. Somehow I found that very comforting.

The owner, a Mr. Badrieh, was related to the shopkeeper in some obscure way and could not have been nicer. He listened to a carefully edited version of my troubles and provided the entire top floor for our use at a very reasonable price. There were four bedrooms and unfortunately just one bath, but Mr. Badrieh assured me that we could use the bath on the floor below if we wished. He also told me in his fluent but careful English that the filigreed iron gates were locked at midnight, but, he added with dignity, if we wished to make special arrangements for special evenings he would be delighted to accommodate us.

It seemed perfect and I was glad of it. It was about time something went my way.

I returned to the Hall of World Peace in a great mood, only to have my encounter with Grey shatter it. Then the kids jumped on me, accusing me of child abuse by abandonment and incipient starvation. It made no difference to them when I tried to explain that I had been gone only a few hours and that it was just twenty minutes past lunch.

I should have noticed that something was wrong when immediate application of great amounts of food did not raise their mood. Instead, I just put it down to tension and nerves and ignored it. More fool I.

We lunched at a chop house in the new part of

downtown. This area looked very much like any city back home, except smaller and cleaner. In places only the bi-lingual signs gave you any indication you weren't on Main Street USA. That, and the heavily armed teenagers in uniform who seemed to be everywhere.

"I've got great news for you. We're moving out of our hotel this afternoon."

To tell the truth, I had expected joy. Or at least gratitude. There were a few weak smiles and a glimmer of happiness, but for the most part it was masked by blank stares.

"A new hotel?"

"Yes. The competition said we couldn't change because of their budget, so I put it on my credit card."

There should have been squeals of excitement. There weren't.

"That's very kind of you, Miss Sabine. Surely this wasn't expected of you," said Gerald.

"No, but then I didn't expect that the competition would give us a hotel like they did. The Badrieh place isn't as new – in fact, it's in the Old City itself – but they're very friendly and understand that we have to practice."

"We were supposed to practice this morning," Carla said with very pointed patience.

"That wasn't called for. I think Miss Sabine is very nice to use her own money for us," Maureen said, then went bright pink. It wasn't like her to speak so forcefully.

"It will be most enlightening to actually stay within the walls of the Old City itself. If one were able to practice psychometry and gain the..."

"Shut up, you damned little perfessor!"

"Tony! I don't want to have to tell you again about your language."

He took a deep breath, then said, "Sorry, Miss Sabine." He didn't mean it.

"Couldn't you and Mr. Hamilton-ffoulkes find us a nice new modern hotel?" whined Carla. "I don't want to stay in a moldy old dump."

"The Bluebird is a perfectly respectable hotel, Carla, and Mr. Hamilton-ffoulkes had nothing to do with it. What makes you think he did?"

She looked away uncomfortably. "Well, he's been hanging around so much... I just thought..."

"Well, you thought wrong. He did offer to find a hotel for us, but I preferred to do it myself."

"Most commendable," said Gerald in a more pompous manner than usual. "If you want something done correctly, do it yourself. You can't be sure of anything unless you investigate it personally."

His words were unremarkable in themselves, but a strange electricity ran around the table, clearing the air as effectively as a crackle of lightning.

Had they quarreled? Or did they suspect Grey of having ulterior motives too? Was everyone else seeing something I didn't? It was maddening.

So was our confrontation with Mr. Feldshuh.

Somehow it didn't seem strange to find him sitting in the little office off the lobby, waiting like a spider in his lair. I had halfway expected him to be there and wondered where Mr. Abramowitz was spending his time now.

"Miss Sabine!" he cried, bounding out of the office and oozing an artificial charm so slimy it was practically rancid. "Back so early? I trust everything is all right."

"It's fine, Mr. Feldshuh. I think I've solved both our problems. Gang, get your stuff together as quickly as possible. We don't want to keep the taxi waiting."

They swarmed up the stairs with alacrity, just as happy to get out of here as I.

"Problems? I can think of no problems." He was smiling, but it looked more like a death rictus.

This was the interview I had been dreading. "You and the Abramowitzes have been very kind, but I know what a disruption our presence has been here, so I thought it was best that we move."

All color drained from his thin face, then he flushed a dangerously dark red. "But Miss Sabine…"

"I do not know if the competition or our sponsors are paying the bill, but if our departure causes a problem, I will settle the account here and now if you will give me a total and discuss it with them later."

"But you cannot leave!"

My eyebrows raised almost of their own accord. "I beg your pardon?"

And for a while I thought he wasn't going to let us go. He argued. He cajoled. He promised. He apologized. He did everything but go down on his knees and fling his arms about my legs. He also tried to hide it, but under his appeal there was an edge of anger. Was he afraid of the Abramowitzs' reactions? I didn't know; from the way things had been going it appeared he had more say in the running of the place than they, but maybe it was just that they didn't want to have anything to do with our contaminating presence.

Tony and Larry were already downstairs with their luggage before Mr. Feldshuh finally accepted that we were really leaving. He named a figure that I privately thought exhorbitant, but handed over my credit card without a murmur. There was no way I was going to start another round and round with him. If the old man objected to my expense vouchers, he could just come over here and go head to head with Mr. Feldshuh himself!

I didn't have time to check if my room had been searched. Thank Heavens I had been drilled in the importance of traveling light, so packing took only a few minutes. By the time everything was thrown willy-nilly into my suitcase all the kids were downstairs waiting. So was Feldshuh. From his expression I almost expected another scene, but he merely stood there, looking at us as we piled into the cab, his face shuttered and cold.

"Spooky," muttered Larry.

"He was really giving you a hard time, Miss Sabine," said Tony.

Larry nodded slowly, rubbing his head where he had banged it against the car's door jam. "Yeah. Like he didn't want us to leave."

"Didn't want us to leave? That's strange." Maureen turned around and looked over her shoulder.

I was looking over my shoulder, too. I watched the strange little hotel get smaller and smaller until we turned on to Ramala Road and it vanished behind a row of buildings. Somehow I had expected to feel relieved when we left. I didn't. I felt strange, as if the malaise of that place were following us.

Chapter Fourteen

Then it was as if the Furies relented, for everything seemed to straighten out and go right. With the exception of a constantly sullen Carla the kids liked the new hotel. Gerald was delighted with the idea of the historical area and Maureen was positively transported with the idea of actually staying in an area of such religious import. She kept sighing and touching the walls, though it was doubtful that in this area they were much over six hundred years old. The rest of the gang just giggled at the place's quaintness. It was better than I had hoped.

We moved in – though there was some grousing about still not having individual rooms – then I took them down the street for a cold drink and a snack. Never underestimate the capacity for teenagers to consume food. Not two hours before they had eaten a healthy meal, but that didn't stop them from putting away an astonishing number of those delicious pastries made of pistachios, honey and phyllo leaves, and cups of hot, sweet tea. We laughed freely and it was as good a moment as we had had. I was to look back on it nostalgically.

After all that sweet pastry I didn't know how they would sing. They needed rehearsal, though, and time was running short. Tomorrow was the next competition and it was getting close.

"Why are they competing on Sunday, Miss Sabine?" Maureen questioned me mournfully. "I would love to attend church here."

We were alone in the hastily converted rehearsal room. I had given the kids a fifteen minute break to clean up before we got down to some serious work. Maureen must not have even paused before coming up to talk to me.

"Saturday is the big religious day here. That's why there were no competitions today. They have arranged things to their schedule." I felt sorry for her. It was doubtful that she would ever come here again. "And they have arranged that early morning service for the contestants tomorrow."

"But that's going to be held in the auditorium at the Hall of World Peace. I was hoping…" She swallowed heavily, longing glowing from every atom of her being. "There's a sunrise service at the Garden Tomb."

Life is rotten sometimes. I wished I could get my hands on whoever organized this competition.

"What time is it over?"

"About eight o'clock."

"Why don't you go, then?"

Her face lit up as if by a searchlight. "You mean you'd let me?"

"Why not? The competition service doesn't even start until then. You could probably make both. We'll arrange for a taxi to wait for you, so you don't have to worry about finding one. Do any of the other kids want to go with you?"

"You'd really let me?"

"I want to, Maureen, and at this moment I don't see why not. If things change, I might change my mind, but for now... I'm only an ogre when it comes to music."

"Miss Sabine!" she squealed joyously, flinging herself at my neck. "I never believed – "

"What's the joyous occasion?" drawled Carla as she drifted into the room. She was still unhappy about something and I made a mental note that I must talk with her more.

"Miss Sabine has said that I might go to the Sunday services at the Garden Tomb!" Maureen looked as if I had promised her the moon.

"Possibly," I added in damp tones. "If everything works out all right."

"Whoopie-do," said Carla.

"What's the matter, Carla? Obviously something's bothering you. Can't we talk about it?"

"I have nothing I wish to discuss with you." She said it with the dignity and hauteur that would have befitted a dowager duchess. On a pudgy teenager it was ludicrous.

"Oh, she's just off on one of her snotty I'm-a-famous-sex-symbol twits." Leading the rest of the group, Tony walked soundlessly through the door. He could move with the stealth of a stalking hunter. "Stupid broad really thinks she's something special."

Carla whirled, her face a contorted mask of unrestrained fury. "What do you know, Mr. Smart-Ass? You're just a boy!"

Almost as her mouth opened Larry grabbed Tony's arm, twisted it painfully behind his back and screamed, "You take that back, you sucker!"

Except he used a different word.

"Stop it! Stop it now!" As I have said, when I wish for volume, I get it. The very stones seemed to shake and there was the thunder of feet on the stairs as Mr. Badrieh and an assortment of his relatives came rushing up to see what was the matter.

It took a few moments to reassure Mr. Badrieh and the others that nothing was wrong. When they finally descended he looked considerably less happy than he had when we had checked in.

"Okay, gang," I said with deadly calm, closing the door and leaning against it like a jailer. Now they were all abashed, even those who had not been involved, and as penitent as they could be. "What in the name of all that's holy do you think you were doing? All we need is to get thrown out of here. Leaving a hotel is one thing, but getting thrown out of one can get us disqualified from the competition!" I was wound up and went on in fine fettle, bringing in every proven guilt-producer I knew, from their parents to American pride. By the time I was finished they were all prepared to crawl downstairs and apologize to Mr. Badrieh and all his assorted relatives individually.

As proof of their willingness to make up the gang rehearsed with a will, working as they seldom had. It was better than their impromptu performance in Jericho. If they sang like this in the semi-finals – ! I held my breath. I wouldn't say that they could make the finals, but I could say that they might. Considering how I had felt when we first started, it was pretty close to a miracle.

The sun was below the wall when we finally stopped. I closed off the final tones of *The Gift of Love* and dropped my aching arms. Silence rushed in, thick and ancient. It hovered for a moment, then shattered at the sound of applause. One pair of hands was clapping; I knew who they belonged to before he stepped through the door and lounged in languid elegance against the jamb.

The silence was not the only thing broken by his presence. Also shattered was the feeling of oneness that had enveloped the kids and me, wrapping us in the comforting blanket of music. Now there were sharp and jagged edges of some kind and once more it was me against them. I didn't know why they should close in upon themselves so at his presence, but I did know I felt uncomfortable about it. I still thought Allen's theories bunk, but... There was always a 'but.'

"Bravo! Such artistry deserves to be rewarded."

"Grey!" My surprise was real. "How did you find us?"

"Find you? I didn't know you were lost. You did leave the name of the place with Stanley."

The glare from the kids was an indictment.

I felt a frisson of unease. Damn Allen Burke! Why did he have to keep my thoughts so upset?

"Of course. I just didn't expect you to come visiting."

"But don't you think impromptu things are the most fun?" He smiled, but I didn't think it reached his eyes. "In any case, I've planned a treat for all us tonight."

"Grey, you shouldn't have," I said mechanically, desperately thinking of something to say, something to buy me some time to think.

"I don't think we want to go anyplace with you, Mr. Hamilton-ffoulkes," Tony said bluntly.

Grey was unruffled. "Well, that's quite all right, because I hadn't intended to take you anywhere with me. What I had in mind was to take Miss Sabine out for a nice dinner. Just the two of us. No children."

The kids bristled at the word 'children,' just as Grey had known they would.

"Thank you, but I can't do that," I said hastily and with a rush of relief. Things were so much easier when you didn't have to make decisions. "I can't leave these guys unchaperoned."

"I never meant that!" Grey threw up his well-manicured hands in horror and only a faint gleam of laughter in his eyes showed that he was not completely serious. "I am dedicated to world peace, an aim that could hardly be helped by turning this crew loose. Actually, I have provided them a singular treat."

"Tea with the flippin' Queen?"

"Tony! Manners!"

Diplomatic training must be wonderful, for the snide remark rolled past Grey leaving no visible reaction. "Actually, Her Majesty isn't here, but for an evening alone with your leader I would try to arrange it if she were. So, I have done the next best thing and fixed you all up with dinner and a movie."

A glimmer of happiness flickered among some of the group, but I had to say, "I still can't allow them to go unchaperoned or with just anyone."

"How about Her Majesty's government? They'll eat at the Embassy, under the protection of the Embassy staff and security. There's a private screening room and a selection of films large enough to keep them busy for a week. And we can have some time to ourselves. Without the children."

I looked at that handsome, smiling face and wondered that I was even wondering. Most women dream of such a romantic encounter – a handsome, attentive man, an exotic city – and I could appreciate it as much or more as anyone else.

At least, I could have until Allen Burke had come along, sowing his veiled hints and frightening allusions, making me see everything through his twisted lens. He had said something once during our halcyon time in England about exploiting coincidence for a desired end; he had been talking about his work, about a string of stories he had been doing about haunted houses. I wondered if he thought I'd remember it. For that matter, I wondered if he thought I might remember almost every word he had said to me during those few, dreamy, perfect days.

"Surely you won't, Miss Sabine!" cried Maureen in a small voice.

"Why shouldn't I?" I asked. "Is there a reason I shouldn't?"

No one would meet my eye. Could they be jealous that I had an interest, however casual, other than them?

More importantly, was I going to let Allen Burke continue to push my buttons? He had not given me one shred of concrete evidence against Grey, just a lot of speculation. Should I believe some vague possibilities and miss a potentially wonderful experience? Even if he were on the right trail, even if there were something suspicious about Grey, should I not investigate and find out the truth?

"That sounds wonderful, Grey. I'd love to go."

* * * * *

The kids weren't happy about any of this, but no matter how I questioned none of them would say why. None of them would say anything other than the most basic sounds necessary for communication, which pretty much boiled down to 'yes' and 'no' and a variety of guttural grunts. This only reinforced my decision; even if I hadn't wanted to go I would have just to show them who was in charge. Perhaps that was juvenile, or just plain petty of me, but quite frankly I was weary of their moods and megrims. Sometimes you have to put your foot down.

Another limousine, similar to the first except for the lack of embassy flags and bullet scars, picked us up, then Grey and I dropped the silent crew at the Embassy. After a few moments of introductions and chat with the unlucky staff members who had drawn babysitting duty Grey and I were off.

Tonight he had hired a car – a stretch Mercedes, which seemed vast when emptied of my gang – but this one was privately owned and came with a driver. I don't care what anyone says, being chauffeured around in a limousine is luxurious and I was enjoying it thoroughly. This was so totally different from my usual lifestyle that if I weren't careful I should find myself enjoying it too much.

"Hungry for anything in particular?"

I shook my head, enjoying the experience too much to put any boundaries on it. "No. Surprise me."

Grey shifted position, stopping short as his leg made solid contact with my purse. He looked down at it balefully. I must admit that in the uncertain light of early evening it did look sort of like a grotesque troll crouching in the shadows.

"Do you take that thing everywhere with you?"

"Of course. I might need something."

He harrumphed. "It's like a date for three."

"It doesn't eat much," I said with a smile. A purse for a chaperone, indeed.

The Jewish part of Jerusalem during Shabbat is the next thing to a ghost town. Most of the big hotels were serving, but we agreed that a hotel is pretty much a hotel anywhere you go. Then we swung by Ben Yehuda, a blocked off area downtown that they euphemistically called a shopping mall, but it was close enough to official sundown that most everything we could see from the street was either already closed or closing, so we came back to the Old City.

Grey had the driver park the car outside the Damascus Gate. It is the most spectacular of the gates; I mean, it actually looks like a gate instead of merely an aperture in the wall. The ground level has risen in the centuries since this part of the wall was made, for to get into Damascus Gate you must go down a series of cunningly designed steps and plazas, each spread with its quota of colorful Arab vendors. This part of the Old City is very much in the Arab sector and were it not for the din of traffic above and behind you and the occasional view of a fugitive power line or television antenna – and a heavy sprinkling of tourists clad in anachronistically modern clothes – it would be easy to believe that time had somehow slipped, that you had left the twenty-first century far behind.

The illusion was heightened by the sinking sun. It darkened the normally honey-colored stones of the wall to a rich old gold. The zig-zag entrance of the Gate was a pool of shadow, but the carved crenellations above it shone as if lit from within. Normally I don't get lyrical about places or views, but if the sheer visual splendor of Damascus Gate doesn't arouse someone's heart, their soul is just plain dead.

Grey was affected too, which as far as I was concerned was a strike in his favor. We walked down the steps and plazas and through the gate in a companionable silence, with no contact save for a gentlemanly hand under my elbow to steady me on the unrailed steps and uneven concrete. If he had spoken or made any flip comment I would have been dreadfully disappointed.

The restaurant was one of the largest in the Old City and obviously patronized by a wide slice of the world's population. In the twenty-odd feet between the door and our simple wooden table I heard at least a dozen different languages, some of which I could actually identify.

Lit by dim wall sconces, the place resembled nothing so much as a cave. Perhaps it wasn't as elegant or fancy as some of the places we had passed in the new part of town, but it was a lot more interesting. Archways and fretted screens separated the different rooms, but it was the tops of other, older arches that fascinated me. They came up out of the floor, like strange decorations at the bottom of the walls. Some were still high enough for a crouching man to pass through, while others would have been a tight squeeze for a cat. Some were nothing but the top of the stones.

"Be fascinating to excavate here, wouldn't it?" Grey dug into the *salatas*, which had appeared on the table almost as the three of us – he, I and my purse – were seated.

"The kids took a city tour. They saw the excavations at the Wailing Wall. There's a dig beside it that they said was forty feet deep with no end to the wall in sight." I tore off a piece of hot fresh pita bread – I could never enjoy the supermarket kind again – and dipped it in the *hummus*. There's no way to really describe *hummus*; it's sort of a pureed chickpea and garlic dip garnished with olive oil, which sounds awful, looks worse and tastes delicious. "I would love to know what's at the bottom."

"Wouldn't it be nice if we could take all the money they spend on fighting in this part of the world and spend it on excavation instead?" Grey asked quietly. He was sampling the *tabouli*, attention apparently intent on the spicy cracked wheat salad, but there was something in the very casualness of his voice that made all the little demons in my mind dance to life again.

"I think that's what any sane person would want, but why restrict it to here? Why not make it all over the world? Just image all the money spent on wars being spent on the arts and knowledge." For a moment I dwelt on the possibility as others have dwelt on the Second Coming; it was a frustrating occupation, especially since you know neither will happen in your lifetime, if ever.

"You sound like you believe that."

"That's a strange thing to say. Why shouldn't I?"

"No reason. Mustn't take everything I say too seriously, Robin. Diplomats are notorious for talking the most dreadful piffle," he said with an engaging grin. It sounded almost like a bad actor doing an imitation of Lord Peter Wimsey. If he hadn't said that, I would have let it slide without much thought; the fact that he was putting so much energy on the subject made me very suspicious.

After that he smiled again as if assuring me of his innocence, took a healthy glob of *hummus* and changed the subject. I let him rattle on about the origins of Arabic cooking, making the appropriate remarks when they seemed to be warranted and occasionally coming up with an intelligent question. I know little about cooking, Arabic or any other variety, and was glad he had chosen a subject which required so little input from me beyond an admiring comment or an occasional word of encouragement.

He had ordered for both of us again, in Arabic again, and when our food finally came I was not surprised to see that it was lamb. Again. I knew it was one of the staples of this country, but even though I liked lamb it was getting a little monotonous.

Then a great number of things happened at once and I'm still not exactly sure how it all came together. Once again I can only remember set scenes, moments frozen in time like snapshots.

The waiter, a tall, dignified man with gray hair, placing our plates of lamb in front of us with a bow and a flourish.

Allen Burke striding in the open front of the restaurant.

The swinging door of the kitchen giving just a glimpse of a man wearing a gold Rolex watch, a man who looked just like the one named Selim who had burned to death in a small and crowded souvenir shop.

The screams of the patrons.

The darkness.

Chapter Fifteen

It seemed like forever before the lights came back on, but in reality no more than a minute or so could have passed. There were a lot of sheepish looks from the tourists who had yelled – I included – and a lot of patronizingly indulgent smiles from long-time residents.

"Don't be alarmed." Grey repeated what he had said when the lights had gone. "It's not unusual. The electricity is often less than stable."

Gently I disentangled my hand from his. He had grabbed it as soon as the lights had gone. Actually, I had been glad, for the darkness had been sudden and absolute in that cave of a restaurant and the pressure of his hand had been reassuring. When the lights came back up, though, the continued intimacy wasn't quite right. It wasn't that I didn't find him attractive, or that I was so much of a prude as to object to holding hands, it was...

Curse Allen Burke! Curse him and the doubts he had put in my mind. Between those and my memories a girl could go mad.

By now Allen was seated. The maitre d' had put

him in the next room, but the fretted wooden screen was really no barrier. I could see him clearly, sitting, watching.

"Who's that?" Grey followed my gaze. "He certainly gave us the once-over."

"Allen Burke. He's a free-lance journalist."

"Does this mean we're going to be front-page news tomorrow?"

I looked Grey squarely in the face. "I doubt it. He only covers the heavy-duty stuff."

"Is that a put-down, Miss Sabine?"

"Oh, don't be that way!" I snapped, trying not to think of all the reasons Allen Burke – a topflight, internationally known troubleshooting journalist – could be so interested in Grey Hamilton-ffoulkes. "You know what I mean."

"Yes, I've read some of his stuff. Some kind of prize-winner, wasn't he? What I don't know is why he's so interested in us."

"It's a personal thing," I said slowly, staring at my lamb as if there were answers floating in the thin sauce. "At one time Allen and I..."

"Oh," was all he said, but there was something in his voice that made me look up. Those incredible blue eyes were focused speculatively on me. "May I assume it is all in the past?"

"Definitely."

"Strange to find him here."

"That's what I thought when I found out he was

covering the competition."

Grey frowned slightly. "A journalist of his reputation is covering the competition? That is odd."

"I guess he was here for something else and since the competition came up – " I shrugged. "I don't know. Until the opening reception I hadn't seen him in over a year."

"Parting painful?" The lamb dinner forgotten, Grey was leaning back, his eyes fixed on mine.

"It was then. Now..." I shrugged a second time and picked at the shredded cabbage salad.

"Some people find things like that hard to forget."

Pointedly I looked at the other table. "Maybe they do, but I wish they would."

"Maybe he just needs longer. Perhaps we can help him."

"How?"

The blue eyes sparkled as he took my limp hand and brought it to his lips. "Oh, I'm sure we can think of something."

Had the circumstances been different, I would have already melted into a pool of quivering emotions. Now I regarded everything as suspicious. "A little obvious, surely?"

That surprised him! Apparently Mr. Grey Hamilton-ffoulkes was not accustomed to having his seductions resisted. He sat back and smiled. "And you don't like the obvious? Or are you not quite so sure of your emotions?"

"What are you suggesting?"

"Women have been known to change their minds," he said with just the hint of a smile.

It should have made me angry, but then maybe you have to be young and foolish to get angry at a simple fact. I threw my napkin easily on the table and smiled back at him. "So have men."

He smiled and gave the ghost of a laugh. "Are you finished here? If so, let's go."

It was completely dark by the time we left the restaurant. Most of the little souks were closed and shuttered. There were few pedestrians and fewer streetlights, giving the place an air of abandonment.

"Let's walk a while," Grey said, stepping to the side opposite my purse and companionably linking my arm through his.

"Is it safe?"

"Are you so concerned about being safe?" Then, misreading my expression, he was instantly concerned. "Come on, we'll go back."

"No. Let's go on. After all, I have you to protect me."

"Don't let all that macho stuff fool you. I am both a weakling and a coward."

I took that badinage for what it was worth, which was probably very little. The arm beneath my hand was hard with muscles and he had the long, athletic stride of a runner. He might be a coward, but he was a fit one.

"But," I said lightly, "they might not know that."

"They?"

"The gang of villains everyone is always afraid of in a strange place, of course."

"Of course."

We turned again into another darkened street and then into another. I recognized where we were; there was the ornamental kiosk in the middle of a joining of five narrow ways. That meant just beyond the next bend and a few yards on lay the Church of the Holy Sepulcher where, in spite of historical evidence that none of the artifacts dated before the seventh century, a great many Catholics believed Christ had been buried. If we kept on this direction we would come out at Jaffa Gate.

I had had several qualms about walking off into the dark with Grey. After all, what did I know of him? I supposed a British diplomat could be a villain just like any other human being. All I had against him was what Allen had told me and, though he could arouse some small doubts, before I believed anything that man told me again I would have to have some hard, cold proof.

I had believed Allen Burke once. That had been enough.

Besides, every feminine instinct I had told me we were not alone. I would have wagered anything that Allen was not far behind us. I wasn't sure if I were happy about that or not.

"They'll concentrate their attention on you, of course," I said lightly, "so I can get away."

"And go running for help, of course," he said with a smile.

"Of course."

Just as I surmised, we swung into the shopping area, now eerily silent and shuttered, right in front of Jaffa Gate.

"Is the car going to meet us here?"

"We aren't going to drive anywhere." Even in the near darkness his eyes twinkled with amusement. "Come on."

I had seen the door during one of my earlier trips to the Old City and the possibilities had been tantalizing. It was a small door, made of heavy wood and covered with another gate of the expected heavy metal filigree, set deep into the Old City wall itself. On the gate there was a sign, invisible in this shadowy light, saying in at least fifteen languages that passage to the top of the wall was prohibited.

Except... Grey produced a ring of enormous, ancient keys and unlocked both gates.

"What are you doing?"

"Surprise. Something that's not on the regular tourist rounds. Come on in, we've got to get this locked back. Don't want just anybody wandering in on us, do we?"

I swallowed hard, suddenly uneasy, then gave into impulse and stepped inside.

The space was small, scarcely more than a landing for a dizzyingly steep spiral staircase. Once inside I could tell that it was lit, though so skimpily I doubted if there could be more than a 40 watt bulb somewhere up there. The grating and clanging of the doors and the locks sounded dreadfully final, as if one were passing from one world into another.

To an imaginative mind, in a way we were, for once those barriers had been refastened we could have been several thousand years back in history. The pale light could have been from a single torch far above, set to guide the feet of the city's defenders. In the perpetual chill of the stone there was the smell of history, ancient history, bloody history, sieges, wars, death...

For a wild moment the space itself seemed to be shrinking, those thousands and millions of pounds of stone and years closing in on me as casually as a human hand closes around an unseen gnat.

"I say, Robin, are you all right?"

I forced my head to go up and down. It bobbed like a broken marionette. Stupid to feel like this! These stones had stood for thousands of years; they weren't going to move right this minute just because I was inside them.

I hoped.

"I'm fine," I lied.

"Good. Let's go, then. Ah," he cried, reaching behind the curving stone pillar and producing a basket with the satisfied air of a conjurer, "just where I left it."

"You left it? What is it?"

"Yes, while I was arranging this, and don't get too

curious. Now... Up! And since I'm going to have to unlock another door and there's not much room at the top, I'm going to be an ungentlemanly pig and scramble up first. Can you manage?"

"Of course," I said through gritted teeth.

I was just as glad that he went first. The steps were tiny, triangular and worn down in the middle until you tilted dangerously backwards even if you weren't carrying a purse the size of Santa's pack. That I had to carry in the middle of my back, because the stairwell was too tiny for it to go by my side. I tried to ignore the closeness of the walls, the tight spiral of the stairs and finally concentrated just on not being overbalanced by my purse. The light didn't help. Beneath its pale glow the rough stones seemed to move, as if part of some great saurian that breathed uneasily in its sleep.

Before the tiny landing, scarcely bigger than the basket it held, came into view I was reduced to an ungraceful down-on-all-fours scramble and was covered in sweat, very little of which was produced by exertion. I've always thought my touch of claustrophobia was minor, but crouching some six feet below the postage-stamp sized landing in that dim well of living stone, waiting while Grey fumbled with keys, I redefined 'minor.'

Then, just as I thought I was going to lose it completely, the low door opened and swung outward onto a new world. As courtly as ever, Grey stepped out, holding the basket in one hand and extending the other to help me over the tall stone sill.

The top of the wall was wider than it appeared from below; four or maybe even six men could easily have marched abreast between the tall crenellations. On one side the brightly lit new part of the city spread out in glittering profusion, while on the other the mysterious, scantily lit maze of the Old City lay almost at our feet. Even up here as below, tiny plants had taken root between the stones, looking like small dark fists against the pale rock. Above all the heavenly full moon washed everything in a sterling-pure silver light. My dress, in normal light a creamy white, seemed to glow like a cool blue flame.

"It's beautiful," I breathed, trying not to gulp the fresh, dusty air and blessed openness. "How on earth did you manage this?"

He laughed softly. "Oh, I have friends. The curator of the wall is an old family friend. The moon was just a lucky bit of timing," he added with a perfectly straight face. "My contacts aren't that good."

I dashed from one side of the wall to the other, drinking in the view greedily. Even the thought of having to get back down that hellish staircase faded before my pleasure.

"Come on, my girl. We've got a bit of walking to do. Watch your footing, some of the stones are uneven." The basket in one hand, Grey once again extended the other to me. I took it without hesitation.

Some moments in our lives are unadulterated

magic. That's how I remember that time on the wall. It seemed as if we walked for miles, but what is distance on a magic night? Grey was as good as any tour guide, pointing out the various things of interest. The Mount of Olives. The golden dome of El As'qua Mosque (or the Dome of the Rock, if you prefer) turned to brilliant silver by the moon. The pristine newness of the Jewish sector – new at least by Old City standards, where some things seemed as old as Time itself. The rough emptiness of Kidron Valley, where the dead of centuries awaited reawakening.

"Now," Grey said at last, indicating a small bench, "we deserve a break."

I sat and watched in wonder as Grey opened the basket and pulled forth two glasses – cut crystal, no less – and a bottle in a thermal sack. "Champagne? How did you manage? It's magnificent!"

"Champagne," said Grey, struggling with the cork, "is always the proper beverage. Did you know the BBC serves champagne to all its guests no matter what the hour? At least it used to; don't know if it still does. So many of the delightful old traditions are dying out." The cork released with the slightest pop and he filled the two tall flutes with a flourish. "I hope it kept its chill."

He handed me one. The moonlight turned him into a black and white image, rendering his eyes as empty dark pools and revealing nothing of his expression. Still, there was something, something I could almost feel, as he looked at me.

Was he going to kiss me?

Did I want him to?

"Wait!" I burst out, unable to face the possibilities. "We must have a toast."

"A toast?"

The moment, if it ever had been, was gone. He leaned back, once more the light sparkling in his eyes and he was the urbane diplomat again.

I made an expansive gesture that took in all that lay below us. "Can you think of a better place?"

"Indeed. Very well, fair lady, make us a toast."

It was only a lighthearted, spur of the moment suggestion, but once made I felt its weight. In this place of so much strife and bloodshed… maybe it was foolish, but I felt that it was important, especially so on this magic night. I raised my glass and touched it to his.

"To peace on earth, and goodwill among men."

Grey's eyes seemed unusually piercing and almost made me uncomfortable. Then we sipped and the mood passed. Had he expected something more personal?

The champagne was excellent.

"It's a shame, isn't it?" I asked at last. "So much beauty, surrounded by so much hatred? Has there ever been a time when there hasn't been fighting?"

"Here in Jerusalem, you mean?"

"No. Oh, at first I guess I did, but it sort of applies to the whole earth, doesn't it? There're always wars going on somewhere. People are always dying."

From the moment he opened his mouth I knew Grey was quoting something and the solemn sound of his beautiful voice with that irresistible British accent in that place at that time sent shivers dancing down my spine.

"'As it will be in the future, it was at the birth of Man – There are only four things certain since Social Progress began – That the Dog returns to his Vomit and the Sow returns to her Mire, and the burnt Fool's finger goes wabbling back to the Fire; And that after this is accomplished, and the brave new world begins When all men are paid for existing and no man must pay for his sins, As surely as Water will wet us, as surely as Fire will burn, The Gods of the Copybook Headings with terror and slaughter return!'" He drained his glass. "Sad, but true."

"You quote poetry a lot, don't you?"

"Too much for most people's taste. Poetry is out of style today."

"What was that you just recited?"

"The last stanza of a gloomy little piece called *The Gods of the Copybook Headings* by that great feminist writer Rudyard Kipling."

I shook my head as Grey refilled our glasses. "Now just wait a minute. I may not know anything about poetry, but I do know Kipling was much more of a male chauvinist pig than a feminist."

"Ah, but wasn't he the one who said that the female of the species is deadlier than the male?"

"Was he? I didn't know. I'll have to re-think my opinion of him. As soon as I form one." I sipped at my champagne as the silence fell.

It wasn't a pure silence, not like at the Dead Sea. Faintly audible was the dull roar of distant automobiles and the mechanical mutterings of televisions and the surprisingly loud voices of late-walking tourists, but up here on the wall it was as if we were separate from all that, as if we inhabited our own little world. With just a little imagination we might have been in any time period. Like the rest of the evening it was a magical silence, and I didn't want to be the one to break it. Instead I simply sat, sipping champagne and waiting for him to quote the one poem I wanted to hear.

When he finally did speak, I didn't want to hear it. "As much as I hate to break this lovely moment with anything unpleasant," he said slowly, "I've tried to find a time to tell you, but there never seems to be a right time for unpleasantness."

"Unpleasantness?" My stomach knotted. What had he found out?

"I knew I had seen that man at your hotel before."

"Mr. Feldshuh?"

"As you knew him. His real name, as far as we know, is Zinneman."

"His real name! Who is he?"

"A very ugly character, I'm afraid. At one time he was with the Hagganah. Do you know about them? They were an outlaw group that called themselves freedom fighters for the Israeli state; toward the end even their fellow freedom fighters repudiated them. The next thing we know he of him he suddenly shows up claiming to work with the Mossad."

"What's that?"

"To a layman, sort of like an Israeli CIA. Then suddenly they disavow him and they part company. The file called the circumstances and situation 'Suspicious.'"

The knots in my stomach turned to rocks. "What does that mean?"

"Haven't the foggiest. That's all that's in the file, but my personal guess would be that he went rogue. Decided to work for himself or whoever would pay him the most."

"You're saying that Mr. Feldshuh – Zinneman – is a spy."

"Right."

"But what is he doing in that little hotel, pretending to be Mrs. Abramowitz's brother? What could he possibly find there?"

"That's just what I was going to ask you, Robin Sabine. What did he want?"

Chapter Sixteen

The sudden attack took me off guard and sent my heart pounding. "What do you mean? How would I know anything about someone like that?"

"You were living in the same building with him. Did you ever hear or notice anything odd?"

"With my gang to look after, when did I have time to notice anything? I hardly spoke to him or the Abramowitzes except about things which affected us. They weren't easy talkers."

"You're holding something back."

Those spectacular blue eyes might be lazy-looking, but they didn't miss a thing. I decided nothing could be lost by being open. "Well, there was a time I thought my room had been searched."

"Did you report it?"

"No," I said, then on seeing his scowl, added, "nothing was missing. I can't even prove it was done."

"But it scared you enough to move your hotel."

"No. Some of the other directors had mentioned their hotels had forbidden non-Kosher food in the rooms. I thought the Abramowitzes had taken it a step further and looked for it. What made me move was the quiet and the restrictions about Shabbat. My kids need to practice."

"And that's the only reason?"

"Isn't that enough? We came to Jerusalem to compete. It's not going to do us much good if we can't rehearse."

He shrugged and to my relief let the subject drop. Picking up the bottle, he scrutinized the level and then poured. "One more glass apiece."

"And then magic time is over?"

"Magic time?"

"This." My gesture could have encompassed the world. "Don't you think it's magic?"

"This time it's my turn to toast. To magic. To shared magic."

We clinked glasses ceremonially. There was more said, of course, but it was as if the magic of the evening ended there. Grey chatted on in his best tour-guide manner as we finished the last of the champagne.

One thing had begun to bother me; I could get almost no personal information on Greystoke Hamilton-ffoulkes. The man seemed to talk incessantly, but on every subject except himself. Since we had met I had found out only that he had been born in Hampshire, that he spoke Arabic, French and German, and that he had a brother two years older than he. Also, he was allergic to peanuts. And that was it. All of it. A small thing, but one I found very bothersome. In my limited experience every man loved to talk about himself and one who didn't was different enough to be suspect. Refreshing, but suspect.

"All done? I suppose we'd best be getting on."

Wordlessly I handed over my empty glass and wished that there were some way to be transported down from this lofty height. As we had been sitting the memory of those horrid stairs had risen again to haunt me.

We didn't go down the same staircase, but the one we did was just about as bad. This time Grey sensed my terror and insisted on going down ahead of me and holding my hand. I appreciated the thought, but he had to carry the basket and that left him no hand to balance himself. Then in a fit of heroic self-sacrifice he offered to take my purse. I declined that, too, remembering what lay wrapped in newspaper and dark cloth in the bottom. Despite the basket he was able to descent the hollowed steps with an easy grace. I finally abandoned all pride and came down the last few yards sitting down.

"My dear girl, I do apologize. I had no idea you were so... so... susceptible."

"It's the steps, mainly," I said, valiantly brushing off the seat of my dress and hoping that the dust of ages was not permanently ingrained. "But I wouldn't have missed up there for anything."

To expiate my cowardice once we were outside I insisted on holding the empty basket while Grey locked the thick wooden door. This stairway had no corresponding grille and it took me a minute to figure out where we had come down. When I did I felt foolish for even wondering. We were in the zig-zag corridor of Damascus Gate, now a tunnel of darkness barely relieved by a few streetlights at each end, and just a few yards from where our car and driver waited. Grey had indeed worked everything out to perfection. I just wondered...

"Isn't Damascus Gate locked at this time of night?"

There was a grin in Grey's voice. "Indeed it is. I see you've been reading your guidebooks."

"Does this mean we're going to have to walk around to Jaffa Gate?"

This time he chuckled, then swore at the recalcitrant key. "Damn this thing! Do they never oil these locks? To answer your question, Robin, yes, Damascus Gate is locked. There is also a small portal which, with the application of a little folding grease, can be opened on appointment."

I shouldn't have worried. Grey was the type who would think of everything.

It was that much more surprising, therefore, when a figure, a red and white kaffiyeh bundled over his face, dashed out of the darkness and without stopping ripped the basket from my hands before vanishing down a small street.

My scream of surprise alerted Grey, who dashed after him into the warren of the Arab quarter beyond the gate and left me alone in that small, dark corner.

If I were the stuff of heroines, those indomitable females who brave storm and danger for the sake of principle, I would have rushed after him to render what aid I could. Sometimes I kid myself that if I had had more time to think, if I had been ready, I would have done something heroic, but isn't it true that heroism is doing what has to be done at the moment when you aren't ready for it?

Whichever it is and however I try to defend myself to myself, I just stood there.

I was still standing there some thirty seconds later when a strong arm reached out of the darkness, latched onto my wrist and pulled.

"Come," said a familiar voice.

I recognized him despite the dim light, just as I had earlier. I even remembered his name. "Selim! You didn't die in the fire. What are you doing?"

"We must get you out of here. Come!" And he pulled me inexorably toward the dark beyond the gate.

Even I heard the crunch. At first I didn't know what it was, but when Selim's handsome face went blank and his grip on my arm loosened I was not at all surprised when he fell into a boneless heap at my feet.

This time I was ready for action. He hadn't even hit the ground before I was off and running. I didn't know where, but as long as I could put one foot in front of another I was going to go somewhere. I heard my name called softly; it was hollow and ghostly and almost unrecognizable in that deep maze of stone. It could have been Death calling me.

My flight had taken me back into the oldest part of the Old City. On the inner side of the wall there was a plaza of sorts with a number of streets leading out of it. I didn't know into which one Grey had followed the basket-snatcher and I didn't take time to wonder about it; instead I dashed across that moonlit plaza as quickly as I possibly could, heading for the nearest dark street as a rabbit will run for cover. In the still of those ancient streets I could hear footsteps behind me.

I hadn't been on this street before. It twisted and turned and grew smaller, and I hoped I hadn't chosen a dead end. Before long it wouldn't matter; the footsteps behind were getting closer. My purse swung wildly, slugging at my body as if it were a live thing struggling to be free.

Had I been able to guess that I would end up running for my life in the hostile terrain of the Old City I would have dressed differently. The light here was faint to non-existent, but the pale fabric of my dress almost glowed. My shoes weren't really high heels, at least not on regular pavement, but they weren't at all suitable for running flat out over dark rough cobbles. Twice already I had saved myself from a nasty fall only by last minute heroic efforts. My breath was coming in painful gasps and this whole affair was painfully pointing out just how out of shape I was.

Well, if I couldn't outrun him, I'd outsmart him. I

sidled into the next cross street and looked for a private house. These generally had double wooden doors leading into a patio. I didn't really think that I could be lucky enough to find one left unlatched, but perhaps the shadows there would be deep enough that I could hide there until the coast was clear.

There was a house; the gate was locked, but the gateway was recessed and it was on the darker side of the street. Besides, I was out of breath. Worse, the pleasant but regrettably slight euphoria from the champagne was eradicated as completely as if it had never been.

I squinched as tightly as I could into the darkest corner and, as if it were some sort of charm, closed my eyes tightly. The footsteps thundered past on the street I had left.

For one moment I was foolish enough to think I had made it.

Then, slowly, deliberately, the footsteps came back. I hardly dared breathe.

Strong hands pulled me into the street so quickly I couldn't make a sound. One arm held me immobile and an iron hand clamped painfully over my mouth. I couldn't breathe, let alone struggle.

"Robin? I'm going to let you go," he hissed in my ear. "Don't make a sound. There're all kinds of people out tonight."

He loosened his grip but didn't let go completely, which made me very glad since I couldn't seem to stand upright on my own.

"Allen… Allen…" I whispered in between little choking sobs, burying my face in the sweet familiarity of his neck.

For a moment he was stiff, as if holding me were uncomfortable, then he relaxed and pulled me closer, our bodies melding together as they once had.

"Shhh," he breathed after a moment. "It's all right. I'm here."

"It was you chasing me? How did you find me here?"

"Your perfume. I kept getting wafts of it. Not too many people around here wear something like that."

I should have known. In spite of teasing by my contemporaries for wearing a 'grandmother perfume' I had worn Shalimar for years. So what if it was a 'grandmother' perfume? It had been my beloved grandmother's favorite scent and was one of my few expensive indulgences. Allen had even bought me a bottle. I still had it.

"Come on," he whispered, peeking out into the street. "It's too dangerous out here. Can you walk?"

"Yes." Pulling free, I repositioned my purse on my aching shoulder and put my hand in his.

"Quietly now," he cautioned and, keeping to the deeper shadows, led me through the maze of streets.

By now I was completely lost. We turned and turned and turned again and once I was sure we had doubled back, retracing ourselves, but it made no difference to me because I had no idea of where we were. Finally he stopped in front of a door that looked just like a lot of other doors, thick and wooden and impervious to just about anything except an armed assault, and knocked. It opened almost instantly and he all but yanked me inside.

Inside what I didn't know. This was nothing but a narrow corridor, a knife slice between two tall walls of stone. At least I could look up and see the stars; that kept me from giving over to an old-fashioned case of hysterics. Allen spoke a single word to the ancient creature of a gatekeeper who sat huddled in a cubby cut into the stone, then led me forward.

Once we got past the single candle that illuminated the porter's hole it was like being in the bottom of a well. I kept stumbling against things, feeling other things brush against my arms, hearing still other things scuttle away as we passed. I was just as glad it was dark.

"Allen, where are we?" I whispered and was silenced by a shush and a vicious squeeze to my hand.

I didn't try talking again until we had climbed a flight of rickety wooden stairs and entered a dark, smelly room. Only after the door was closed did he say anything and that was only for me to stand still while he found the lights. Several sinister thuds and one rather pungent curse later, a single bulb, probably not more than twenty-five watts and hanging unadorned from the center of the ceiling, flickered to life. The shadows its weak light cast were not much more reassuring than the darkness.

I had thought the Abramowtizs' hotel had been basic; this place redefined the term. In this light the walls had no color, but I could see a rickety-looking single bed shoved against one wall. Underneath the dangling bulb was a crude table and two chairs. A fuzzy blanket of an indeterminate dark color hung on one wall, presumably covering a window. Everything looked gritty.

"Allen, what is this place?"

"An old house. It's in the process of being remodeled into apartments."

"But what are we doing here? How did you know about it?" Despite my reluctance, I eased down gingerly onto one chair. It creaked alarmingly beneath my weight, but it didn't matter; my legs simply wouldn't hold me up any more.

"I did a story about it. New development in the Old City, that sort of thing. We're here because there are too many people out there."

"Allen..." I stopped and shuddered, biting my lips until I could gain control of them again. "What is going on? Where is Grey?"

"Covering his tail, I suppose. He'll be found with a gentlemanly bruise and a good excuse for losing you."

"What are you saying?"

"That man wasn't taking you to a summer social tonight! My God, Robin, what have you gotten yourself involved in now?" Reaching across the table, he held my hands with a painfully sincere grip.

"I don't know. I don't know that I'm involved with anything!"

"Robin..." It sounded like a groan. His hazel eyes were filled with a pain so deep that I would do almost anything to relieve it, but it was one of Life's crueler jokes that I could do nothing. "You knew that man."

"The one you hit? I met him in a souvenir shop. I bought some trinkets from him. There was one I was undecided about and when I finally went back there to get it I found the shop had been burned. The man who owned the shop across the way asked if I had known Selim, that his body had been found in the shop," I babbled, words spilling out on top of each other. "That's all. I was happy to see that he hadn't burned."

Which brought up another question in my inconvenient mind – whose body had been found in the shop?

I couldn't think about that then, since Allen was regarding me speculatively. "And that's all?"

"Of course that's all. You keep seeing me as some sort of villainess and I'm not, Allen, I'm not!" Despite all my good intentions a few tears seeped out of my eyes. Even as I dashed them away he was out of his chair, around the table and holding me close. "I never have been."

"It's all right, Robin. I'm here. I'll take care of you."

I sank into the luxury of his embrace. When we had

Janis Susan May

parted so acrimoniously I had expended a great deal of energy on fantasies of him crawling back to me and my disdainful repudiation of him, but real life doesn't work that way. I was alone and frightened and his shoulder was so tantalizingly familiar. If Grey's Gods of the Copybook Headings take off points for being human, I was doomed.

Thinking of Grey was a mistake. Allen felt me stiffen and immediately released me. He stepped back only a foot or so, but that distance was as great as it had ever been between us.

"What is it?"

"Grey. We've got to find out if he's all right."

He made a sound of disgust. "You still don't see, do you? Hamilton-ffoulkes staged that little snatch and grab to protect himself."

Well, I didn't see that and said so.

"He's got the stuff now, you're out of the way – he thinks – and he's in the clear."

"What stuff?"

"Whatever was in the basket."

"There was nothing in that basket but some glasses and an empty champagne bottle."

"Robin!" he growled and began to stalk the room like an angry bear, clawing at his hair until it looked like a mare's nest.

"Don't you understand that man has been using you as a screen?"

"For what?"

"I'm not sure," he said after a moment's hesitation, "but I'm sure you're in danger. He's up to no good and he won't stop at anything."

"Allen this is all ridiculous! We've been over and over this before."

"You just won't believe me, will you?"

"Give me one good reason why I should."

For a moment he looked so exasperated I thought he might strike me. When his hand shot out I actually flinched – a fact he noted with pain in his eyes – but he only grabbed my wrist and yanked me to my feet.

"If it's reasons you want, it's reasons you'll get. God, I wish I could get you out of my system, Robin. I wish – "

He didn't say any more, biting off the words as if they had been a licorice whip. With grim determination – and without letting go of my wrist – he charged out of the room, back down the stairs and out the tiny corridor onto the street again, dragging me clumsily behind. The porter's cubby was dark and deserted.

This trip through the Old City was nowhere near so tortured, but I still had no idea where we were. These were residential streets and all frighteningly anonymous. Not until we turned one last corner did I realize we had returned to Damascus Gate by yet another route. Losing by comparison to the brilliant moon, one lone street lamp burned over the open plaza into which the gate opened. By day it had seemed much smaller when crowded with people and donkeys and handcarts and vendors and tourists; now it looked vast, like a frozen river cascading down the odd bits of step here and there that spread out into the streets of the city. The silence was profound. Here you couldn't even hear the sullen roar of traffic outside the wall. Our footsteps sounded unnaturally loud even though we were trying to go softly.

"Hush," Allen hissed, then caught himself as he made hard and noisy contact with one of the big heavy rubbish barrels the city placed around. He winced as much in pain as at the sound which whistled between the stone walls.

"Where are we going?" I asked under my breath.

"To find you some proof," he answered in an odd voice.

"Are you hurt?"

"Just a bump." He even made it another step or two before faltering.

I grabbed at him. "You are hurt."

"Just hit a tender place. I'll be all right in a moment. Let's just stand here a sec." There was tension in his voice. I wished I could see his face. How badly was he hurt?

His arm tightly around my shoulders, he wedged me into a tiny doorway where we could have a full view of the plaza.

Allen was wrong. It was a full five minutes before he could even stand without leaning on me and the wall. Twice he tried to put his weight on the leg he had hit, but each time his face twisted with pain and if I hadn't grabbed him he might have fallen. When I demanded that something would have to be done about getting him an ambulance he shushed me vehemently. Just about the time I was ready to disregard him and go for help he stretched out his leg and took a tottering step.

"See? Good as new."

I doubted that. He had made only a single baby step and his face was grimly set. In the leaching moonlight it was not a pretty sight.

"Okay, lean on me and we'll go out and find a cab. You need to get to bed."

He grinned. "That's even a better idea."

Oh, he was so full of himself! "Dream on," I said. "Come on…" I put my arm around his waist, prepared to support him. It wouldn't be easy, getting him up and down the meandering steps of Damascus Gate, and I didn't know if cabs even ran at this time of night, but we couldn't just continue to stand here.

Allen grabbed me and we fell back into the shadows so abruptly that I thought his leg had collapsed. He clapped his hand over my mouth, effectively stifling any questions about his welfare.

"Look," he whispered on the slightest breath. Releasing my mouth, he pointed a shaking finger across the plaza.

I sometimes wonder what would have happened if we had gone on and met them. However, wondering what might have happened *if* is one of the most ridiculous timewasters ever devised. I could never have predicted what happened.

While we stood there in the darkest of shadows the impossible happened.

The red of her hair defying even the silvering wash of the moonlight, Carla dashed into the plaza and ran across, out of our line of vision. I would have called to her, but Allen must have heard my intake of breath and once again clamped iron fingers over my mouth.

"Quiet!" he hissed in my ear.

Such was the force of his order that even when his fingers loosened enough for me to breathe I still whispered, "But that's Carla! What's she doing here? She should be with the rest of the kids. I – "

"Just a second. If I'm right, I think you'll see what's been going on."

He was right, for in a moment two figures walked back across the plaza. Grey's blond head was bent solicitously over Carla's red one and their arms were entwined in a perfect picture of lovers.

I remembered another time when they had been together like that, when Carla had disappeared after the semi-finals announcement dinner and Grey had brought her back. I also remembered how the kids said Carla had always been vanishing to meet a man. None of it had seemed very important then, but now I saw it in a new and very ugly light as, Carla held tightly in Grey's arms, they walked quickly across the plaza and disappeared into the shadowy mouth of Damascus Gate.

We were so intent on them neither Allen nor I noticed the man with the gun.

Chapter Seventeen

D on't move."

It was a useless order. Allen was holding me so tightly I couldn't have moved if my life had depended on it. Which, since Selim was pointing a very large gun at us, it might.

"You." He gestured at me. "Come here."

"Leave her alone," Allen said while trying to get between me and the gun in the best heroic tradition.

There was a dark line down Selim's hawkish face; in this odd black-and-white world it looked like chocolate syrup, but could only be blood. He was not too steady on his feet; the gun, however, didn't waver. It was pointed right at me.

"I said come here!"

More still photograph memories. Allen leaping for the gun. Selim, surprisingly agile, dodging. The butt of the gun coming down on Allen's skull with a horridly final thunk like an overripe melon splitting. Selim's propelling me forward, one hand cruelly around my upper arm, the other holding the gun that was digging a hole in my back.

"Let's go," he muttered, walking past Allen's

crumpled body without a second glance.

Allen wasn't dead; at least, I didn't think so. He had fallen on his back, sprawled across the cobbles as if in sleep. It seemed as if his chest were going up and down, but in that unreliable light I couldn't be sure and there was no chance to check. Selim and his gun saw to that.

I went wherever he pointed me without argument or even hesitation. I didn't have the slightest doubt that he would use that gun with no thought of consequences and I had no intentions of dying quietly in a dark, deserted stone street. Anyone who has ever watched some of the more melodramatic television shows would know that the gun had a silencer on it. He could kill me with little more sound than it would take to crush a mosquito.

That is not a comforting feeling.

We walked through anonymous streets that were dark and narrow, turning twice and stopping before yet another blank wooden gate. At one time I had admired the secretive architecture of the Old City, but by this time I was finding it annoying. I had been all over a great chunk of it tonight and yet I'd never be able to tell exactly where I had been or find any place again. It was maddening.

Selim used the butt of the gun to pound on the rough wooden door, then sagged wearily against the stone jamb. At first I was just glad to have that hard metal thing removed from my backbone, then I took a second look at Selim. The light was bad – there was just a single streetlamp some twenty yards away – but it was obvious that he was in a bad way. The dark streak down his face had grown wider, but even where it wasn't bloody his skin gleamed with a sickly moisture.

"Are you – ?"

The gun waved in my face, just missing my nose. "Be quiet. I do not know what you think you are up to, but..."

The wooden door opened with a mournful creak and I was unceremoniously pushed inside. At one time this must have been a reasonably prosperous house; now it appeared to have fallen on bad times. A single oil lamp burned in a corner niche, showing scabrous walls surrounding a small courtyard full of unidentifiable rubbish.

Keeping his feet with an effort, Selim followed and babbled something in Arabic to the slight figure whose face was masked by a *kaffiyeh*. This creature nodded and – slight though he/she/it might appear – grabbed me in a hold stronger than Selim's. Without ceremony I was shoved up a crumbling staircase that shook and creaked alarmingly under our combined weight, then thrust through a dark doorway. The door was slammed and uncompromisingly barred, leaving me alone *(hopefully!)* in an impenetrable black nothingness.

* * * * *

For a moment it was all I could do not to panic. A thousand fears each more hideous than the next crowded into my brain, all the old horror movies I had ever seen leaping to life. What if there were some sort of monster – human or otherwise – waiting to do who knew what? What if I had been pushed to the brink of a well or chasm of some sort, where one false step would send me into the bottomless pit just waiting to swallow me up? What if there were sharp things waiting to impale me if I moved?

Worst of all was the darkness, a darkness so thick and impenetrable it seemed to be a thing in and of itself. To a claustrophobe utter darkness is the most hideous kind of confinement of all, one that enveloped you, clung to you, swallowed you...

Well, at least that was something I could do something about!

Crouching very carefully, I dug in my purse until – after making contact with an inordinate number of surprisingly sharp things – my fingers closed around the slim barrel of the little pocket flashlight.

Amazing how much different even a tiny bit of light can make. The unknown chamber of horrors dissolved into a small, cluttered and very dirty room. There were boxes almost to the ceiling, some of them appearing not to have been touched in a generation or more. Except for the small, dusty island where I stood, what was left of the floor was covered with more rubbish – bits and pieces of metal and wood, stacks of paper, sinister lumpy sacks. Everything was filthy and there were probably enough germs in there to wipe out most of the civilized world if they had put their minds to it. After my panicky fantasies, though, it seemed blessedly normal.

I was glad that something did!

So Selim too thought I was 'up to' something. I didn't like that. Entirely too many people thought I was 'up to' something and that made me uneasy, especially since they all seemed to think that I was 'up to' something different!

Maybe it was time I did get 'up to' something, something like getting out of here.

I really needed to stop and think things out, but I had the feeling that would be an ill-afforded luxury. It was surprising they hadn't taken my purse before throwing me in this bargain-basement Black Hole, but if I had had a partner or friend or whatever who looked to be as bad a shape as Selim did, I would certainly tend to him first if my quarry were securely locked up.

But was I?

This time I really searched the room, climbing on boxes and kicking aside the most unimaginable amount of rubbish, much to the detriment of my shoes, stockings and dress. There was a window, heavily shuttered and hidden behind a monstrous stack of boxes; it was so hidden that I had missed it the first time around and even after finding it dismissed it. Only after another search of the room showed no other way out did I go back to it. The only other opening in the walls was the door, which was of heavy wood and securely fastened from the outside. I couldn't even make it wiggle.

So the window it had to be; I didn't know how much time I had left.

Luckily the boxes were fairly light. Any other time I would have been curious as to what was in them, but right now time was the most important thing. *Curiosity had killed the cat,* my grandmother had told me again and again during my childhood and I had no intention of proving her right.

The only thing which came close to undoing me was when one of the boxes slipped and slithered to the floor, its aged tape splitting and allowing a fountain of filmy, jewel colored fabrics to spew out. I love beautiful fabrics and for a moment they sang to me with a siren's lure. Why did I always run across the neat stuff when there was something else that had to be done?

There was a very welcome thin edge of breeze coming around the edges of the wooden shutters. They were old and splintery and very sturdy shutters, but they fastened on the inside. Heaven only knew when they had last been opened, for the catch was both rusty and stiff, but by now I was beginning to get frightened at the amount of time that had gone by and when I get frightened I get very strong.

The lock and the hinges finally gave over with just a small amount of angry screeching and swung outward. At one time this window had been glazed, but the glass was long gone, leaving an empty sash with only a faint saw-toothed rim of shards around the edges. Suddenly that became very important.

The window opened above the street, but it was a street that went up one of the hills and it was at least two and a half floors sheer drop below the sill. In the uncertain light it looked like the cobbles went downhill pretty steeply. If I could have hung by my hands out the window I might have considered just dropping, but the glass made that impossible. It would have cut my fingers to ribbons even if I did have the courage to drop over two floors onto sloping cobbles, which was a pretty desperate thing even to think about.

At least the moon was still up; its light poured a little of the way into the room and I could turn off my fading flashlight.

I had to get out, and soon, before I dissolved into a groveling, screaming heap of pure fear! Gnawing my lower lip, I went over the possibilities. I even considered trying to go up and get on the roof, but the wall was one of the old ones, worked smooth by ancient craftsmen. It would take a human fly to get up that wall.

Believe it or not, it took me two whole minutes to come up with the solution and another five by the dying light of the flash to implement it.

In the rubbish on the floor there had been a length of sturdy wood, about the size of a two-by-four; it was exactly six inches longer than the window was wide. I'd have preferred a bigger margin, but time was passing and I didn't dare risk waiting to search for a hypothetical longer piece. Already it seemed like hours since I had been shut in here and sooner or later someone was going to come back.

I didn't intend to be here when that happened.

Using the end of the wood, I knocked out the remaining shards of glass until the bottom of the window was as smooth as I could make it.

The next part was the hardest, but not for the obvious reason. I can tie a knot as well or better than the next person, but it seemed obscene to be tying knots in lengths of silk and brocade that back home would cost a week's salary just for enough to make a simple dress.

Still, you do what you have to do and, tying one end of my gaudy rope to the wooden bar and wedging it against the stone window jamb, crawled out the window. In the movies stunt men make walking down a wall look so easy; it wasn't. The material burned my hands, my arms felt as if they were being pulled out of their sockets and my purse hung from my shoulder in dead weight. All in all, it couldn't have been more than a minute or a minute and a half that I hung like a bug on that wall, but it seemed like ages. The lumpy street cobbles had never felt so good.

One of the most amazing things was the silence. In my own ears my breathing (all right, panting) and heartbeat sounded at least like an earthquake, but other than that the silence was profound. Coming down the wall there had been only the small scrapings of my shoes against the stone and there was no sound in the street.

I had done it.

I paused only to take a deep breath before tip-toeing quickly away in the shadows.

* * * * *

What to do now?

A good hundred yards and half a dozen turns away from my erstwhile prison I stopped in a deep shadow to catch my breath and think. There was really only one answer to that question.

I had to get back to the kids.

Carla's appearance tonight had shaken me to my foundations. Still, even if she and Grey were somehow involved (*How?* And in *what?*) where were the rest of them? How had she managed to get out on her own?

Maybe I was wrong; maybe I should have thought of myself, of getting out of this country and somehow getting hold of the old man in spite of his orders, but I just couldn't. Those maddening, irritating, sullen, uncooperative kids were my responsibility and whatever anyone said I took my responsibilities very seriously. Right now they were more important than anything else; if I had to explain it later, I would explain it later.

First of all, I had to get out of the Old City or at least find a telephone, both of which were more difficult than they sounded. The Old City is walled, and where they have walls they have gates, and gates are to be locked. I knew I was probably closest to Damascus Gate, but that would be locked. Grey had said that there was a portal which could be opened by appointment, but I was not going to bet on that. Even if the 'appointment person' were still there, the fewer people I saw the better.

The other gates? I didn't know if any of them were locked or not except for Jaffa Gate, which in modern times is not truly a gate but just sort of a big hole in the wall. It would be open, but it was in the Christian quarter, almost completely across the Old City. At least, I thought it was; for all my running around I felt sure I was still in the old Arab quarter near Damascus Gate.

In the end Lady Luck compromised with me. I had been completely turned around and when I struck out for Jaffa Gate had walked in almost the opposite direction. By doing so, however, I ran into Herod's Gate, one of the smaller portals and blessedly unbarred. It opened onto Suleiman Street, a wide thoroughfare that ran almost the entire length of the northern wall, all the way to Damascus Gate.

Even outside the wall this part of town tended to go to bed early. This four lane thoroughfare was deserted. I knew there were a few of the old luxury hotels such as the King David in the area ahead, but not exactly where they were. I could waste lots of precious time in fruitless search. Better to head toward the new section of town and keep my eyes out for a cab or someplace

234 Janis Susan May

open.

For those of you who have not jogged on concrete in even semi-high heels, I have but one thing to say – don't. My feet felt as if they had been systematically beaten, but the road was so rough and gritty I didn't dare take off my shoes. Besides that, if I did even for a moment I'd never get them on again.

I was back on Jaffa Road and almost up to the Central Post Office before I found a small open coffee bar. Even so, the surly owner was just about to close and would not let me use his telephone; after seeing myself all scraped and filthy in the light, however, I couldn't blame him. He did point out a rank of public phones across the street, though, then quickly locked himself inside until I had walked away.

Israeli phones don't take money; they take a special kind of plastic calling card. There had been a courtesy one included in the information pouch handed out by the competition when we registered. It took a good five minutes to excavate it – still tucked in the rather battered envelope – from the bottom of my purse.

"British Embassy," said a woman's voice as alert and crisp as if it had been high noon.

"This is Robin Sabine…" was all I got out.

"Miss Sabine! Where are you? We've all been so worried!"

"Are my kids still there? Are they safe?"

"The choir?" she asked slowly and my stomach began to sink. "We haven't seen them since you sent the car to pick them up."

Oh, my God!

"I didn't send anything. Where were they going? Do you know..."

Another voice, a well-known, beautiful voice, came over the wire as he snatched the receiver. "Robin? What the devil do you think you're doing?"

"Grey..."

"I don't know what you think you're doing or what you're involved in, but it's time to come in, girl."

Someone else who thought I was involved in something!

"Where are my kids?" I shrieked.

"Robin, where are you? I'll come get you."

"Stay where you are. Just tell me where those kids have gone."

"You should know. You sent a car for them."

"I did no such thing!" My control was slipping as my hysteria rose. "You just let them go with any old car that happened to drive up?"

"I was with you at the time, Robin."

"Your people, then!"

"Are you telling me you didn't send a note?"

"Yes!"

There was the sound of rattling paper. "Robin, I have it right here. I know your handwriting, girl. Look... let me help. This has to end."

I slammed down the receiver. Grey's asking me to trust him was a siren lure, but at the moment I couldn't afford to trust anyone but myself.

Besides that, I knew that back home a telephone call could be traced almost instantaneously; it was probably the same here and I wasn't about to risk anyone finding me until I was ready to be found. Shouldering my purse, which seemed to be growing bigger, heavier and more unwieldy by the moment, I dashed down a side street, made two random turns and hid in the shadow of a fire escape. This part of town was much too well lit for my comfort.

Who had the kids? Was it Grey? Possible; if I had been completely honest, I might have said probable.

Why had Carla met Grey? What was she doing away from the others? Was that before or after the gang left – or was supposed to have left – the embassy?

And mainly, *why*? They didn't know anything. They were just with me.

That was the answer. It was so simple.

If I had had anything in my stomach I would have thrown up.

The kids were nothing more than a tool to reach me.

It was a big city and a bigger country and a great big world and I didn't know of anyone whom I could trust. Even if I called the old man – assuming of course that I could reach him, which was doubtful; he called people, people didn't call him – there was nothing he could do. I was on my own.

I didn't know who had the kids or what they would

do to get to me, but I did know – and I surely did wish I didn't – was that the only way I could get any answers would be to be very visible, to be out there where they could find me.

Whatever else was going on, whatever else anybody thought was going on, whatever needed doing, whatever...Whatever! The kids must come first. They were my responsibility. I had to get them back and safe before I could do anything else.

I was going to have to make myself into a target.

Chapter Eighteen

Just how did one go about making oneself a target? And considering the number of factions that seemed to be involved, what could I do to make sure that I made contact with the one who had the kids?

The only thing was, there were no clues as to who that might be.

There had to be another way.

But what? I was absolutely sure that the kids were in danger. Some sort of latent maternal instinct? I don't know, but I was positive.

All of which did not contribute to my peace of mind.

I sat on the rough metal step of the fire escape and rested my head on my knees. I was desperately tired, my feet hurt terribly and I had to make some of the hardest decisions of my life. Why do the worst crises always occur when we are the least prepared to deal with them?

The obvious solution was to go to the police. Except, I would have to convince them I wasn't some sort of crazy vagrant. And, if they did eventually accept my *bona fides*, would they have the capability to deal with the situation? It seemed that there were some very heavy types getting their fingers in this pie; were the locals on their level? Somehow every nerve in my body told me that going to them would be a mistake.

Grey? I didn't know. There was every reason to distrust him, but somehow I couldn't picture him as a villain, which only shows the foolishness of trying to mix logic and chemistry.

Allen? I didn't even know if he were alive or not. Part of me was feeling extremely guilty about not even trying to go back to look for him while the other part shrilled that my first loyalty was to the kids, that by going to look at him I might be putting anybody or everybody in more danger.

Another choice was Maestro Kaminsky. Of course, it would kill any hopes we had in the competition – and how unimportant that all seemed now – but first I had to reach him. He wouldn't be at the Hall of World Peace at this hour and I had no idea of where he lived or even how to contact him. Maybe that was for the best; what could he do besides call the local police?

The American Embassy? All travelers abroad were told to regard them as the ultimate problem solver, sort of a surrogate mother and father who were there to look after you. The old man had warned me against getting involved with the embassy, calling them less than useless.

But...

Given the choices, they were the most logical. I didn't have any idea of where the embassy was, but somewhere in this town there had to be a taxi. If I kept to the main streets I could probably find one or at least a hotel with a taxi rank. I would go to the embassy, tell my tale and pray that they would back me up when I went to look for the kids.

Jaffa Road was still deserted. Accustomed to the twenty-four hour pace of American cities, I had never seen a major artery completely empty. At two-thirty in the morning at home there was always some traffic, no matter how light. Here it was like being in one of those horrible sci-fi movies where everyone was dead except for the hero. That was hardly a cheering thought for a long walk down a lonely deserted street. If I hadn't been so tired and thirsty I would have sung just to have the noise; as it was, it took all my energy just to keep putting one aching foot in front of another.

I had walked three blocks – three long blocks – when the incredibly beautiful sound of an engine broke the uncanny silence. It was behind me; I watched it turn from a side street far down Jaffa Road and drive toward me as I would have watched for Santa Claus as a child. Perhaps, here of all places, there was something to be said for the power of prayer, for – wonder of wonders! – it was a taxi. The light was off, but it obligingly pulled over at my hail; I was glad, since I was almost prepared to fling myself at it to make it stop.

"American Embassy, please," I said, leaping in the

back.

"I think not," said a deep, heavily-accented voice as its owner placed the muzzle of a very large gun next to my cheekbone.

* * * * *

I was really getting quite tired of having firearms shoved against various portions of my anatomy. Unfortunately, at the moment I was not in a position to do much about it. Gently I turned my head until I could see who was sharing the back seat with me. The gun never left its place, but it moved as I did. Maybe, if I were very good, they didn't intend to kill me right at this moment.

The man was a stranger. I had never seen him before. Swarthy, heavily bearded, clad all in black, he was not too easy to see now. Whose side was he on?

"I don't suppose asking you questions would do any good," I said bitterly.

"No, madame."

"Tell me this; are the kids in my choir all right?"

Something in my voice must have touched him, for after a moment of blankness he gave a quick glance at the impassive back of the driver, then an even quicker tiny affirmative nod. It cheered me as much as anything had in quite a while.

"Where are we going?"

"No questions, madame."

"Do you really think it's going to make a difference?"

As an answer he reached up and cocked the gun. I shut up. As he implied, at the moment it really didn't make much difference.

We drove away from the downtown area; by now I was pretty thoroughly turned around, but I would have said we were going west. The downtown area faded behind us and we kept driving, even though by now even the suburbs were getting thin.

Then suddenly I knew where we were and where we were going, well before the taxi stopped in front of the small shabby hotel with the dusty walled garden and single tree in front.

I'll say this for my captor, he used no force. Perhaps that's faint praise, but after an evening of being grabbed and shoved and wooled around by a variety of semi-Neanderthal types it was refreshing to be allowed to move and walk on one's own. Oh, the gun didn't drop and the muzzle was never more than half a dozen inches from my person; still, it didn't touch me and I was grateful. Once the door was closed behind him, my captor stood in front of it with his arms crossed, as impassive as a statue.

"How nice to have you here again, Miss Sabine."

I should have known; he walked across the marble lobby with the silent grace of a predator.

"Good morning, Mr. Feldshuh. Or whatever your name is. I forgot your real one."

He smiled urbanely and indicated one of the hard benches in the lobby with a courtly gesture. The character of retiring, scholarly Felshuh had been cast aside as easily as a sweater. "As Shakespeare said, what's in a name? I have been called many things."

"I'm sure you have," I said with a smile and took the seat he indicated. I could think of a few pungent things myself. It was strange that no one had yet tried to take my purse, but I wasn't going to mention it. Instead I kept it slung over my shoulder and clutched the strap as if it were a lifeline.

How could I ever have thought this man frail? He was old, to be sure, but it was a strong and vigorous age. There was a lean, wiry strength about him that would have made him fair competition for men with only half his number of years. Now that the air of querulous old scholar was gone, he was quite attractive. In his youth he must have been devastating.

"Where are my kids?"

His smile did not change. "I would rather talk about your activities."

"And I would rather find out about my kids!"

"I gather you would, but that does not interest me at the moment. You have caused me a great deal of trouble, my dear Miss Sabine, and I do not have much time left to bother with you."

Did he even know where the kids were? Had the man in the taxi – the big man with the big gun now blocking the exit – given me that little sign just to help keep me quiet? My heart fell, but I didn't dare let it show. Instead I lifted my chin and charged on.

"Where are the Abramowitzes? Are they in this with you?"

"Those religious fools?" He smiled. I don't care if he had to be close to eighty, he was a handsome rogue. That meant I had to be extra careful, because I have always had a soft spot for handsome rogues.

"They weren't part of your scheme?"

"Hardly. They are just what they appeared to be. As you know, when you are on the job it is best to be as close to the truth as possible." He looked at me speculatively, then as I remained silent, went on. "Your fears are unfounded. I am unlike those new young people who use killing as a normal mode of operation. The Abramowitzes were fools and cost me a great deal with their meddling."

"That bit about keeping Shabbat."

"That bit about keeping Shabbat, as you say. However, rather than remove them permanently, I have sent them to Eilat for a well deserved holiday."

"Bully for you."

"You sound unimpressed. Are you one of those who thinks killing is an answer for everything?"

"I am not one of anything and I don't think killing is an answer for anything!"

His smile thinned but remained affable. "It is easy to criticize from a place of safety, Miss Sabine. One does what one has to."

I don't know if he meant it to be or not, but I found it as chilling a threat as I had ever heard.

There was a thudding down the staircase. Amazing how unadorned marble could make two smallish feet sound so thunderous.

"Is she here? Have you found it?"

He looked very different from our last meeting. Then he had been groomed and proper and very much the international gentleman. Now he was casually dressed and a little rumpled, the perfect picture of a great man at ease. This time his yarmulke was black, edged in a dingy-looking cream. Only his eyes, cold and haunted and hungry, didn't fit the picture. He was just about the last person in the world I had expected to see there, but his presence did solve a number of questions.

"Good morning, Mr. Sternberg."

At first I had been startled to see him, but almost instantly it all made sense – my troubles with the contest personnel, our being placed out here in this prison-like little hotel, his trying to get us thrown out of the country. So many things became clear, all except for why.

"Has she told you yet?" He was talking to the erstwhile Feldshuh, but his eyes never left me. His gaze was both appreciative and apprehensive, like those people who brave an exotic reptile house, and barely glimpsed beneath that there was something else, something unwholesome and very scary. "Why is she sitting down here? Make her tell us!"

Languid and elegant, all traces of the fusty old scholar gone, Feldshuh frowned slightly. His voice was just as urbane as his attitude; only his eyes showed his annoyance.

"Miss Sabine will tell us everything."

"When?" Sternberg's expression turned feral. "She must have it on her."

Quick as a striking snake he grabbed my purse. I tried to hold onto it, but he struck me across the face and my instinctive recoil – plus the sight of the goon at the door – made me sink back on the bench.

Sternberg yanked open the top zipper and rooted through the contents like a pig going for truffles. I watched, hoping everyone would think my anxiety was for my person rather than my purse.

If he just dug, stirring up the contents, the Crown and the gun might go undetected. They were both wrapped in cloth and securely zipped in the hidden bottom compartment. If he dumped everything out, though, there was no way he wasn't going to notice the weight and bottom-heaviness of a theoretically empty purse.

"It's not here," he cried in fury and dropped the bag on the floor. It made a horrifically loud *thump!*, but perhaps I was the only one to think it had a metallic clang. A few items – my comb, a flier from a tour bus company, a couple of receipts, a mint, the new lipstick called Jezebel – spilled on the floor.

Thank goodness for safeties. I couldn't imagine what would have happened had my purse shot at someone.

"You have the mentality of a Visigoth, my dear Avrom," Feldshuh said coolly. It was obvious he disliked the great man of international music much more than he did me, for what that was worth. "Surely you cannot think anyone would be so stupid as to carry it around with them!"

"She must tell us where it is!" Sternberg spluttered, looking hungrily at me, as if he would like to shake whatever he wanted out of me physically.

"Miss Sabine is a civilized young woman, Avrom. She will see things our way."

Something ugly passed over Sternberg's heavy features. "We are not paying you to make her see anything. We are paying you to deliver!"

"Which I will, in my own time and in my own way. No one dictates my methods!" Feldshuh's words were a beautiful example of steel wrapped in silk.

"Why are you wasting time talking to this..." Sternberg then – thankfully - switched to German. I didn't know what he was saying, but I could guess, and the look of distaste that passed over Feldshuh's aristocratic features made me think that they might be even worse. He replied in the same tongue and for a moment they were involved in a vicious quarrel that I suspected had its true roots in things far removed from me.

I considered trying to sneak out during their heated exchange, but quickly discarded the idea. Even if it hadn't been blocked by a very large man with a very large gun, the door was too far away and the two old men weren't arguing enough to be completely oblivious. Besides, their exchange had given me a valuable bit of information. Sternberg had mentioned an 'it.'

What did he mean by 'it?'

"I apologize, Miss Sabine," Feldshuh said calmly, though his eyes were practically shooting sparks. Sternberg looked as if he might attack something – anything – without warning. "Mr. Sternberg unfortunately lacks finesse in things not musical."

Not musical? I thought this was rapidly developing into the kind of melodrama most often found in grand opera and said so, which elicited a throaty laugh from Feldshuh. I didn't dare look at Sternberg.

"Well put, my dear, well put. What a shame we could not have discovered this felicity of minds when you were here and we could have had more time to talk. Now, however, I am afraid that time is a commodity in very short supply, so I must ask you to tell us the truth."

"About what?"

"Don't be smart with us, you…" Sternberg snarled, spouting more and more guttural German. The man made me positively happy I had never studied the language other than learning the correct pronunciation for singing.

"I'm not being smart," I said with deliberate reasonableness. "What are you talking about?"

"Let me make her tell," Sternberg breathed, a queer kind of hunger in his eyes that made me as fearful as anything that had gone before.

"You have something we want, my dear Miss Sabine. We intend to get it. How difficult that becomes is up to you."

"But I don't know what you're talking about!" I answered, an all too real quaver in my voice.

Sternberg gave an inarticulate growl and paced the lobby like a frustrated wolf. I had the distinct feeling he would prefer and probably enjoy throttling whatever he wanted from me.

"You had better make her talk, Zinneman, I'm warning you. Amateurs! Never depend on amateurs! You couldn't even make her stay here so we could keep watch on her! I had to make a deal with that idiot Kaminsky, saying I would drop my complaint if he could make her stay here." Sternberg looked both angry and affronted. "I had to tell him that those idiot Abramowitzes were my cousins and they needed the money! Then you let her leave anyway!"

Feldshuh couldn't restrain a chuckle. "But they got the money. Miss Sabine most kindly paid the outstanding bill."

Uttering an inarticulate roar of rage, Sternberg started to move towards us, and I don't know which one of us he wanted to attack, but he was almost foaming at the mouth. I nearly dived under the bench, but Feldshuh didn't even flinch. He just snapped his fingers and the statue at the door animated, coming forward a few menacing steps.

It was enough for Sternberg; he stopped dead, gnashing his teeth.

Unruffled, Feldshuh turned his attention to me, leaning forward and smiling ingratiatingly. All of a sudden the urbane sophisticate was gone, magically transformed into a caring and concerned grandfather/uncle/father confessor. What a pity the man had chosen this field; he was a magnificent actor.

"Of course you must say that, Miss Sabine, but we are all professionals here. Help us and we will not have to do things that none of us except perhaps the honored Avrom Sternberg will like."

"But I really don't know what you're talking about," I cried. "Until just a minute ago I didn't even know that you two knew each other or that you were looking for something."

"She's a liar!" Of course that was Sternberg. "We've known all along that the director of the Trans-Texas Canticle Society was coming here to pick something up. And we want it!"

What? Boy, was I going to have a talk with the old man when I got home! How dare he send me into a situation like this!

"But I'm a last-minute substitute," I said, trying to keep my voice steady. "Surely you knew that. The original director was taken ill just days before the competition. I was asked to go just at the last minute."

From their quick glance at each other I realized I had scored one for my side, for whatever that was worth.

"You can," I went on, pushing my advantage, "check that out with the competition. I almost didn't get my competition credentials because of the short notice."

Instantly the avuncular elder vanished; pure rage flashed from Feldshuh's eyes and he whipped his gaze around to Sternberg with the force of a lash. "Is this true?"

"I don't know," stammered Sternberg, taken aback. "She could be making it up."

"Something so easily checked? An amateur's trick!"

"We can make her talk." Little flecks of foam were gathering in the corners of Sternberg's unlovely mouth.

Feldshuh stood up. It was like watching an emperor end an audience. "Unlike you, Avrom Sternberg, I get no pleasure out of violence for violence's sake. I was engaged to obtain a certain piece of property, not commit atrocities against a young woman who may not know anything."

Unhealthy-looking sweat was starting to pour down Sternberg's face. "But now she knows..."

"In which case she will be dealt with, but properly. Your desire to inflict pain is really most disgusting."

It is not very heartening to hear your own death being discussed so efficiently, so dispassionately.

"You have been hired..." Sternberg began, but

Feldshuh silenced him with a glance.

"And I will use my own discretion. Miss Sabine will just have to be our guest until you can check her story tomorrow morning. My dear?"

For some reason one of the madder scenes from *Alice in Wonderland* popped into my head. After discussing my impending demise with no more – and perhaps a great deal less – emotion than he would tomorrow night's dinner, Feldshuh bowed with the courtly grace of a Regency beau and offered me his arm.

What else could I do? Thanks to him I had at least until that rat Sternberg could get down to the Hall of World Peace and check out my story, every bit of which was true.

As if it were the most natural thing in the world – even though my knees were turning to water – I bent over and scooped up my purse and belongings, which sent Sternberg into another froth of wordless rage.

"My dear Miss Sabine..." Feldshuh began, but I took a gamble and interrupted.

"Whatever it is you want is not in here; even Mr. Sternberg said that after he went through my possessions with all the delicacy and concern of an enraged water buffalo!" I glared at him. If he stayed that color much longer maybe he would have a heart attack and one of my worries would be taken care of. "And, as a woman, there are certain... things... I need. Unless either one of you gentlemen would care to go and purchase some for me?"

I had read their personalities correctly. Both men instinctively shook their heads with a violent negative. It had been a risky ploy, but generally men of their age and religious upbringing did not want anything to do with some aspects of a woman's plumbing. With the sense of a small victory I swung the purse over my shoulder and placed my hand on Feldshuh's extended arm in the grandest of manners, allowing him to escort me up the stairs. He apologized most civilly that due to security reasons I could not be given my old room, but that he hoped I would find the accommodations comfortable.

It was one of the more fascinating facets of his personality that although he might kill me without a blink tomorrow, tonight he was truly concerned about my comfort.

Move over, Alice.

The accommodation in question was what appeared to be a tiny maid's room on the flat roof at the back of the hotel. Scrupulously clean, it was just about the size of a closet and monastically furnished. The single tiny window was uncompromisingly grated and – should anyone be foolhardy enough to consider removing the filigree – above a sheer three story drop to a flagstoned yard below. Even the roof above was out of reach.

One thing that did interest me was a tiny sink in one corner of the room. As soon as Feldshuh had bid me his formal farewell until the morrow (his word, not mine), the door closed tightly and there was the unmistakable sound of a hasp closing, then a padlock snapping shut. Apparently I wasn't the first person to be locked in here, a thought I found most uncheering. Then his footsteps crunched across the roof and I could barely hear the clicking of his heels on the marble floor of the hall. Instantly I was in the corner, turning the sink's taps and letting the heavenly cool water rush over my hands.

There are those who say it is unwise for tourists to drink Jerusalem tapwater; they are probably right. At that moment I was so dusty and thirsty that no virus or amoeba could daunt me. Like that apocryphal Texas Ranger of legend, I would have happily drunk muddy water from a horse's hoofprint, but there was another consideration which held me back. Like all dedicated fiction readers I knew of the theoretical existence of mind-controlling drugs, of mysterious poisons and strange potions slipped into the bedside carafes that proliferated in English murder mysteries; those frightened me. I didn't know if they could be dispensed through a running tap, but after what had happened in the last twelve or so hours I wouldn't have discounted anything, up to and including Martians occupying Akron.

The clear water splashed over my hands like a benediction. No wonder springs in the desert were always regarded as holy places.

I compromised. I let the tap run full blast for over five minutes, then figured that if any drug still remained after that time it wouldn't make any difference. I had to have something to drink. Nothing in my life before or since ever tasted as good as that plain tap water.

After I had slaked my thirst I tried to clean up a bit. It didn't help much; by this time, though, anything would have been an improvement. I was hungry, too, but there was nothing to do about that. I wished I hadn't passed up so much of that wonderful lamb at dinner with Grey a hundred years ago last night. Usually I carried a granola bar or two in my purse; however, I had eaten the last one on the plane and was too tired now to dig through and see if I had miscounted.

Tired? That wasn't the word. I was exhausted, so sick with fatigue that I hurt. Even though the room was tiny and only a faint sheen of light entered through the window I was too tired even to feel closed in. At the moment, I almost felt that things were being closed out, coming to some sort of climax. I knew I should be planning an escape, that I should be trying to find out where my kids were and make sure they were safe. Instead I was doing good to keep my eyes open. My arms were so heavy it was all I could do to wash the last of the dirt off my legs.

There was nothing else I could do. I had to have some sleep, or I'd be of no use to anyone about anything. On the other hand, to be so fatigue-sodden would make me a sitting duck for Feldshuh and Sternberg and who knew who else.

Quickly I searched the room. It was an excellent prison, being nothing but a small square box. There wasn't even a big armoire, just a tiny one that would have been crowded by half a dozen garments. The bed was little more than a cot and jammed into a corner.

That iron-steaded little bed was the most attractive thing I had seen in a long time. I could fall across it and sleep for hours, which was just what I couldn't do. That would be little better than serving myself up to Feldshuh and company like an hors d'oeuvre.

Finally my sodden brain kicked in with the most basic kind of animalistic, self-preservationist thinking. If I couldn't really disappear, perhaps I could appear to. Every second of surprise I could gain would be one more second I could use to save my life and the kids'. Though it was hard labor, like trying to jog through gelatin, I remade the bed so that the thin cotton coverlet hung down to the floor on the side facing the room. Then I and my purse crawled under it and stretched out on the cool, slightly dusty tile. It was far from comfortable or even sanitary, but at that moment I could have cared less.

Hopefully Feldshuh would glance in the room and, not seeing me, might assume that I had somehow escaped. If he went to look for me, I might...

On that pathetically optimistic note I fell asleep.

Chapter Nineteen

I awoke with a jerk, banging my head against the sagging spring that hung only inches above my sleep-crusted eyes. For a moment there was complete disorientation and I had to consciously remain still until memory returned; even that, when it did come back in horrendous fullness, was not helpful. It was definitely daytime, but only a narrow band of sunlight lay directly at the foot of the shuttered window. My watch confirmed that it was almost eleven o'clock.

I had slept for almost eight hours.

What had happened?

Where were the kids? Were they all right?

Gently I eased out of my improvised hide and peeked around the room, half expecting to find a smiling Feldshuh waiting for me. He seemed to have that kind of humor.

The room was deserted.

As glad as I was to be alive and undisturbed, I didn't quite understand why. Surely by this time Sternberg could have gone to the competition officials and been back a dozen times over. I had no illusions

that he would still kill me even after finding out my
story was true, so – ? Had my little camouflage ruse
worked better than I had hoped? Were Sternberg and
Feldshuh and company out right now looking for their
mysteriously vanished prisoner? Or were they merely
being gentlemanly, sitting downstairs laughing at such
a desperate move while waiting for me to awaken
normally, a delicate kindness before removing me from
their way?

Either way, I didn't like it.

Trying to be as quiet as possible, I slithered from
under the bed and tiptoed over to the door. There I got
the second shock of the morning. I had definitely heard
Feldshuh lock the door last night; now it was hanging
open by a few inches. The open padlock even drooped
from the hasp.

My heart sank. Now my second little scenario made
sense. Feldshuh had come upstairs, seen me asleep
under the bed and decided to let me finish my earthly
rest before giving me my eternal one. He was probably
downstairs right now, probably fully appreciating the
macabre overtones of his gesture. For all the good my
diversion had done I could have slept on top of the darn
cot and been a little bit more comfortable.

Well, I wasn't going to go docilely downstairs like a
lamb to the – literal – slaughter. I was going to creep
out, find an unguarded way out of the place and then
run like the devil. At least, I was going to try.

I was alive and I intended to cause all the trouble

necessary to get my kids and me to safety! I don't like guns for their own sake, but they have a time and a place. I dug down and pulled the 'gift' Selim had given me from the hidden bottom compartment, then carefully unwrapped it and laid it right close to the top of everything, where it was out of sight but available for easy access should it be needed. Though it went against all standard safety rules, I put the safety off. I might need it in a hurry, and this was most definitely not a standard situation.

I blinked, struck by a sudden question I had ignored before. Why had Selim given me a gun? If he were one of the bad guys (whoever they were) why would he give me means to defend myself? Unless it was supposed to cause me a problem. The Israeli government had very dim ideas about gun possession, I believed, and being found with this on my person could mean the beginning of a very uncomfortable round with the police. Or, I thought gloomily, it could be rigged to explode if I tried to fire it, thus removing me when whoever wanted me dead was far away.

Oh, dear Heaven, what was going on here? Who could I trust? What could I trust? I felt like sitting down and weeping, but knew that would be a waste of time. In order to get any answers – in order to find my kids – I had to get out of here.

It went well until I got down to the second floor landing and saw who was there. At first I wondered if Sternberg, not trusting Feldshuh, had decided to sit guard himself and then fallen asleep on the landing. There was no other way down; could I creep past without waking him? Fists clenched around the straps of my purse – in case I had to battle my way out – I tiptoed as quietly as possible until I was next to his outflung arm. Then I saw that I didn't have to tiptoe at all.

His eyes stared sightlessly up. There was a nasty-looking red hole in the side of his head. What I had thought was a shadow was really a pool of rapidly drying blood.

I had never seen a dead body before, at least not that kind of a dead body. Elderly relatives heavily made up and lying in peaceful repose were a totally different thing from a casually distorted body with a piece of its head missing.

For a moment I considered going back up to my little prison and trying to lock myself in, but that was stupid. On the other hand, going on didn't seem to be much more intelligent. Whoever had killed Sternberg might still be lurking around.

I forced myself to take another look at Sternberg. What a strange and tragic death for one of the most respected names in choral music! Who had he been working for and how had he strayed so far from the apolitical idealism of music? What's more than that, how would his death be explained? Would the powers that be expose that he had been part of a dirty espionage scheme or would the whole thing be swept under a metaphoric rug? I didn't know and at that moment I didn't much care.

The blood that pooled beside his shattered head was thick and dark, not fresh. I couldn't even guess how long he had been dead, but judging from that dark blood I knew it had to be some little time. Had this happened right after I went to sleep? Where were Feldshuh and that charming companion of his who had snatched me off the street? I didn't know and didn't particularly want to be found here if they were still around. Gripping the stair rail with both hands, I crept down the broad marble steps on trembling legs.

Feldshuh was in the foyer, lounging elegantly on one of the hard benches just as I had pictured him, except that he was dead. There was a tiny hole, neat as a caste mark, right between his staring eyes.

I didn't bother to look for the man in the taxi. I wasn't even smart enough to look for a back entrance. All I wanted was out and out right then! Policeman, American Embassy, whatever, I wanted to find some authority figure and tell my tale.

At least I did have the good sense to peek outside first and, seeing no one in the dusty garden nor any suspicious cars at the curb, let myself out into the uncomfortably warm, wonderful sunshine.

* * * * *

This time I made it almost to Ramala Road before they (*who this time?*) got me again.

There was no warning, no finesse; a car merely

pulled alongside me, I was snatched roughly inside and before I could even scream an absolutely revolting rag was stuffed in my mouth. Then an equally revolting bag was dropped over my head, I was shoved down to the floor and we sped off towards an unknown destination.

I read lots of detective stories. I know you're supposed to listen to any clues your captors might drop while they converse among themselves and for any clues the car itself might give you – stop lights, railroad tracks, road surfaces, traffic noises, etc. It is a vastly overrated theory. First of all, my captors said absolutely nothing except for one garbled cry of alarm, which was quickly followed by a violent braking and a squeal of a number of tires. Then we drove sedately on, which told me absolutely nothing. Near-misses and minor accidents happened every day on almost every street in Jerusalem's crazy traffic.

Finally I deduced we were heading out of town simply because the traffic noises thinned out and then just about died altogether, but I had no idea of where we were. By that time, frankly, I was concentrating more on not throwing up than on road surfaces, traffic noises or anything else. The rag in my mouth was truly foul and that, combined with the uncomfortable strain of lying face down in the floor of the back seat, draped around an inordinate number of feet and legs, plus the lumpy mound of my purse, made my empty stomach positively roil. I could only pray that something wouldn't make the gun discharge into my stomach.

We must have driven for half an hour after leaving the city. After a while I dared enough to straighten my position as much as I could;. I had no choice – my muscles were screaming. By then we had to have been out of the city, because my captors took pity on me – or perhaps they were just tired of my inarticulate whimpers. In any case, they lifted me up and let me sit between them. It was an improvement... not much, but some.

After a much longer while, when there had been no noise of any other traffic for quite a time, they took the bag off my head and pulled that hideous rag from my mouth. There were three of them; one in front driving, two in the back, one on each side of me. All three wore the *kaffiyeh* brought around and tucked up so that it made an efficient mask, allowing only their eyes to show. At first glance they appeared to be Arabs – probably as I had been supposed to think – but one of them was slow in lowering his eyes. They were pale blue.

Well, whoever they were I was still very much their prisoner. Then, when I looked up and saw where we were, that seemed even more true. We were out in the country all right, so far out that we were almost to the Dead Sea.

"Is this a sightseeing trip?" I asked in a cracked voice.

"Quiet," the driver growled.

"I've always wanted to see this part of the

country..."

"Quiet!" the driver repeated and this time the tone of his voice convinced me that I should.

We drove for at least another twenty minutes in a thick, uncomfortable, unnatural silence. Perhaps I had been around teenagers too long, but the idea of four people trapped in a smallish car for almost an hour and no one saying anything seemed downright unnatural. It did, however, give me time to study the area. We were going down the same road where Grey had taken us the day of our Jericho lunch.

The day the sniper had tried to kill us.

Or had he?

Definitely he (*she? it?*) had shot at us, but surely on such an open road he could have done a better job of it. I began to think. Even if the glass had been bulletproof, he could have shot one of the tires; we had been going so fast that would have just about guaranteed a crash. Then a shot to the gas tank and... boom!

I gulped.

Not that I was sorry he hadn't done a more thorough job of it, yet I couldn't help but wonder if someone desperate enough about something to take shots at an embassy car wouldn't make sure he had completed the job. Unless he didn't intend to kill us, just frighten us.

Allen had said something like that and I hadn't really listened to him. Of course, I did have the excuse that quite a lot had been happening at a horrendous pace, but that didn't negate the idea's validity.

Just a short way before the road dropped away to the Dead Sea shore – just about where the shooting had occurred – we pulled off the paved road onto a narrow dirt track. Even though the driver slowed considerably it seemed that we would be jolted to death, bouncing in and out of potholes the size of hot tubs and over rocks as big as lawn mowers.

Of course I thought of waiting until he was really going slow and then making a jump for it, but decided that would be foolish. First, I could never free my purse from under all our legs even if I did make it out of the car at all, which was doubtful. Then, if miracles occurred and I did escape, where would I go? It was miles and miles over some of the roughest, driest, most desolate terrain in the world to the first human habitation I knew of, and even if these men didn't catch me my chances of getting even one quarter that far were pretty slim.

The road began to climb and for the first time I was glad of my bookend guards. As the car bounced from side to side up the heart-stopping road they were a lot softer to land against than the car doors. I even took a small pleasure every time they grunted as I was slammed against them.

Finally the car slowed to a stop and when the engine shut off the silence descended like a blanket. This time, though, I had no chance to appreciate the stark grandeur of nature; no sooner than the car had stopped the back doors flew open and I was yanked out.

There was nothing man-made in sight. Grunting slightly, one of my *kaffiyeh-ed* captors shoved me forward. Apparently from here on we walked.

I wondered if I would ever return from this desolate place, or would my bones bleach forever in this lonely wasteland? For a moment I came close to breaking. There was so much left to do, so much life to live, and I wanted to live it!

Well, I wasn't dead yet!

Then two small miracles happened.

As I left the car I automatically grabbed my purse, as women will do. My captors noticed and grunted a questioning communication in some language I didn't recognize. Quickly I slung it over my shoulder and hung on for dear life, fully expecting to have it ripped from my grasp. The driver gave me a quick once over, then gave and almost Gallic shrug and shook his head. I was to be allowed to keep my purse.

The second was they didn't tie my hands; I was grateful, because I needed every hand I had and could have used a few more for hanging on. One man in front of me and one behind in single file, we started slithering down a steep and rocky trail that was little more than a scratch against the cliffs. I never noticed what happened to the third man; probably he stayed with the car, but I was too busy trying to keep my purse from overbalancing me and sending me head over teakettle down the steep slope.

Our destination wasn't far, but when we got there I wasn't sure it was any kind of improvement. In fact, at first I didn't even see it. We stood at the top of a large U-shaped gully, where the rocky scree fell away at a sharp angle. Above us was almost a sheer rock wall, sheer only in that it was directly vertical. The surface itself was fissured and channeled as if some gigantic beast had scored it while trying to climb up. Clinging to the rough cliff, our feet almost sliding out from under us, we inched our way past the point of safety.

Then there it was, right in front of me. Where there should have been rough and fissured stone, there was wood. Heavy, flat wood, crudely painted to resemble stone and fitted with hinges and locks that would withstand anything up to a direct mortar assault, all set back deep in a wide crack until it was all but invisible.

Who would put a door in a rock cliff in the middle of the desert? Later I would learn that the door had been put up originally by archaeologists half a century or so ago when the place had been used as a field office and storeroom, but since then it had been commandeered and used by everyone from religious hermits to smugglers to terrorists.

The man in front unlocked the door, opened it and shoved me inside. Caught unawares, I staggered and then sprawled out on the gritty rock floor as the door slammed and locked behind me.

If it had been dark I don't think I could have taken it. I would have burst out screaming and flung myself against the door until it or I had given way. As it was, it was none too good, but for the moment bearable.

The room was a small cube cut out of living rock. At the far side was a seat-like shelf cut into the rock, probably where the body of the original tenant had been laid. All the workmanship appeared to be rough and crude, with great knobby lumps of matrix rock making every surface in the place uneven. That impression, however, may have been exacerbated by the light. A single camper's lantern sat in the middle of the floor, casting a weak and distorting light.

All that I noticed later. The first thing I saw with heartfelt thanks was the six faces of my kids. They were on the shelf thing in the back, huddled together like a nest of abandoned kittens in spite of the airless, sticky heat. They looked dirty and uncomfortable, but they were alive and apparently unharmed. My heart sang.

"You're all right!" I cried, stumbling to my feet. "Thank Heavens! How did you get here? Are any of you hurt?"

A strange glance flashed among them and it was as if a wall had suddenly arisen between us. Tony, after a confirmatory look at the others, slid from the shelf and looked me square in the face. In this strange half-light he looked like a grown man.

"Stay right where you are, Miss Sabine. We know all about you now."

"What?"

"I said we know what you've done and we don't

want anything to do with you."

Chapter Twenty

I don't understand." My arms dropped to my side. "What are you talking about?"

"You dirty spy," spat Carla. Her face was a mask of angry contempt, but there was hurt on the other faces, hurt and sorrow and – in Gerald's case – curiosity.

"How could you, Miss Sabine?" asked Maureen. She was almost in tears.

"You hardly seem the type. It would be most interesting to know if your motives were political or purely monetary." That was Gerald, of course.

I looked blankly from hostile face to hostile face. "What are you talking about? I don't understand."

"What made you do it, Miss Sabine?" growled Larry, his voice taking on the rumbling bass tones that betrayed emotion. There was a new bandage on his forehead, almost covering a swelling and rapidly discoloring cut. "You seemed so nice."

"Do what? Please tell me what you're talking about."

"Sell out our country, you... you Benedict Arnold!" Carla screamed. The sound echoed most uncomfortably in the confined, rocky space.

Betty Jean reached out and put a restraining hand on Carla's arm. "Not so loud, please. Screaming doesn't do any good."

"It makes me feel better," she snapped back, but her volume was lower. Her glare at me was lethal.

"Larry – your head," I asked, truly worried. If these people (*who?*) had started beating up on children...! "Did they – ?"

"There was no violence against our persons," Gerald said, manfully ignoring the baleful glances of the others. "Larry stumbled getting out of the car and hit his head on a planter. The planter," he added with an odd relish, "broke."

"Only a chip!" Larry snapped, giving Gerald a murderous look. "And why would she care anyway?"

"Larry!" I cried, surprisingly hurt.

"Maybe we should let her explain. Maybe there are reasons..."

"There are no reasons for selling out your country, Maureen," Tony said firmly.

"You're just too nice, Maureen," Larry rumbled. "You can't find an excuse for being a traitor."

"Traitor!" I shouted when at last I got enough breath. "What kind of bull are all of you talking? I'm not a traitor."

"Of course you would say that," Carla snapped. "We know better."

"Carla, what are you talking about? What do you think you know?"

"Mr. Burke said…"

Oh, damn!

"And you believed him?"

"Why shouldn't we?"

"Why should you?"

She seemed to have no answer, instead opening and closing her mouth several times before calling me a very unladylike name.

"Did he give you any proof?" I asked. "Because if he did I can guarantee you it's a phony. I would never sell out my country."

My impassioned statement hadn't convinced them; there was still suspicion and hurt in their faces, but there was also a glimmer of doubt. I still had a chance.

Sometimes the best way to state a point, especially with teenagers, is to say nothing. Let them think for a while. I could feel their eyes on me as I sat down gingerly on the rubbly floor, then busied myself with homely tasks.

Being careful to shove the gun out of sight, I dug through my purse with my usual enthusiasm, which Allen had once compared to a terrier going at a rathole.

Allen.

Why on earth had he told Carla that? He couldn't seriously believe…

If he had told her that. Perhaps someone else had told her and then told her to say that it was Allen.

Stop that! It was a bad sign to start making excuses.

Pulling out my makeup case, I grabbed a brush and mirror and tried to set my hair aright. This was the first time I had even thought about my appearance. I didn't even look into the little compact mirror until I had brushed some sort of order into my unruly mop and then I still looked bad enough to scare small children.

I rubbed some lotion onto my parched face and hands – rubbing off a lot of dirt in the process – then held the bottle out. "Want some?"

Again that flash of uncertainty among them. It was Maureen, gentle Maureen, who finally reached out and took it from me.

"It's so dry here," she said.

"Indeed," I replied, not watching as she and Betty Jean used some of the lotion. When it was offered to her, Carla just sniffed viciously and turned her back. Apparently as far as she was concerned even my hand lotion was suspect. What on earth had I done that she should hate me so?

The lotion didn't help my lips. They were cracking painfully. I had covered my entire upper lip with lipstick before discovering it was the wrong one. Well, I thought, that was the least of my worries now. Jezebel would keep my lips moist as well as anything else.

"Why did you send that car for us?"

"I didn't, Gerald."

"But it was your handwriting on the note!"

"No, Carla, it was not. It may have been a good forgery, but I did not write any note."

"So you say." Even in the pale lamplight her eyes glittered.

Somehow, the emotional atmosphere in the room changed indefinably. Maybe the kids weren't so convinced of my guilt after all.

"Why don't you believe Miss Sabine?" asked Maureen.

"Yes, Carla," Gerald chimed in, "you seem most intent on proving Miss Sabine to be in the wrong. What do you have against her?"

"That's not fair!" Larry snapped. "Why are you picking on Carla?"

"You must admit that she does seem very anxious to make Miss Sabine look bad," Gerald said.

"And it was Carla who first told us about Miss Sabine's being a traitor," said Betty Jean.

"Such eagerness toward one who has not done her or any of us any obvious harm is in itself suspect," Gerald said somewhat pompously, even for him. "As the Bard says, 'Methinks she doth protest too much...'"

"You shut up, you little toad!" Without warning Carla flew at Gerald, all claws out. It was a thoroughly unequal match, taking both Larry and Tony – with varying degrees of gentleness – to pull her off Gerald's cowering form.

"Stop it this minute!"

There was still enough residual respect for my position as their leader for them to respond to me. Either that, or my sheer volume in that small space stunned them in to momentary immobility. In any case, it gave me a small advantage and I used it ruthlessly.

"Don't you see that's probably what they want? To set us at each others' throats? If we're fighting each other we can't work together."

Slowly, uneasily, they broke apart. Carla looked at me venomously, but settled on the shelf quietly enough.

"Them who?" asked Tony.

"I don't know."

"And she wouldn't tell you if she did."

"What have I done to you, Carla? Why do you want to believe the worst of me so badly?"

She wouldn't meet my eyes. "You know what. You can fool them, but you can't fool me."

"I wouldn't try to, Carla."

"Where have you been, Miss Sabine?" That was Larry, chivalrously taking up his beloved's point even though his reluctance showed. "Can you explain this?"

"I can tell you what I know," I said carefully, seeing the surprise in their faces. "Remember the day you went on the city tour with St. Anselm's I said I had some paperwork to do? Well, I did do some, but I also fibbed a bit. I had some very special souvenirs I wanted to pick up, stuff for my parents and my best friend, and the man I work for back home had asked me to pick up something for his wife, so I made a small shopping trip to the Old City before going back to work."

Carla snorted as if the admission of such a minor culpability were proof of complete guilt.

"Maybe," I continued without a break, "it wasn't quite the thing to do, I admit, but I knew that on the days we had set aside for shopping and sightseeing I'd be more interested in looking after all of you than seeing to my own purchases. Anyway, I found the perfect thing for my boss' wife... or so I thought. I bought it and that's when all the trouble started."

"What is it?"

"How did it start the trouble?"

"A full-sized copy of the Crown of the Virgin of Janóch, Maureen, and I don't really know how it started the trouble, Tony. I just know that ever since I've had it all kinds of weird things have been happening."

"Like Mr. Hamilton-ffoulkes," said Carla.

"Among other things," I replied evenly, "like running into Allen Burke again."

Carla harrumphed, then turned away, which alarmed me no end. Just how well had she and Allen gotten acquainted? And what had she been doing in the Old City with Grey last night?

"So you think these guys are after that Crown?" Tony asked.

"I think that might be it."

"But the Crown of the Virgin of Janóch has been found," protested Gerald. "They were talking about it at the Hall of World Peace yesterday. Day before yesterday the Zurich police found it in the possession of a dealer known to handle stolen artworks. They believe it was being sold to a private collector in Japan."

"Maybe they don't know the one Miss Sabine has is a fake," suggested every practical Betty Jean.

"Don't be silly," Gerald said patronizingly. "It's been all over the papers and television."

"Lots of people might not see it," Maureen answered.

"And maybe they think it's a trick and don't want to believe it," Tony said. "Or maybe it is some sort of a cover up."

"The one I bought is definitely a fake," I said, feeling I should at least try to keep some sort of control over the conversation. I don't know why; it had never worked before. "It's pretty, but the workmanship gives it away."

"Of course," Carla dripped innocence, "you could still be part of it. Maybe you double-crossed your partners..."

"That's not true, Carla. No matter what you think, I have no partners to double cross. Now to go back and answer Tony's question of where have I been..." I told them of my adventures for the last twenty or so hours, leaving nothing out, not even Sternberg's and Feldshuh's deaths. I also included Carla's meeting with Grey.

All eyes swung to her and she met them with a coolness worthy of a seasoned celebrity twice her age.

"Now," I said quickly, before tempers could erupt, "why don't you tell me what happened to all of you."

Somehow it had evolved that Tony, one of the least articulate of the bunch, had become the spokesman with Gerald acting as sort of a hyper-verbose counterpoint. Each of the others – with the exception of the icy Carla – threw in their own viewpoints and experiences, which made it all a pretty incomprehensible mish-mash.

When I finally got everything straightened out, it was pretty much as I had imagined. The car, accompanied by the forged note, had picked them up from the Embassy and driven them to a large private house on the outskirts of the city. They had been separated, questioned one by one, then locked up alone. Although no one said anything, this must have been when Carla had left the house and gone to meet Grey.

This morning they had been reunited, though under a heavy guard. After a good breakfast they had been put into a closed van, driven here and left. Aside from being frightened to death they appeared to have been treated fairly well, which put some of my more lurid fears to rest.

"But what did they question you about?" I asked with a blithe disregard for grammar.

"You, mostly," Tony said, a definite edge of accusatory suspicion still in his voice.

"Where you were," added Maureen.

"How well we knew you," ditto Larry.

"They seemed to be interested in all of our

movements and plans, and most especially in yours, Miss Sabine." Gerald looked around, almost as if waiting for someone to tell him to shut up, then continued. "You definitely seemed to be the focus of their inquiry, though I was queried about each of the others."

"So was I." The refrain ran through the group with the notable exception of Carla.

"What if we just give them the old Crown?" Maureen asked. "They they'll let us go."

"Stupid," Tony said. "We can't."

I knew where his mind was going, because I had already thought the same thing. Once whoever it was who had us got the Crown – if that were indeed what they wanted – they couldn't let witnesses live. Was that why we had been left in this filthy stone box in the desert without any water? Were they going to let us die of heat and thirst and madness, then come in and take what they wanted? Our bodies could be left anywhere in the desert and, if we were even found, I would be blamed as an irresponsible teacher leading her charges into a danger from which we were not rescued.

The scenario was so pat it was terrifying.

"It seems," I said quickly, the second thing in my mind spilling out, "that we have at least two groups to deal with."

"How do you deduce that?"

"It's simple, Gerald. Why would they be asking you where I was if they had me?"

His round little head bobbed. "True, unless they were trying to mislead us."

"Why would they do that, dummy?" Tony asked. "We ain't of any importance."

The lamp had been sinking, pulling the shadows in closer around us, then it popped twice and almost went out.

"We're almost out of oil," Maureen said unnecessarily.

"Is there any more?"

Tony shook his head. "Nah, there's nothing in here."

"When we first got here we searched the place all over," Larry said. "We were looking for a way out. Believe me, there isn't anything in here."

"Not even any water," Carla complained.

"Do you have any water in your purse, Miss Sabine?" Maureen tried to disguise the naked hope in her voice, but failed.

"My pocket flash is getting low," I said, diving into my purse once more. I was unable to answer and would not let myself cry. "But I think I have some spare batteries in here."

"Is that where you're keeping the Crown?" asked Gerald and Tony replied contemptuously, "Do you think she'll tell you, dummy?"

I ignored the conversation, as if that were possible in a rock chamber no more than eight feet square, and continued to dig. The business of finding the batteries and replacing them took long enough to kill all conversation and once the little beam was strong again it did not revive, which was just fine with me. I was working hard to think, to plan, and, most of all, to keep my relentlessly encroaching claustrophobia away.

"Why don't we use this and turn out the lamp?" I suggested neutrally. "It might make it cooler."

Somehow whatever our differences we became a unit against the dark and its attendant unknown. I turned down the wick of the flickering lamp, then set the little pocket flash in the middle of the floor like a candle. It made almost as much light as the lantern and a great deal less heat, both of which we appreciated. If they suspected I had any other motive for the switch, they didn't show it.

In this ageless place time literally had no hold. We might have been in there for hours or days. Several of us wore watches, but they seemed to cease to matter as time took on an entirely new dimension.

There was a large boulder protruding from the wall, sort of over to the other side from the shelf. It was too irregular to have been used for any practical purpose; perhaps it was formed of a rock too hard for the mason's primitive tools. Perhaps... I really didn't care anything about it except that it made a dandy backrest. The kids had sprawled over the shelf and on the ground at its foot, leaving as much space between us as possible, even though it wasn't much. I had not yet convinced them, though now there were glimmers of uncertainty among them.

I had worse worries than if they believed in me or not. The heat in here was rising and the air was getting very stale. What there was of it. In ancient times this rock-cut tomb would have been sealed with a great rock, perhaps with the cracks filled in with rubble. I don't know how air-tight that would have been, but the modern door was pretty good. Oh, I don't mean air-tight in the scientific, vacuum-creating sense, though what we had was good enough. I was just worried that it was tight enough not to allow in sufficient oxygen to replace what we used.

If the lamp hadn't guttered when it did I would have said something, but I didn't want to alarm the kids. They had enough on their plates at the moment and I wanted to spare them any worry I could. Maybe I was wrong... but from the drowsy way they were lying around I didn't think so.

We were in very real danger of suffocating and I was powerless to do anything about it.

Chapter Twenty-One

An unquantifiable length of time later the atmosphere of the tomb was definitely getting thicker. I had been trying to think, to try and make some sense out of all these incredible incidents, but my brain simply would not work. The little flashlight's new batteries hadn't started to weaken yet, but the air was getting fouler and fouler. I looked at the gang, my six charges, my responsibilities, and remembered how cocky I had been about being able to keep them safe. Surely somewhere a malign god was laughing.

The gang was drooping, almost asleep. Or unconscious. I wondered if we could really die from being shut up in here or if we would just suffer irreversible brain damage. I had looked at the door; the wood was incredibly thick and definitely locked. Whoever had cut it had done a wonderful job, for there was scarcely a quarter inch opening at the most all the way around the edge between the wood and hard rock. Air was coming in, but would it be enough to keep us alive and sane?

I thought about trying yet again to open it, but the

idea of moving away from my rock seemed too much to bear. Wasn't that one of the symptoms of oxygen starvation? Everything was just too much trouble...

Perhaps it was only a fantasy, the offshoot of a fuzzy brain's wishful thinking, but there was a sound, a scraping like that of bolts being drawn back.

Although it was desert-hot and blisteringly dry, the flood of fresh air was as good as a wave of cold water to bring life back to my mind. I never remembered anything that felt so good and when the blazing light of sunset (*only sunset? of the same day?*) poured in it was like a benediction from a merciful deity.

And when Allen Burke, his face pale and rigid with urgency, scrambled in through the opening I felt positively elated. In spite of all I had feared he was all right, Allen was all right and in the long romantic tradition of heroic white knights he had come to rescue me.

"Allen!" Carla cried, scrambling to her feet and trying to look very grownup and desirable despite her filthy jeans and smudged face.

"Hey, man, where've you been?"

"Thank Heavens you've come..."

Apparently my group was much better acquainted with Allen Burke than I had believed.

"Hush, guys," I said quickly, my mood evaporated by the ugly 9 mm automatic he was pointing at me.

"Hey," Tony snarled, his fists clenching, "what's all this?"

"Shut up, kid!" Allen growled in a voice that sounded totally unlike his own.

It was perhaps the first time anyone had ever said 'shut up' to Tony when he had been unable to beat them up for doing it. He obviously did not like the sensation. "What's this guy –?"

"Tony, please be quiet!" I cried and to my relief for once Tony did what he was told. Everyone saw the gun now and the old stone room fairly sang with tension. "Allen, I'd like to know that, too. What are you doing? What's the meaning of this?"

"Always the wide-eyed innocent, Robin," he said in a harsh tone. "Give it over."

In the faint light of the pocket flash Allen's expression was cruel and feral and utterly unlike I had ever seen it. He resembled nothing more than a particularly nasty cat toying with a cornered mouse.

I had once loved this man. I had dreamed of spending the rest of my life with him. I thought I had known him well and tried to excuse the little doubts that had sprung up from the beginning. How could I have been so wrong about someone? I felt not only grief for the death of an old love, but embarrassment for having been so criminally stupid!

There was something else, too. I had taken charge of six teen-agers – rowdy and ill behaved and self centered, yes, but still little more than children – and now they were being made to grow up in a quick and unforgivable way. After facing a gun in the hands of a man like Allen Burke was proving himself to be they could never really be children again. I could only hope that they would be allowed to be grown-ups somewhere else besides this hot and stinking hole in the rock.

"Where is it?" he asked and suddenly everything became crystal clear.

There was really no reason to be coy, but I was going to buy as much time as I could. Whatever happened, I would go down fighting.

Do not go gentle into that good night...

For all that I hate poetry, why did I have to think of that just at this moment when above all I had to be clear headed?

"Damn it, Robin, don't stand there like a scared rabbit," Allen said, sounding more like himself. "I don't want to hurt any of you, but I've got to have it! *Where is it?*"

"Miss Sabine, what's he talking about?" Maureen piped, her voice reedy as a piccolo. I could only guess at what courage it took for her to speak.

"Goddammit, dummy, be quiet!" Tony roared. He was unaccustomed to not being in control and his face was contorted with impotent rage. At all costs I must keep him from doing anything foolish.

"It's obvious that he wants the Crown," Gerald said with the same patronizing air of superior intelligence that he displayed with such dreary regularity, not realizing what a stupid move he had made. I had never disliked him so much as at that moment.

"Gerald!" A chorus of despair rose from six throats – mine included – and Tony, set on fulfilling a dream that had been in his mind for the entire trip, forgot the gun and stepped forward, swinging at Gerald with a clenched fist and sending him sprawling.

"Why couldn't you keep your dumb trap shut, you frigging bird-brained genius? Now he knows that we know about it."

More frightened than actually hurt, Gerald made no move to rise. He looked as if for the first time in his life he thought he might possibly have been in the wrong. It was not a pleasant expression, but the others didn't have time to savor it. Allen waved his gun in a seemingly casual motion and suddenly Tony sprawled limply on the dusty stone floor.

"Tony!" Betty Jean called in her throaty voice, all pretense of uninvolvement gone. What a pity Tony couldn't have seen the expression on her face as she fell to her knees beside him, gathering his dark head into her lap. A thread of blood seeped from his forehead and, having seen too much blood in the last few hours, I almost panicked until I could see the regular rise and fall of his chest.

"Now all of you shut up! Stop right there, Robin."

Again the gun was pointed unerringly at my midsection. I had been easing to the side, trying to get away from the kids, so at least I wouldn't have to worry about their being in the line of fire. He seemed to read my mind, though, and stepped to his right, putting the entire bunch of them squarely between us. The ones still standing, that was; at the moment the fallen made that little tomb look more like the final act of some of Verdi's more bloodthirsty operas.

"I'm tired of playing games, Robin. It took us too long to find out that what we wanted was the Crown, and we've chased you all over this damned country and a damned merry chase you and your friends have led us, too. Now this Crown..."

"We?" I asked brightly. I was on uneven ground; I spread my feel slightly further apart and flexed my knees as much as I dared in case a chance to move should come.

"Of course," he said contemptuously, killing one of my hopes. "Only fools would come on an assignment like this alone." He made it sound an indictment.

"Allen, let the kids go."

"As soon as you give me this Crown. How very like you to choose a Crown, romantic little Robin!"

"It's just a souvenir for my boss' wife," I said, desperately trying to deflect his attention.

"The Crown?" Even flat on the ground Gerald was still Gerald and, Heaven help us, he probably always would be. "It was in all the papers."

"Shut up, kid!"

Gerald never did know when to quit pressing his luck. "But it's a fake! The real one is in Switzerland..."

Allen swung the gun to within inches of his nose. "I said shut up!"

Gerald blanched and for a moment it looked as if he would be explosively sick. It was understandable. The muzzle on even the largest handgun is less than an inch in diameter, but when that small dark void is staring directly at you it is the biggest, scariest pit in the whole world and anyone who tells you different is a liar!

It was a small chance, a minuscule chance, and the only one I had, so I took it.

The instant Allen's eyes left me I jumped as far to the left as I could, hoping that I would get far enough to keep the kids out of the line of fire. The floor was filled with small (and some not so small) rocks as well as grit and debris and I could feel all of it scraping ruthlessly at my bare legs and arms as I hit the dirt in a sliding dive that any pro baseball player would envy.

As it turned out, my heroics were all for naught because I had underestimated Tony. When he had fallen I hadn't noticed that his outflung arm was right next to the flashlight. He had been watching everything through slitted lids and when Allen's attention had moved to Gerald, he snapped the light off, plunging the interior of the tomb into a nightmare chiaroscuro of red and black.

Outside the sun was just about gone, leaving behind a sky stained the color of fresh blood. Desert sunsets are short; in just a few minutes it would be black dark outside. Shoving Betty Jean aside, Tony knocked Allen's legs out from under him and made a manful attempt to try and take the gun away from him. No matter how great a heart or an intention, however, they are no match for an old pro who knows his job.

Allen sent him flying with almost no effort and Tony's body made a sick thunk against the stone wall.

"Now don't," he said in a hard voice as he scrambled to his feet, "any of you try anything stupid like that again." His gun was brightly nickel plated and in the uncertain red light seemed to glow like a laser. Everything else was shadow and suggestion, but that gun was brilliantly visible as it pointed directly toward Maureen.

"Now light that lantern."

"I don't have any matches," she said, then Allen threw a packet of them at her knees. His head swung back and forth like some sort of radar, his eyes attempting to probe the darkness where I was trying to be so quiet.

Maureen's hands shook as she tried to light the lantern.

"Robin?" Allen said in a deceptively gentle tone. "You can't get out."

Now that there was sufficient oxygen, the wick flared and caught and the room was bathed in brilliant light. It showed unmercifully how dirty and disheveled we all were, except for Allen., He looked as he always had, corduroys, multi-pocketed jacket, long sleeved shirt with cufflinks and all, which only added to the unreality of the scene. He must be sweltering. The light outlined the rough walls of the tomb and the sharp edge of the shelf. It highlighted the ancient scratchings in the rock and glinted coolly off the blue steel of the revolver that had been Selim's little gift.

"I wasn't trying to get out."

"Miss Sabine!" someone breathed in awed tones.

Allen's lips curved upward in an admiring smile. "So you are a professional. I knew it!"

"Put the gun down, Allen."

"Why should I? I just want what I came for."

"Put the gun down, Allen!"

"I'm not leaving without it, Robin. Now if it's part of that Crown, just give it to me and we can..."

"No way."

"Think, Robin. You can try to kill me, but I can kill you. Or one of these kids."

I had positioned myself well; the kids were well to one side of us, but just the thought upset me and, curse him, he would know that. Still, he would have to turn sideways both to aim and shoot if he were going to try for one of the kids and if I were very quick and very lucky...

And if I could shoot a person, even Allen Burke, at all.

"Why, Allen? Why do you want the Crown? Everyone knows it's a fake and not worth more than a hundred dollars or so."

Once again his pistol's deadly eye was looking directly at my stomach. I tried not to think about it.

"Don't try to be cute, Robin. You know as well as I that the Crown is just the carrier. I never thought you'd sell out your country, Robin." His voice shook just the tiniest bit. "Let me help you. There's still time..."

"Do you know what's in the Crown, Allen?" I asked, ignoring the kids' gasps. Their belief in me was plummeting visibly.

"I'd kind of like to know that myself," Tony said carefully. He had stayed on the ground. Ruefully one hand rubbed his jaw, which now had its own decoration of blood, while his other arm protectively cradled a white-faced Betty Jean, though whether her concern was more for our predicament or for Tony's wounds was a questionable point.

"And what do you mean about Miss Sabine selling out her country?" Larry asked in a voice that cracked with pain.

"Yeah," piped Maureen defiantly. "Miss Sabine wouldn't do anything like that."

Allen's expression changed to one of sorrowful understanding. He was good! "All right, kids. I'll level with you. Some of you know who I am and I'm going to trust you not to break my cover. I'm with the CIA. I've been keeping Miss Sabine under observation ever since you landed in Israel."

"I've been trying to tell you about your precious Miss Sabine, but you just wouldn't listen!" Carla said with a repellent smugness. "Now maybe you'll believe me."

"I still don't think Miss Sabine is a spy!" That was Maureen, bless her!

Allen spared her a glance. He was so realistic I could almost believe him myself. "This isn't the first time I met your Miss Sabine, little girl. Last year..."

"Allen! No!" I couldn't help myself and it cost me belief.

"I even fell in love with her a little. Until I found her trying to take sensitive documents out of a safe."

"Miss Sabine is a safecracker?" asked Larry, but Gerald merely nodded.

"She has perfect pitch. It must have been one of the new sonic sequence types."

Allen looked startled, as if that fat boy were another agent. "One of the prototypes," he confirmed uneasily.

"But how," Tony asked, gingerly shifting both Betty Jean and himself into a more comfortable position, "does that tie in with us and the competition?"

"About three months ago a deep mole at the Pentagon broke his cover trying to get a batch of missile plans into the hands of an unfriendly foreign power..."

"Who?"

"Russia?"

"China?"

"Russia's our friend now, stupid."

"It would seem that since the Soviet Union has broken up that Russia alone would be unlikely purchaser. Logic would dictate a more probable destination in one of the Middle Eastern countries."

"Like Iran? Al-Qaeda or the Taliban?"

"What about Pakistan? Especially if they have a civil war?"

I could almost feel sorry for Allen. He wasn't used to the rapid-fire dialogue of teen-agers and it rattled him.

"Sorry," he said quickly. "That's all classified. Anyway, we got them all back except one. It's a device that makes anything it is attached to immune to all conventional radar and sonar systems. Theoretically it can be put on anything – planes, subs, missiles, and nobody knows anything about it until there is visual contact."

"The Invisible Man," Gerald said smugly. "Professor Callender lectured on it. I didn't know it had ever become practical."

Allen's eyes widened. "Well informed, aren't you? Believe me, it's practical," he added in grim tones, "and there are countries out there who would pay almost anything for the plans. We got a tip that Robin Sabine would be picking them up, so it appears that they're on that Crown. Give it to me, Robin," he snarled.

For a long moment we stared at each other. Once he got his hands on the Crown, with or without the information (*a missile cloaking system? fantastic!*) I was a dead woman for sure, and probably the kids would be too. He was a very thorough man. The fact that I had once loved him turned the tears I had shed into galling acid. Sucker, sucker, sucker!

"Would you believe me if I said I don't have it?"

"Come on! Your stuff has been searched, so you've got to have it. You've been watched, so you couldn't have put it anywhere, and those clowns Zinneman and Sternberg didn't have it."

"So it was you who killed them?"

"They wouldn't give me the Crown. I'd like to know how you got away from them. Smooth move, Robin."

I didn't feel like enlightening him. Just the thought that this murderous creature had looked into the room where I slept unprotected by anything but a length of screening fabric made me ill. "That doesn't necessarily mean it's here."

"You haven't had a chance to do anything with it. Don't push me, Robin."

"Miss Sabine, it's our duty as citizens to help the CIA..." Carla said throatily. She was back to posturing again. I was wondering exactly what it was he had told her.

"Allen, we can talk..."

"I don't want to talk. I want the Crown."

I had not forgotten the gun I had pointed at him. I raised it in what I hoped was a menacing gesture. "Let the kids go."

"Don't want them to see that you're a traitor? Robin, Robin... Your government doesn't want..."

"How dare you speak to me about the American government!" I snapped. My nerves were starting to stretch and snap. This really wasn't the way I had planned for things to go, but if anything were to be done, if anyone were to get out of here alive, I should have to start doing something.

"The Crown, Robin. Now."

"All right."

Chapter Twenty-Two

My purse was open beside me, where I had dug in it for the gun after my scrambling dive. Keeping both the gun and my gaze squarely on Allen, I knelt down – at great cost to the painful scratches on my knees and legs – and rummaged in its capacious depths until the cold ring of metal and glass was firm in my hand.

Fake it might be, but when the light hit the Crown the stones erupted into a glittering fountain of colors – red and blue and green and yellow – as if it had been illuminated from within. Legend had it that the original had been designed from an ecstatic vision of the Virgin's halo; it was easy to see where a people less sophisticated and more devout than our learned, cynical, greedy race today might have taken such beauty for a sign of Divine Favor.

Only one person in the room was unaffected by its radiant glory, his mind instead occupied by the idea of a black smudge on one of the gems that to the uninitiated might be nothing more than a flaw in the stone. Allen wet his lips and held out his hand.

"Hand it over."

"In exchange for your gun."

"You are something else, Robin. You know I'm going to have to take you in."

I had no illusions about my chances of surviving the trip if he took me anywhere, but there were other things to think about besides myself.

"Let the kids go and we'll talk about it."

"I'm sure these guys are loyal Americans. They won't stand still and let a traitor get away."

That was hitting below the belt. I had never thought that he would actually use my own kids against me – or that he might succeed at it. On the other hand, there was Carla, and now the others were regarding me with almost hostile speculation. They had no way of knowing what a risk they were taking. I took a deep breath.

"You're right. Okay, I'll go with you. But just to make sure nothing does fall into the wrong hands, I'll destroy this."

It was no small feat to pop one of the jewels out of its setting with just one hand, but once the colored glass hit the ground, looking like a piece of light itself on the dusty floor, it crushed easily under my heel.

"My kids will testify to what they've heard and seen. If these plans are as volatile as you say, they'll be safer destroyed."

Another jewel gave way to my insistent fingers and crunched underfoot.

"Stop that!" Allen screamed in a high, almost

hysterical pitch (*an e-flat, I think*) that sounded nothing like him.

"Why? This way the plans will be safe... from both of us."

"But not from me."

Incredibly enough, we had been so intent on watching each other that three men had slipped in the doorway and none of us had noticed. All of them were armed, too, and at the sight of so much steely-eyed firepower aimed at all of us my stomach just sort of rolled over and died.

"Grey..."

"An interesting situation, Robin." The lamplight glittered on his blond hair, turning it into the golden helmet of an ancient warrior, which didn't go at all well with the modern pistol he was holding. It was an automatic of a make I didn't recognize, large and deadly and very efficient looking. It was also pointed negligently between us, which meant that it was aimed directly at the kids. I felt no fear for them, however, for no bullet from that gun would ever dare go anywhere except where Grey Hamilton-ffoulkes wished it to and he had nothing against the children.

At least, I didn't think so.

"Now put your guns down," he said pleasantly. "Both of you."

Reluctantly both Allen and I let our hands fall to our sides.

"I can handle this. This is an American affair,"

Allen said through clenched teeth. "We don't need any of you British glory-grabbers coming in at the last minute to take the credit."

"And good evening to you, too, Mr. Burke," said Grey at his smoothest. "Might I ask what this bizarre little party is all about?"

I would have expected the kids to erupt into babble at that, but apparently they had been frightened into silence. I tried to think of something to say, but Allen spoke first.

"Miss Sabine is in the possession of a stolen article. It's my duty to get it back."

"That Crown?" Grey asked, glancing at the mistreated object in my hands. "It's a fake, and rather the worse for wear, but I daresay you know that. Robin, are you always that hard on everything?"

"This is not time to be urbane, Grey."

"Agreed," he said easily, the pistol wavering carelessly between Allen and me. The men with him I dismissed as either stalwart co-workers or hired goons who could be dealt with, but at the moment Grey Hamilton-ffoulkes scared me as much as Allen Burke ever had. "But it will have to do until someone gives me a reasonable explanation."

"The Invisible Man," Gerald said with unprecedented brevity.

"What? The missile masking system?" Now even Grey was shaken.

"You know about that, too?"

"Yes, I do, Tony. It's not all that secret, especially in diplomatic circles. I presume it was in the Crown? Yes, that would explain why half a dozen people have been killed over that rather gaudy piece of costume jewelry. A pretty thing, or at least it was. What have you been doing to it, Robin? Still, hardly worth all those lives."

"It's United States property... My duty..." Allen was sweating now, more than the dropping temperature of the tiny room would warrant. The temperature outside was falling as rapidly as the sun. I suppose I was sweating, too.

"The CIA..." Carla began, but her worshipful voice was cut short by a vicious glance from Allen.

"Will you keep quiet, you dumb bitch?"

"Allen, you told me..."

"Goddammit, I can't trust anybody!"

Carla's eyes welled and spilled over with tears. "But you said that you loved me, that I could help you..." she blubbered.

It explained a great deal, but it didn't make me feel any better. My heart ached for her betrayal, even as it ached for my own over a year before.

"Calm down, Mr. Burke!" Grey said and the ice in his tone seemed to bring the temperature down even more alarmingly. "It is no secret that the U.S. government has an operative in this affair."

"Well, that's different." Allen smiled and once again appeared as innocent and ingenuous as he had that first afternoon we had met by the ornamental garden pond at Ravenhurst Castle. At the time I had thought it a serendipitous accident. Now I would bet it had been anything but. "I'm sure you understand that this is purely an American security matter... Hey! What are you doing?" he snarled and his face became ugly as one of the men tried to take his gun. His hand tightened and there was a horrible moment as the muzzle waved toward the kids until he relaxed and let it be slipped from his fingers.

I let the other young man take mine without resistance. I knew when I was overmatched.

"And who are you with, really with?" Tony asked Grey. He was standing up now and behind that sullen face I could see the wheels of intelligence turning.

Grey smiled. "The British Embassy. Unlike almost everyone else you have met during your stay in Jerusalem, I am exactly what I claim to be."

"Well, that's good to know. If you'll help me..." Allen grinned and I felt a thrill of fear. He was going to pull it off, curse the man!

"Just a moment, if you please, Mr. Burke. I said it was no secret that the Americans had an operative on this; what is unclear is just who that operative is."

"What? That's ridiculous. I've just identified myself."

"Indeed you have, Mr. Burke, but I'm an old-fashioned kind of a fellow. However, I have always thought that the best place to get information is from the source, so I contacted the head office. Talked to a very efficient man named Brubaker."

My stomach knotted and lurched.

"Who's he?" Tony asked.

"You're a young man full of questions, aren't you, Tony? A good trait. Mr. Brubaker is head of interior security for an agency which, by the way, is not precisely the CIA, but rather a small elite offshoot that is officially non-existent."

"How do you know so much about it, then?"

"Friends. And a high security rating. Even so, I probably wouldn't have gotten through if they hadn't been having quite a flap about a breach in security. They thought I could help them."

"A breach in security?" Allen breathed. "Do they know who...?"

"Anyway," Grey went on, sublimely ignoring Allen and playing shamelessly to an audience of open-mouthed kids, "I called this Mr. Brubaker, who for your information is a devilishly tempered fellow when he's awoken in the wee hours, and got clearance. So, I suppose, in a way that makes me an official operative for the American government."

I eyed him speculatively. He looked thoroughly amused at the situation. It could all be bluff. The existence of such an agency and even a man's name wouldn't be too difficult for someone of his credentials to discover. Or, he could have made some clever deductions and made the rest up out of whole cloth. So far he hadn't really proved anything.

"Well, I'm glad of that," Allen said heartily. "Did I get a clean bill of health?"

"Brubaker said he had assigned one of his best couriers to the job," Grey replied with an enigmatic smile.

The kids were all staring at me with eyes brimming over in sorrow and shock. I wished that this could be easier for them. I hoped that someday I would be in a position to explain, to let them know the whole truth.

"He did? That's nice of him." Allen was expansive. He had always liked compliments. "Now if you'll just take these guys back to Jerusalem, I'll take Robin here and start processing the evidence."

"No hard feelings?" Grey asked almost shyly. "After all, 'When comrades part, 'tis never known they will meet again,'" he quoted casually and my heart almost stopped beating there and then.

Allen smiled. "Oh, I wouldn't be too sure we won't run into each other again, Hamilton-ffoulkes. It's a small world."

"'When a year passes, nought can bring it back again.'" My throat was dry and my voice felt as small as Maureen's at her most frightened, but I enunciated every word perfectly.

I can't describe it, but the atmosphere, the very air itself in the tomb changed at that exact moment, becoming as charged and dangerous as an electrical storm. Grey whirled around and although his face didn't change there was a look in his eyes that turned me to melting butter. My heart was beating so hard it was a wonder that it didn't deafen everyone in that tiny rock room.

"'But whence did it go, this year that is dead?'" he intoned, his voice a shade deeper.

I answered, "'Surely a place far beyond the mind of man.'"

"'It is part of an endless river flowing to the west.'"

"'But empties like all into the encompassing sea.'"

By then Allen had caught on, if not to the exact mechanics of the operation at least to the spirit of the thing and started a vigorous protest. It was just as well, for I could never say that line about my neighbors carving potatoes without giggling.

"What's going on?" he roared, diving into one of the many pockets in his jacket. "I've got proper identification..."

But it wasn't identification, it was a small revolver that suddenly appeared in his hand. Amazing how that little gun could make so much noise. It filled the confined space, bounding and rebounding on sharp claws until it seemed that it was the noise itself that smashed through my flesh instead of the deadly soft-nosed bullet they dug out of me later.

Chapter Twenty-Three

Voices.

"She's lost a lot of blood."

"Messy wound. Lucky that rib deflected the bullet or she'd never have made it."

Lucky? I thought vaguely. *Lucky to feel like this? He was crazy!*

But thinking was too much of an effort.

Later. More voices.

"All I want to know is when can you tell us something?" Angry. "It's been hours."

"I'm sorry, but she's not responding." Placating.

"Well then, bloody well do something!" Angrier.

Long lovely black silence. So nice, so comforting, so easy to slip into...

If...

I floated content on that dark sea, tethered by only one strand, one annoying strand that stuck and grew and grew until its whiteness lit the sky and burned my eyes while its creaking took on many sounds that stamped at my ears and no matter how I tried I could not find the dark sea again.

There were things around me now, things with

teeth and fingers that bit and stuck and pulled... I cried out for them to go away.

"Well, we've got a positive response."

"It's about time. I was afraid we were going to lose her."

"No. This lady is special," said a familiar voice that I couldn't quite place but still something within me thrilled at the pride it held.

The darkness swirled in again, taking me once more to that place of silence.

I kicked and fought and my mind at last thrashed free of the darkness.

A woman's voice; soft, urgent. "I know it's late, but thank you for coming. She's been saying things, repeating them over and over, and getting quite upset. We thought you might know what they meant. That you might help calm her."

"I'll try."

Once more a hand touched me, but this one was gentle and I clung to it.

"Tell me," said a soft, beautiful voice. "Tell me what you said."

Once again I sent out my signal, "' When comrades part...'" the same three words I had repeated until my throat was raw and dry.

"'...'tis never known they will meet again...' Come back, Robin. Come back."

* * * * *

On the second evening after that horrible episode

in the rock tomb even I began to think I might live. That's not as easy a thing to believe as one might think, especially when you can't move, you're bandaged from here to there, half the time you're in pain and the other half you're out of your head with drugs and you have more tubes and needles stuck in you than a mad scientist's experiment.

Anyway, on that third morning I was delighted when the nurse took out two of my tubes and began straightening my hair.

"We must look our best when we have a gentleman caller," she chirruped, and suddenly I didn't feel so good.

I was still under a ban on all visitors, so it could only be Grey, to whom it seemed no rules applied. At first I said I wouldn't see him; the disgustingly chipper nurse seemed to think that I was worried about my looks and kept saying how they didn't really matter, not with a man who seemed determined to send me half the flowers in Jerusalem.

Well, it did matter – even with my hair tidied I still looked like death warmed over – but that wasn't the reason. The drugs they had given me had been pretty efficient, but I had fairly good memories of repeating my identification code over and over again and only being quieted by Grey's repeating it back to me... over and over again. It was not the sort of memory one liked to recall.

However, it appeared I had no say in the matter,

for not ten seconds after the nurse's starched back had disappeared through the door Grey entered, smiling lightly.

"Well, how are we doing today?"

"We've been talking to the nurse, haven't we, so we know that we are doing just fine!" I said peevishly.

He laughed at that, his careful smile exploding into mirth, and pulled the single straight chair next to the bed. "Thank God! I thought to find you all soggy and emotional. What a relief to find you already back to your usual bobbish self."

I wouldn't have described the way I felt as 'bobbish,' but it certainly beat being regarded as a Camille-like flower teetering on the verge of extinction. People didn't tell the truth to sick people and there was too much I had to know.

"How are the kids? Are they all right? Who's looking after them?"

"Wait a minute..." he threw up his hands and his uncomfortable expression could not quite hide the laughter in his incredible blue eyes. "I'm only here on sufferance and you're supposed to be resting."

"How can I rest? They're my responsibility and no one will tell me anything except that 'They're all right, they're all right.'"

"They are all right, Robin. In fact, they have a number of people fighting to look after them – the competition people and my people at the embassy, to say nothing of your own embassy people. They've been fêted, toured and entertained as much as we all can. When we can pry them away from the waiting room here, that is."

"Here?"

"They are all worried about you, girl, and undergoing the most exquisite guilt because they doubted you."

"Well," I was surprised to hear myself saying, "what choice did they have, after all that bastard told them? What about Carla?"

"The prematurely lubricious Miss Parkinson has been submitted to a rather extensive debriefing by just about everybody involved. It will be a long time before she meddles in things adult again. Thank the good Lord."

"The poor thing."

"You are entirely too kind, my dear."

"He used her, just like he used me."

The blue eyes were kind as he held a finger to my lips. "Read me no details, please. I know what you were doing, by the way. You didn't want to terminate Burke in front of the children."

I was silent. Was that what I had been doing? I didn't know. Frankly, I didn't know if I could have terminated Allen or not, and it had nothing to do with the fact that we had once been lovers. Shooting at real people is very different from taking shots at tin cans and circular targets and paper cutouts. I didn't know if I could have done it. The only thing I knew for sure was that my job was to protect the kids, to protect me and to do what I had been sent here for. I tried to wipe it all out of my mind; if I hadn't any clear idea of what to do then, how could I be sure now?

"Thank you for the flowers."

"You're welcome."

I looked around the room. Every flat surface, excepting the bed and including most of the floor, sprouted with incredible arrangements.

"You didn't have to send so many."

"I didn't. That one is from Brubaker, your 'old man.' That one is from the British Ambassador, that one from Stanislaus, that one from the American Ambassador, that one from the President of Israel, that one from the President of the United States..."

"And the rest are from you?"

He leaned his elbows on the bed. "Guilty. Except for..."

"Grey, you didn't have to be so excessive."

"Dear girl, you have no idea of how excessive I can be." He smiled and his eyes twinkled and suddenly I saw a world of possibilities. "However, that one over there," he pointed to an exuberant profusion of poppies and tulips and every kind of flower you could imagine, "is from your choir. Paid for with their own money, I might add. They insisted, even though I offered to help them with the ready."

Knowing how much flowers cost in this desert country, and knowing how little money most of them had, I was so touched that my eyes welled with tears. "I wish I could see them," I said a little plaintively.

"Then you shall," Grey said, rising with a flourish.

"Really?"

"As long as it doesn't overtire you. The instant you start to get tired, out they go!" Then the flip expression on his face changed. "They have been wanting to see you most awfully. They're a nice lot, you know."

It was an entirely different group of youngsters Grey ushered into my room than I had met in Dallas just days ago. They looked older, harder, and – conversely – touchingly vulnerable, and not just because of Larry's two new bandages. After one quick glance not one of them could look me in the eye – remembering, I suppose, those horrible minutes when they had believed me a traitor to my country and probably worse.

"Hi, gang."

They mumbled a greeting and my heart went out to them. It just wasn't fair! Being an adolescent was hard enough and then to miss the semi-finals and the concert and get involved in all this...

"I'm sorry."

Tony looked up. Responsibility set well on his shoulders and already he looked much more mature. "You're sorry? Hey, Miss Sabine, it's us who should be apologizing to you."

"Are you all right?"

He smiled slightly. "Wasn't nothing. That guy

couldn't hit at all."

"It really is we who should be apologizing to you, Miss Sabine." That was Gerald. Of course. "It was really most foolish of some of us to believe that you would be a traitor. Such behavior is quite out of character with you. For a certain person to believe what that obvious liar was saying simply because he pretended to be romantically interested in her, and for her then to try to make us believe it was unpardonable."

Cruel little beast. I wondered how hellish they had made Carla's life during this time. Not that she wasn't guilty of some pretty bad judgment, but – nobody's perfect. I was a number of years older than she and I had fallen under Allen Burke's spell too.

Carla was lurking at the back of the group, all hangdog and sad. I wished I could make it right for her.

"That's enough, Gerald. Allen Burke is just about as convincing a liar as I have ever seen. I was completely taken in by him and I'm a great deal older and wiser than any of you."

They all looked uncomfortable. It was Grey who finally broke the spell.

"Was, Robin."

"Was?" A tight knot suddenly formed in the pit of my stomach and I wasn't quite sure why. "Is he dead?"

"Yes."

"Did you kill him?"

"My God, woman!" Grey exploded, half in exasperation and half in amusement. "You sound like you're asking if I took him to lunch. Don't you care?"

"For you, if you did it, yes. To take a human life must be a horrible thing."

"It was dreadful, Miss Sabine," Maureen said, her gentle face tight with remembered horror.

"You... you all saw it?" I stared, Oh, these poor children! Not only did they have to endure the stress of these last days and seeing me shot, they had had to watch Allen die. Poor Carla especially; he had entangled her and used her without mercy.

Tony nodded. "When you and Mr. Hamilton-ffoulkes started talking in that funny poetry way we knew that we were all wrong and that you were okay, but everything happened so quickly. Mr. Burke had a gun hidden somewhere and then he shot you... He tried to say something about protecting national security, but Mr. Hamilton-ffoulkes..."

Grey laughed. "Why don't you call me Grey, Tony? It's much less of a mouthful."

Tony's eyes beamed. Grey's action had set the final seal on his new-found adulthood. "Really? Then Mr. – Grey's men jumped him. He tried to get free, but when he saw they had him he ate his cufflink."

"A suicide pill?"

Grey nodded and I saw remembered horror in his eyes. Instantaneous poisoning was not a very nice death.

"I didn't know anyone ever really carried those. It's like something out of a spy novel," I said in amazement, then started as Grey began to laugh.

"You are priceless, Robin, absolutely priceless."

"If you are a CIA agent, why don't you?" Carla had raised her head and her expression was hateful. Somehow I was afraid that Allen Burke had set her on a path from which she would never come back. I didn't know what to say to her.

"One thing I would like to know," Larry said slowly to Grey, "is how you just appeared in the tomb like some sort of super-hero or something..."

"A super-hero?" Grey asked in horror. "Good God!"

"How did you know where to find us?"

"Simple enough. I didn't. When you all disappeared and Robin disappeared I simply didn't have a clue. I remembered how interested Burke had been in Robin at the restaurant, and then I remembered some of the tales about him, so I put out feelers on where to find him. When we did, we followed him, and he led us to you. Finding him wasn't all that difficult. His reputation is none too savory and I guess by then he'd gotten sloppy with overconfidence."

Carla made a strangling noise, but her face was as hard and defiant as ever.

"So you knew that Mr. Burke was a crook?" Tony asked.

"No, just suspected. However, at the time I was sort of suspecting your Miss Sabine, too." He softened the words with a smile. "That didn't last long, though."

"Grey, haven't you told these guys anything?"

"No, because I don't know enough to tell. Brubaker was madly discreet and let me in only on a need-to-know basis. I'm nearly as much in the dark as they are."

I swallowed twice. Somehow I had come to think of him as omniscient, an undercover operative of the highest level who knew everything. "Then you are just a diplomat."

"As I said in that tomb, I'm perhaps the only person in this whole mess who is exactly what he says he is, and I'm just a simple, lowly diplomat in the service of Her Majesty's government."

"But the old man... Brubaker..." If the old man wanted to use that name, I would too.

"I have friends. And, I have a pretty high security clearance, but not high enough to break your cover officially. That's why I had to use the code contact to ascertain the agent's – your – identity. That was given me under the table, so to speak, so you would have the option of revealing yourself or not."

"So you really are a CIA agent," Tony said slowly.

It would be foolish to try and deny things now. I had longed for the opportunity to tell the truth and paid dearly for the privilege. I would tell them what I could.

"Not really. I work occasionally as a courier for a branch of the government which is definitely not the CIA. In fact, I'm not sure it exists officially."

"Then that bit Mr. Burke told us about you breaking into the safe was true?" Tony asked.

"Yes. I was trying to rescue some politically

sensitive documents from someone who would have sold them to the highest bidder and caused our government a great deal of trouble."

"So Allen told the truth. You are a spy!" Carla hissed.

"No. I really am a music teacher and choral director. As I said, I'm just an occasional courier. This competition provided the perfect cover for me."

"That means we weren't really in the competition," Gerald said.

"You were indeed entered and you got into the semi-finals on your own merit, but I admit if we hadn't needed the cover you wouldn't have been put together as a group or brought over here. That's why the late registration and all the problems. I think it's a stinking deal for you."

"Oh, no!" cried Maureen, her eyes shining. "We got to come when we wouldn't have otherwise."

"I'm glad you feel like that. Anyway, it was supposed to be so simple. The agency arranged for you to be entered in the competition and sponsored by one of their shadow companies. Then they arranged for me to take the place of your leader who got sick at the last minute, presumably so whoever might be watching wouldn't have time to check me out."

"Fat lot of good that did," Grey said wryly.

"They had no way of knowing that Allen Burke would be here. The minute he saw me the cat was out of the bag."

"So Miss Wilberforce isn't really sick? That was all planned?"

I nodded; it hurt, but it was a good hurt. You have to be alive to hurt, and I liked proof that I was alive. "Yes, Larry. Miss Wilberforce isn't an operative or even a courier; she's just a choir director like me, hired by the agency. After we got over here and finished the competition, I was supposed to go to a certain shop and buy a present for my boss' wife."

"The Crown?" Grey asked.

"The Crown, although I didn't know what it was until I saw it. I disrupted the whole thing by going early, because when we went shopping I wanted to be able to concentrate on you all. I was supposed to take the Crown home as a souvenir and turn it over to the old man."

"It sounds so simple," Maureen said.

"It was supposed to be. I don't know when things went wrong. No one was supposed to know what was going on. Even when I ran into Allen I had no idea that he was anything more than the journalist he pretended to be."

"An excellent cover for someone who needed to move around the world without suspicion," Grey said in solemn tones. "We've been finding out a lot about him. He was notorious, and getting sloppy. He'd worked for too many people, crossed too many people, made too many enemies."

"What was that you and Mr. – Grey," Larry used

the name shyly, "were saying in the tomb? It sounded like poetry."

"It is. It's part of a poem called *The Dying Year*."

Grey reached out and carefully took my hand, lacing his fingers with mine. "By Li Wong Su."

"Who?"

"I never heard of it."

"You're not supposed to." Sensing my fatigue, Grey took over. "Rather clever idea, using poems as recognition codes. There's always the chance an agent looking for a contact could run into a poetry buff, so obscure poets are chosen for contact codes. And they always start with the third line of the poem, never the first. Each agent is given a new poem on each operation. Identity cards can be forged, faces changed, but an obscure poem... It's a good system."

"Indeed, except when you hate poetry."

"My dear Robin!" Grey was scandalized.

"I had to memorize half a dozen of the things to cover the contingencies of this operation. I couldn't even get the Crown until I had given the right poem. Grey... what about Selim and the man in the fire?"

Grey squeezed my hand. "Later, dear girl, later. Now I am going to play villain and throw all of you out of here. You need your rest, and these children have a plane to catch this afternoon."

"This afternoon!"

"The competition is sending us home by way of Paris!" Betty Jean said, her eyes sparkling.

"And we get to stay a few days." Maureen grinned from ear to ear.

"Sort of a consolation prize," Tony added.

"And a marvelous chance for intellectual advancement. Mr. Hamilton-ffoulkes has promised us an introduction to the director of the Louvre." Gerald's face beamed.

"I can't wait. Where did you go in Paris? I went to the Louvre!" mocked Larry and Tony joined in the laughter.

"Enjoy it," I said. "Enjoy all of it. You've earned it."

"All right, youngsters," Grey said with a snap of authority in his voice. "Miss Sabine is tired. Say good-bye and be quick about it."

One by one the kids left, each one except Carla with a private word of farewell. She just turned and walked out; I wished I could say something to reach her, but I couldn't think of a thing that would even dent her hatred.

The other five kept their farewells short, for Grey stood beside me and watched them with a commanding eye. It didn't matter, for whatever their words were I got the message from their eyes – the respect, the affection, the apology. It was quite touching and after the last of them was gone I began to weep.

Grey misunderstood completely, immediately leaping to the conclusion that I was in pain. Before I could protest a nurse was summoned, a needle stuck into my IV and I was drifting off to sleep again in spite

of my firm yet fuzzy knowledge that it wasn't over yet,
that there was something urgent I had to tell someone.

Chapter Twenty-Four

It was late the next afternoon before they would let me have visitors again. By then I truly was feeling what Grey would call bobbish and when the chipper nurse came in to tell me I had visitors I happily let her fix my hair.

"Good afternoon, Robin." Grey took my outstretched hand and – careful of the tubes I still trailed – gently kissed the back. "You look better."

"I feel better."

"Enough for a little serious talk?"

"Of course. What's wrong? Didn't the kids get off all right? Is anything wrong with them?"

Grey settled on the side of the bed without relinquishing my hand, his blue eyes dancing with laughter. "Unnatural woman! Is all you ever think of that group of pre-delinquent brats? I meant about us."

"Is there an 'us'?"

"I would be most interested in exploring the possibilities. What about you?"

Suddenly it was difficult to breathe. I've never been a femme fatale type and to have such a man as Grey express an interest in me so blatantly was startling, even more so when you considered that at the moment I looked more like a science project gone wrong than anything anyone would desire. "Indeed."

Grey's eyes twinkled. "Indeed. I presume you aren't going to take another 'assignment' soon."

"I hope never again."

"Good. Now in another week or so you should be on your way home. Your embassy is arranging stretcher transport on a military plane."

It certainly wasn't what I had expected to hear. And, drat him, he was so businesslike about it!

"If you take care of yourself and do what the doctors say, you should be completely back to normal by October. At least, I hope so."

He might be a very good diplomat and adept at showing a calm countenance to a bunch of other diplomats, but the man hasn't been born who can completely conceal all his emotions; at least, not from a woman very interested in them. He was up to something.

"Why October?"

"Quick, aren't you? Well, I've heard a rumor that you are to be offered the position of Director of Choral Music at the Wellington Conservatory in Washington, DC."

For a moment I couldn't breathe. The Wellington Conservatory! Small, private and very exclusive, it was perhaps the best music conservatory in the United States, if not the world. To become Director of Choral

Music at the Wellington was harder than becoming President. Of the United States, that is. The idea was too big. I couldn't get my mind around it.

"And," Grey was going on, "I am being transferred to Washington in October on a special assignment. Since we are going to be in the same city, I thought perhaps you might be interested in continuing this courtship under more conventional circumstances."

"Oh," I said slowly, the earth dissolving beneath me, "this is a courtship, is it?"

"I would like it to be. I am an old-fashioned man, Robin, and I like to do things in an old fashioned way. I believe a successful relationship has to be carefully built and that isn't done overnight. I would like to have a very long relationship with you, perhaps even for the rest of my life, but I want to go slowly and make sure that everything is right."

Unable to speak, I nodded. It didn't hurt a bit.

A smile spread across his face as if I had given him a present and he didn't even try to hide the twinkle in his eyes. "That is, if I can trust you to stay out of other people's safes and not to run around playing spy and breaking up perfectly good copies of the Crown of the Virgin."

"Never again, I swear!" I said and started to laugh. "I just hope you won't be bored by a simple music teacher who has no aptitude whatsoever as a spy."

"It will be a relief, dearest girl, believe me!"

My bandaged ribs hurt a little when he took me

gently into his arms, but I was just glad my lips weren't bandaged. I thought I had been kissed before, but never by anybody who could kiss as well as this man could! He was right; I would need at least until October before I was in any sort of shape to be courted by him the way I wanted to be courted by him!

"Um-humm!"

A smartly dressed and somewhat embarrassed older man stood in the doorway.

"I'm sorry. I did knock."

Grey was more equal to the occasion than I. While I could only lean back and blush, he rose and shook hands with the visitor, then led him to the side of the bed. "I bring you yet another guest. This is Mr. Wilson of your State Department."

Wilson? I had seen this dapper little man more than once and his name was not Wilson and he did not work for the State Department! The old man sometimes showed a dreadful lack of imagination. You'd think he could do better than that on the first trip I had ever known him to take out into the field.

"How do you do, Mr. Wilson?" I asked absolutely straight-faced. If he wanted to pretend we had never met before, I could too.

He took one look at my attachments and declined to shake hands. "Fine, Miss Sabine, but the question is, how are you?"

"I'm feeling well enough, thank you, well enough to want some answers."

Grey laughed and, gesturing to 'Mr. Wilson' to take the uncomfortable-looking straight chair, once again sat beside me. "What did I tell you, Mr. Wilson? Robin is one-of-a-kind."

"Very well, then, I suggest we speak frankly. Mr. Hamilton-ffoulkes is here at my invitation, Miss Sabine. He has become, if you will excuse the expression, intimately involved with this incident and as his security clearance is of the highest... I take it you don't mind?"

Pompous idiot! I glanced at Grey and could almost hear him saying it. "No, I don't mind at all."

"Where would you like us to begin?"

"With Allen Burke. Was he really an agent?"

"Yes, had been for years, though he really didn't have a master. Worked free lance for whomever had enough money. He had been approached by the KGB when young, but apparently thought he could do better working for himself."

"As Mr. Wilson has been telling me," Grey said gently, "Burke had been making quite a name for himself delivering ... er...hard to find merchandise to the highest bidder."

"Ruthless creature he was, too," Wilson added. "He was getting something of a reputation for that."

"I think it's a little bit of coincidence that he was here after last year in England."

The old man's eyes flashed. "We thought so too, and instigated an inquiry. We knew that you knew each other..."

"We were lovers at one time," I said bluntly. "Was he here because of me?"

"Not really, any more than he was in England last year because of you. Both times he was after something else – Lord Mugoran's papers and the Invisible Man plans. He probably regarded your presence here as just a bit of serendipity. Until he started to suspect that you were here as an operative."

"And how did you get in involved with this, Grey?"

He looked cherubically innocent. "I was at a big party and saw a very interesting-looking woman with an enormous purse whom I thought I should like to know better. Later, when things became so suspicious and involved, I of course reported it to my superiors and my involvement took on a more official tone. It's a happy man who can mix business and pleasure."

"Mr. Hamilton-ffoulkes has been of inestimable help," said Mr. Wilson and then clammed up.

I had decided that Gerald was an embryonic 'Mr. Wilson' and proceeded as I would have with him; it was a new sidelight on the old man. It took a little ruthless interrogation, but finally the major part of the story came out. There had been a security leak in the agency – one of the desk types selling off little bits of information, such as who was going where, or that a certain piece of information was going to be passed at a given place and time.

"And apparently our leak had no sense of honor at

all," Wilson finished with a sneer. "He sold the same information to several different people."

"Well, they could hardly complain," Grey said. "From what we've found out, Robin, your name was never mentioned. The leak just said that the director of the Trans-Texas Canticle Society..." he grimaced.

"I know. It's a horrible name. You'd think they could have done better. How surprised Allen must have been to see me."

"Delighted, I should say. He would have thought it an extra bit of luck."

"But I didn't cooperate."

"You certainly didn't! In fact, Miss Sabine, you brought this whole thing on yourself."

"What?"

"Why did you go and pick up the Crown on the first day until waiting until the sightseeing day that was arranged after the competition?"

"The kids."

Grey frowned and Wilson looked confused.

"Once I met them I knew I wouldn't dare leave them alone in the Old City, even for a few minutes to buy a 'souvenir' for myself. Plus, they were so sharp I knew they'd notice when I gave the code sequence. So I decided to go early."

Wilson gave a rusty little laugh that was only slightly forced. "We thought of just about every contingency but that one."

"I knew it was a problem, since I was sent from one

shop to another."

"It was kept there as a safety measure. We thought we could keep a secret in this town." The old man shook his head sadly.

"Grey? Did you know about it?"

"No. No one was supposed to, but Mr. Wilson is right about keeping secrets in this town. Apparently one of the coffee boys saw or heard something. Word filtered up to me that there was a rumor about the Crown of the Virgin of Janóch being seen in the Old City. That was before the real one was found. We didn't know anything about the Invisible Man, of course. I went just to check out the rumor about the Crown and ran into you. I never had any idea you had something hot with you. I just thought it was my lucky day."

"And when the shop burned? Who was the man who died?"

Grey stroked my hand and once more interlaced our fingers. "Apparently the coffee boy was just as free with his information as our leak. Of course, the opposition knew the Crown itself wasn't real, but they knew what it held. They went to get it, but it was of course gone. They started the fire to cover the fact that the shop had been thoroughly and rather roughly searched. Selim was there; they intended to have him burn with the shop, but they underestimated him. The man who died was one of theirs. Selim, by the way, is one of yours."

I blinked at that, and looked to the old man for

confirmation.

"A top man," Wilson muttered.

"Is he all right?"

"Yes," he said somewhat shortly, "though still nursing a headache. He did have his doubts about you, however."

"You did seem to have a great number of unusual people interested in you, Robin. Do you always attract such attention?" Grey's tone was almost facetious. Almost.

It took some more hard questioning on my part, and some occasionally reluctant answers on theirs, but it turned out that I had two separate groups – that we knew of – after me, though I never did learn exactly who was backing whom.

There was Allen, of course; except for a few hired goons he worked pretty much alone. He had arranged for the snatching of the picnic basket, thinking that whatever the information was on might have been hidden in there, as well as being a handy way of separating Grey and me. He couldn't tell how much we were involved, but he daren't take a chance. The fact that I was out with Grey at all was a wound to his ego, so he played the rescuing hero to the hilt. I didn't kid myself that he cared about me; he just wanted me to care about him.

Allen also sent the car for the kids. He knew my handwriting very well, well enough to forge a credible note, and had choreographed both Carla's return with

Grey at the Hall of World Peace and the oh-so-elaborate scene where I had seen Carla 'meet' Grey in the plaza of Damascus Gate. Both were designed to make me disavow Grey and come running to Allen for comfort.

Allen had seen our little group that first night at the Hall of World Peace reception and, sensing Carla's willingness to be corrupted by an older man, had obliged by romancing her shamelessly. And used her shamelessly, feeding her a rigmarole about working for the CIA and needing her help to catch that master spy and consciousless traitor Robin Sabine. Grey told me later that at their meeting in the plaza Carla had told him she had snuck out of the Embassy for a date with a singer in another choir and was afraid of going back to the hotel alone. Then at the hotel she had refused to let him come in and, after he was gone, had been picked up by a properly grateful Allen, who had then taken her back to where he was holding the rest of the carefully separated group. Grey had given up searching for me and gone back to the embassy where he found the kids gone. Then, he said later, was when he had his worst doubts about me.

The whole scenario was masterly and it had worked, only Allen hadn't planned on Selim. Selim and his men had seen me with Allen several times, and since they knew his reputation, had rightfully begun to doubt my trustworthiness. They were just keeping an eye on me and putting me safely out the way for a while when they locked me in that storeroom. Perhaps it's tacky of me, but I would love to have seen Selim's face when he returned and I was gone.

We never knew, or if the old man did he never told me, who or what Sternberg was working for. Was he free-lancing for the money, or involved with some sort of political organization or maybe a radical religious sect? We'll never know, because his comrades all vanished and neither he nor Feldshuh (I could never think of him by any other name) were both too professional to leave any evidence behind.

Sternberg had an advantage over the others; being an integral part of the competition he not only knew I was coming, he knew my position and had some say in our disposition. He had insisted we be put in that grim little hotel and installed Feldshuh to look after us. We think his was the group that ransacked and burned Selim's shop trying to get the plans while Sternberg himself tried to get me out of the country before I was supposed to pick it up. Their main mistake had been not to send the Abramowitzes to Eilat in the beginning, never dreaming that their restrictive rules would inspire me to move.

It was, of course, Allen who had killed Sternberg and Feldshuh. When Selim carted me off to lock me up until he could contact his superiors, Allen had panicked, not knowing who had me. He had started searching the streets for me and by sheer luck – and the deserted streets – had seen Feldshuh's associates pick me up. Then he just followed us to the hotel. The armed goons out front had kept him at bay for a while, then he had come in and shot both men. Apparently my pathetic attempt at camouflage with the sheet had fooled him and he thought that I had gone. Maybe he thought I was in league with Sternberg and company; I don't know. In any case, he had arranged to have the place watched and when I finally did leave, his goons had picked me up.

"A most exciting story," Wilson said at last. "What a pity it was all for nothing."

"Hardly nothing," Grey said. "At least the plans didn't fall into any unfriendly hands. And that reminds me of something, Robin. How did you know on which jewel the plans were? I admit it was a clever idea to destroy the microdot just in case one of our little friends got their hands on the Crown, but I saw nearly all of your little performance and I don't see how you could find the right jewel without looking, since they're all the same size and shape."

Of course! It had almost surfaced last night, but I had been too tired and too doped to realize it. I was the only one who knew.

"But I didn't destroy the microdot."

That got both of them! Grey leaned back and regarded me with veiled eyes while 'Mr. Wilson' looked as if he had just swallowed a frog.

"Robin…"

"But you must have, Miss Sabine! We have had a

laboratory crew taking that Crown apart to find it. We've even had people sifting the dust on the floor of that tomb trying to find proof that it was destroyed! Are you trying to tell me that the microdot was never on the Crown? That Selim...?"

"No, of course not."

"Robin," Grey asked in a terrible voice, "what have you done?"

"Would you hand me my purse, please?"

He rummaged in my closet and pulled out the battered canvas tote. Scruffy and stained, it looked even more disreputable against the sterile surroundings of my pale pink hospital room. Then, a lump rising in my throat, I realized that those new, rust-colored splotches were my own blood. Somehow that made everything different, sharper, even more so than my bandaged body.

"You know your wallet and papers and valuable things are in the safe at the embassy," Grey began, but I shook my head. I wasn't interested in those, not now at least.

"Look in the make-up kit. There's... oh, just hand it to me, please. "It's a blue striped zipper bag."

Grey eyed the bulging canvas warily, regarding it as he would a hostile bulldog. "Is it safe to go digging in there?"

"Probably not, but you have my permission to bite anything that bites you."

That did not seem to reassure him. Grey was a lot

more timid about rooting around in all that stuff than I, but he persevered manfully. "What on earth are you doing with.... Never mind. I don't want to know."

Which was just as well, because I couldn't think of anything in there that would provoke such a reaction. Finally he unearthed my pathetic little make-up kit and handed it over gingerly.

It took some doing before I finally got things arranged the way I wanted it, with the table over my lap and a clean bath towel draped over it. Unfortunately having various tubes trailing from your arms does not increase your dexterity. I had barely opened the make-up kit when my glucose drip sent it flying, scattering the various tubes like buckshot. Wilson, his nerves already overstretched, almost screamed. Grey, practically, began to gather up the debris.

"We can get the rest later, Grey. I just need the lipstick called Jezebel."

His eyebrows arched upward. "Jezebel?"

"I bought it for the trip. Considering, it seemed appropriate." I took it from him. "My pocket knife is in the zipper pocket of my purse. Would you get it, please?"

After taking a long look at my purse, Grey reached in his pocket. "Here. Would you consider using mine?"

I waited until he had opened the blade and handed it to me, then I screwed the lipstick up as far as it would go and began to scrape at the base.

A look of amazement washed over Grey's face as he

suddenly understood. "When did you do this?"

"The night of the sniper. That was Allen, wasn't it?"

"We surmise so. Apparently he wanted to make you believe it was dangerous to be with me."

"We'll take that up later." I removed another thin curl of waxy pink. "Anyway, as you know, Mr. ... Wilson, I didn't know what it was that I was to pick up. I was to take whatever was given me by the person who knew the sign and countersign of the contact poem, who turned out to be Selim."

Grey gasped. "You mean you didn't know that a microdot was involved?"

"Not at all. We couriers aren't encouraged to ask questions or allowed to know too much. We just transport what we're given. You can't tell what you don't know. When I saw this, especially after meeting you, Grey, and your mentioning it right there when I picked it up... That went a long way toward making Allen's accusations seem true."

"Pure chance, I assure you."

"Anyway, I didn't know what to do except keep it in my purse and keep it safe, although it was obviously a fake. Then, after the sniper attack, I decided that either someone didn't know it wasn't valuable or there was some value there that I hadn't seen. I went over it until I found the microdot."

"And the plans for the Invisible Man have been lying around inside your lipstick ever since then?" The old man looked as if he might have a stroke at any moment.

I nodded, intent on shaving away the thinnest possible layer of lipstick. I hadn't gone through all this just to end up scratching the microdot with a penknife!

"After all, the Crown was so showy... If Allen hadn't had the kids and if I'd have a chance to hand it over and live, I'd have given it to him. To anyone. Without a thought. This seemed safer."

"Safer!" Wilson shrieked. "Your purse has been lying around here and God knows where else..."

"It was foolish, Robin," Grey said, but his eyes were full of admiration.

"No, it was really quite brilliant," I said without any false modesty. "This was one of the safest places I could think of. Do you Brits ever read any of our American authors? Poe, for instance? *The Purloined Letter*? Nothing is safer than when it's in plain sight. Ah! Almost got it now."

"I'm not sure I agree with that."

"Don't be stuffy, Grey. You see, it wasn't any trouble to cut a chunk of this stuff, put the dot in, put the chunk back, then heat the edges so they sealed. Even if I couldn't make it smooth or even make it look like a mold mark, it really doesn't matter. No one ever twists a new lipstick up all the way."

Carefully I lifted the small black dot from the lipstick shaft and handed it over to Wilson, who took it as if it were some sort of Grail. Still smeared with bright pink, it sat on his fingertip like a piece of ash. "An archaic technology," he muttered, "but still most efficient."

"And you say you have no aptitude," Grey said wonderingly.

"You can be sure that my report will reflect on you most favorably, Miss Sabine," Mr. Wilson said, putting the dot safely away in a small plastic envelope. "I am sure that we will be calling on you much more often in the future."

"Oh, please don't," I said. "I have other plans. I might be going to Washington in October."

After the old man floated out, buoyed up by his recovered plans, Grey looked at me and asked, "Did you mean that?"

"I said I might."

Then he spent a great deal of time trying to convince me.

I let him.

About the Author

Janis Susan May is a seventh-generation Texan and a third-generation wordsmith who writes mysteries as Janis Patterson, romances and other things as Janis Susan May, children's books as Janis Susan Patterson and scholarly works as J.S.M. Patterson.

Formerly an actress and singer, a talent agent and Supervisor of Accessioning for a bio-genetic DNA testing lab, Janis has also been editor-in-chief of two multi-magazine publishing groups. She founded and was the original editor of The Newsletter of the North Texas Chapter of the American Research Center in Egypt, which for the nine years of her reign was the international organization's only monthly publication. Long interested in Egyptology, she was one of the founders of the North Texas ARCE chapter and was the closing speaker for the ARCE International Conference in Boston in 2005.

Janis and her husband live in Texas with an assortment of rescued furbabies.

www.JanisSusanMay.com
www.JanisPattersonMysteries.com